RECLAIM

BETH YARNALL

RECLAIM

1

NOLAN

I'm kind of a fuck up. It's not something I aspire to. It just sort of happens. The effort's there. It's the execution that's lacking. I'm not a total loser. I have a few things going for me. I'm told I'm good looking, but my appearance hasn't delivered a single date for months. I've never had a steady girlfriend. I went to school—a good school—and got a college degree, but that didn't translate into a job in my chosen field. I bought the winning lottery ticket once and lost it. I don't play the lottery anymore. The company that manufactured my first new car went out of business less than a year after I bought it.

I joke a lot about having bad luck and being cursed. That's not what it is. I'm just one of those people who have to work harder than anyone else. Nothing comes easy to me. I get what I'm after...eventually. Usually on the third or forth try. Never the first. I envy people who coast through life thinking about wanting something and then BAM. They have it. My best friend Dominic is like that. He thought about settling down and getting married. A week later he met his wife. They talked about having children. She was pregnant within a month.

I don't get people like that.

If it weren't for my obstinate determination I wouldn't have achieved a single thing in my life. Stubborn to a fault. That's how my friends and family describe me.

At least I learn from my lessons. My friend Mike is one of those guys who keeps doing the same thing over and over, lamenting all the while about how he can never catch a break. You gotta make your own breaks. At least those of us who don't get things handed to them. I'm always looking out for the next thing, the next whatever it's going to be that'll take me where I want to go. However circuitous the route. No straight lines to anything for me. Nope. The road to all of my achievements has been twisty and windy, filled with flooded potholes. Every once in a while something will fly out in front of me, forcing me change course to avoid it.

It's those unexpected detours that have lead to the most interesting things in my life. Take my new job at Nash Security and Investigations. Totally not what I saw myself doing when they handed me my college diploma for my degree in criminal justice. I was going to be a police officer. Or maybe a sheriff. Okay, a small part of me kinda hoped the FBI would recruit me right out of college. That didn't happen. Also it turns out that I'm not cut out to be a cop. A little more than halfway through the entrance application I had the sudden, overwhelming realization that I didn't want to go into law enforcement.

After that revelation—another something leaping across my road, making me jerk the wheel to avoid it—I found myself on an unfamiliar street, fenced in by unfamiliar surroundings, driving along at a snail's pace. That was the year I wandered aimlessly through job after job, looking for

The Thing. *My* Thing. Who and what I was meant to be. And then I came across the story of how this PI firm, Nash Securities and Investigations, had helped to clear a man named Beau Hollis who was wrongly convicted for the rape and murder of his ex-girlfriend. That sounded like a really cool job. I mean, freeing someone after years in prison. Giving them their life back. That's a fucking incredible thing.

I wanted to be a part of *that*.

It was the first time I ever had that feeling about anything. I sure as shit didn't have it about selling cars or driving a delivery truck or in customer service for an electronics company. Even the free pizza I got to eat doing deliveries for an Italian restaurant didn't give me the sensation of being imminently *useful*. Contributing to society. Doing good. Making wrong things right. That's what I want to do.

Expect as usual I managed to screw things up the first chance I got.

Backing up.

I got the job at the agency that I wanted to work for, Nash Security and Investigations, nailing the interview. That never happens to me. I should've known it was too good to be true. Like I said, nothing's ever been handed to me. Definitely not something as big and as sought after as this job was for me. The very first assignment they give me on my own I screwed up. Like huge, major, no-going-back-from-this, lives-in-danger kind of fuck up. It should've been a cakewalk. Watch this retail center. See if this guy shows up. Follow him. See where he goes. Simple, right?

Not for me.

I got close enough to get his license plate. I followed him, thinking I was cool and important, then the guy lost me. One minute he was there then the next POOF. Gone.

When I got back to the office to give my boss, Cora Hollis, the car and tag info the client, Vera Swain, pointed out that if I got close enough to get the guy's plate then I was close enough for him to get *my* plate. And son of a bitch if he hadn't. That's how the asshole found Vera—through me. Finding her resulted in the bastard killing her sister and nearly killing Vera and Cora's brother Beau, the guy who'd just gotten his life back after spending years in prison.

All of that shit was on me. Why Cora didn't fire me on the spot I have no idea. Hell, *I* would've fired me. A young girl died because of me. I almost got Beau and Vera killed. All because I can't get anything right the first time out. This was one case where the effort and the thought didn't count. *I tried* didn't mean shit. *I'm sorry* wasn't enough. *I didn't mean to* was useless.

Cora insisted there was nothing to forgive. An honest mistake, she called it. Could've happened to anyone, she said. You'll do better next time, she placated. Would I though? Second and third tries were iffy for me. Nearly as dicey as the first time. And that first time was a giant clusterfuck of epic proportions. I know it'll get better from here on out, but that's not much consolation. Like a category five hurricane downgrading to a three or a four. Still a major disaster. There will be damage, it's just a matter of how much and who it will effect.

I show up at the office and keep my head down. I do as I'm told the way I'm told. I try to absorb as much as I can from Jerry one of the old-timers whose unenviable job it is to show me the ropes. I hope the guy has good life insurance. I joked about that once with him. He didn't laugh.

Cora hasn't been in the office much the past few weeks. She visits Vera in the hospital pretty regular. So does Beau. Now that he's out of jail after being accused of shooting

Vera. That guy's luck is as shit as mine. No. Shittier. *Way* shittier. I've never been in jail for anything let alone being accused of hurting the woman I love...twice. That's some powerfully bad karma he's carrying around. When I think about all he's been through I can't feel too sorry for myself. If I don't think about how he wouldn't have gone to jail that second time because of me and how Vera wouldn't have gotten shot and how her sister wouldn't be dead.

Yeah. I try not to think about that. I do my job. I put in my best effort. I pray it'll be enough. Maybe one of these days it will be. I'm not sure why I'm here except that because Cora's not around a lot there's a ton of work that needs to get done. I owe her that at least. Whatever she asks I do. Take out the trash—it's out. Run a few copies—they're done. Pick up lunch—I get the order *exactly* right. All I have to offer is my best effort. What happens after that is a complete and utter mystery. Could be good. Could be bad. Who knows? It's me we're talking about.

I'm running a computer search for client—a job Beau held for a while before the shooting—when Cora walks in, muttering over the open file in her hands. She's really pretty, like make you drop your sandwich and stare like an idiot kind of pretty. She doesn't even know it. That makes her sexier. Even if she weren't my boss she'd be way off limits to me. She's dating the son of the owner of the agency. I don't even exist to her on any level except employee. That's okay though. I'd screw that up too. She's not the kind of person you mess around with casually. She's an all-in kind of woman. The kind you marry and never cheat on. Her boyfriend is a lucky son of bitch and he knows it.

"You almost done with that search?" she asks me.

All I get is the top of her blue and black streaked head. I can't help but stare at her when she's not looking. Leaning back a little in my chair, I crane my neck to check out her legs in the skirt she's wearing. Nice. High heels look good on her, making her legs longer somehow. It's one of those tricks only women know that make a man forget his name and apparently the question they've just been asked.

"Nolan?"

Shit. My gaze snaps up to hers. Busted. "Ah, yeah. Just about."

"Good. I have something here I want you to take a look at."

My mind spins her innocent words into something lurid. I give myself a stern lecture about workplace decorum and about not horning in on another guy's woman. That's not cool. That's not who I am or who I want to be. I just wish my boss were a little less hot.

"Oh, yeah?" I ask.

She slides the folder she's holding in front of me and leans in with a hand on my desk. "The Freedom Project sent these cases over for our review. Every year we choose one and work it pro bono. I wish we could work on them all." She sighs. "I see Beau in every face and it's hard to say no. I need an objective opinion."

She separates the three pages, spreading them across my desk. Her arm brushes mine briefly and I instinctively flinch away. If she notices it doesn't show in her face. All of her focus is on the papers in front of her. There's a crease between her brows and her bottom lip is pinched between her teeth. This is important to her. Even if I didn't know her brother's story I'd know it in the look on her face and how she touches the black and white mug shots of the three incarcerated people staring back at her.

"What do you want me to do?" I ask.

"Read the case summary and the notes from the

Freedom Project's staff. We need to choose one and I just can't decide. It feels like I'm handing down a sentence to other two if I don't select them."

And she thinks I won't get the same feeling? I glance up at her.

"We're not," she amends. "Their cases will get handled by another PI firm, but it won't be us, you know?"

"Yeah, I think I get it. That makes me feel better about choosing." That's a lie. I'm lousy at making decisions. She should already know this about me.

"Have a look and let me know what you think. I need to get back to them by the end of the day."

"Sure thing."

She leaves her scent behind and the lingering sense of doom that I'll make the wrong choice. God, really? She's leaving this up to me? Someone's life's in my hands, the hands of a fuck up. Does she have *any* idea what she's doing?

I pick up the first sheaf of paper. Bruce Swanson was convicted of the brutal murder of his parents, Doug and Nancy Swanson. As the only child he stood to inherit his parents' vast estate, which entailed a personal fortune of close to eleven million dollars, a company worth twice that, and various real estate properties worth millions more. The conviction hinged on hinkey DNA evidence and a questionable witness—a cousin who inherited everything when Bruce went away. As an only child I'm tempted to choose poor Bruce who should be sitting on fat stacks instead of a thin prison mattress.

I force myself to put the paper down and pick up the next one. D'Shawnte Devon was convicted of attempted murder for the drive by shooting of a rival gang member based on faulty eyewitness testimony. Three people—who also happen to be members of his gang and thus deemed unreliable—said that D'Shawnte was at a bar-b-que at the time of the shooting. There was nothing to tie him physically to the crime and although the eyewitnesses later recanted, D'Shawnte remains in prison for a crime he didn't commit.

That one sucks. D'Shawnte reminds me of me and my bad luck. I'm starting to see what Cora was saying about not being able to choose. You only have to have a smidgeon of empathy to want to do something that could change these people's world.

The third page has a photo of a woman. A *young* woman. Nineteen. Dang. She looks younger. Like maybe fifteen. Carla Ruiz is an undocumented immigrant in prison for the murder of her son. Even though the coroner declared the boy's death an accident the district attorney filed murder charges and won. There's a note about a witness that wasn't called by the defense who could've corroborated the coroner's report. She was convicted for a crime that wasn't even a crime. That's harsh. She lost her son then her freedom. I wonder what will happen to her if she's freed. Will she be forced to go back to Mexico or will she get to stay in the U.S.?

I set her sheet next to the other two, my gaze bouncing from one to the other then the other. Who to pick? Eeny meeny miny mo? Roshambo? Put their names in a cup and draw one?

Cora's depending on me to make a decision based on something real not something arbitrary. I'll probably have to justify my decision. It would be pretty tough to defend rock, paper, scissors.

I look at their faces. They're all young. Under thirty when they went inside. They're older than that now.

D'Shawte is in his forties. Bruce is thirty-six and Carla is nearly thirty. I should pick D'Shawnte. He's been in the longest. But Bruce reminds me of myself except for the rich parents. Carla lost her son. That's a horrible thing. Uuuugh. I just don't know.

I set the pages aside and try to go back to the computer searches I was doing. But my gaze strays. With I sigh I tear up little pieces of paper, write their names on them, and shake the folded scraps in my hands. I hope this is the right thing to do. I close my eyes and choose. Carla. I'm disappointed and yet not. I take her page out and look at it again.

"Well?" Cora stands in the doorway ankles and arms crossed. "Were you able to pick one?"

As subtle as I can I scoop up the little pieces of paper and ball them in my hand. I can't let her know how I couldn't come to a decision. That I let fate randomly decide. I don't know why I did it. Fate has never been anything but a bitch to me.

I hold up the page. "Carla Ruiz."

She unfolds herself and comes toward me. She takes the sheet and nods. "This one got to me too. What made you choose her?"

I *knew* it. "She lost twice—her son and her freedom. That's too much for anyone let alone someone so young."

"Yeah. I thought the same thing." There's a look in her eyes that I don't like seeing. Sadness. She's too pretty to be sad. "Beau was a year younger than her when he went to prison."

"That must've been awful."

She nods, her focus on Carla's photo.

"How's Vera doing?" I have to ask. Then I hold my breath, waiting for the answer.

Her bright blue gaze slides from the paper to me and it's

a warm wave crashing over me, making my breath catch. It's the same blue as the streaks in her hair. Startling. Mesmerizing. Totally off limits.

She smiles. "She's coming home today. That's why Beau isn't here. He's getting her settled in."

"That's good. I'm glad." So, so glad. It's like someone just lifted a stadium off my shoulders.

"Thanks for taking up the slack." She motions with the paper. "And for helping me choose."

"Sure. Any time."

She starts to turn away, then comes back. "We're still a little short around here. You've been so great about working over time and filling in I hate to ask…"

"Whatever you need."

"Since you helped me pick the case I'd like you to take lead on it. I'll help. It's not like I'd be leaving you on your own. It's just that the work you've been doing has been really great and I'd like you to start heading up a few cases. Jerry's been making noises about retiring and with Mr. Nash in semi retirement already we really need another lead investigator around here. You've more than shown you can handle it. This could be a training case. Leads make more money and you'd get out of the office more. What do you say?"

I open my mouth to speak—because she clearly expects a response—but nothing comes out except a squeak. A horrible, embarrassing squeak. I cough to cover it up. She caught me totally off guard. Her eyes are hopeful and before I form the thought I'm nodding my head. *What am I doing? Make it stop.*

"Sure," I say, completing the humiliation. My brain is having a meltdown. While it burns the rest of me goes on automatic, responding totally separately from my brain. I can almost smell the smoke that is surely bellowing out my ears.

"Oh, *thank you*." Cora says. Her smile fans the flames. Sirens go off in my head. "I'll set up the appointment for us to meet with the Freedom Project staff attorney," she continues, totally unaware of the mass casualties in my skull. "You're going to do great. Just great." She backs away toward the door. "I'm looking forward to working with you."

Before I can stop her she's gone.

What have I done?

2

LILA

I'm late. I hate being late. I hate people who show up late even more. Now I'm one of them. There was a jam up at the coroner's office so it took me forever to get a copy of Diego Ruiz's autopsy. I've got it and am now racing across town to meet the private investigator that will be helping with Carla Ruiz's case. I'm lucky. Nash Securities and Investigations has a stellar reputation. Carla deserves the best.

I've never worked with them so I haven't been to their offices. Recently they were instrumental in freeing two men who were wrongfully convicted. I'm hoping they've got what it will take to free Carla too. I hope *I've* got what it takes. I've never encountered a case that touched me the way this one does. The form she filled out to have her case considered by the Freedom Project reads like a note one of my parents might have written. The sentences are all in English, but they're broken and the word order is wrong in places.

I felt her pain in each carefully chosen word. I also felt her confusion, her anger, and deep sense of betrayal. She illegally crossed the boarder from Mexico to the United States with her family when she was a small child just like I did. And just like Carla and her family my father, my mother pregnant with my sister, and I came to America with the hope of a better life. That wasn't what Carla got. That's not exactly what I got either.

The end of her story hasn't been written yet. She can still have the life she dreamed of. Or at least a close approximation. I can't give her son back, but I can possibly give her life back. We're not supposed to make promises to our clients at the Freedom Project. That wouldn't be fair. But I make one to myself—that I'll exhaust every avenue, pursue every lead, I won't quit until I've done everything I can to free her. I am her. She is me. We are one in our shared experiences. I can give her something she may have never had—hope.

When she's free I can help her through the process of getter her paperwork to stay in the U.S. We speak the same language and know the same fears. I can help her rebuild her life. Through my ties to the immigrant community and can help her find a job and an apartment. But first I have to fight for her freedom.

Tomorrow I'll visit her in prison. It will be our first meeting. I don't know if I'm excited or afraid or an unsettling combination of both. This is my first case for the Freedom Project and I fought hard to win the privilege to help Carla. I just hope I'm up to the task. Wanting something and achieving it are two totally different things.

I pull up to the building with the offices of Nash Security and Investigations and park. It's unassuming. Not at all flashy. I appreciate that. The inner office is simple. A blond receptionist sits at a desk talking on the phone. She holds up a finger to let me know she'll be right with me. I turn my attention to the framed newspaper clippings on the wall. They feature the two men that Nash Security and Investigations helped to free. I picture a similar tribute for Carla placed right next to the other two.

"Can I help you?"

I turn to the receptionist. "Hello. I'm Lila Garcia with the Freedom Project. I have an appointment."

"Oh, yes. Pleased to meet you." She comes around the desk and offers her hand. "I'm Savannah."

"Nice to meet you."

"I'll let Cora know you're here." She goes down the hall then comes back. "She asked me to direct you to the conference room." I follow her and take a seat at the large table. "Can I offer you something to drink? Coffee? Tea? Water?"

"Water would be great. Thanks."

"Cora will be right with you."

Alone, I pull out all of the information I have on Carla's case. I made copies of everything for the PI except for the coroner's report. I'm sure they'll want a copy so I set it aside. I got a copy of the trial transcripts. Her defense attorney was an incompetent ass. This case never should've gone to trial let alone ended in a conviction. There was no crime. I flip open the coroner's report and skim down to his finding—accidental death. Not murder. So why did the district attorney file charges in the first place? And why didn't the defense attorney get the charges dropped? It just doesn't make sense.

"Lila?" A woman with black hair streaked with blue enters the room followed by a dark haired guy. "Hi, I'm Cora Hollis. This is Nolan Perry. He'll be lead on this case."

We do the shaking hands thing and sit. Savannah comes in with bottles of water for everyone. Cora and Nolan sit across from me. He looks nervous. She looks composed.

And familiar. I'm trying to figure out where I know her from and then it hits me—she's Beau Hollis's sister. She started working at Nash to help free him. That was a hell of a case to crack. I'm impressed.

"Thank you for taking this case." I slide a folder across the table to her. "I made you copies of everything I have except the coroner's report, which I just obtained." I hand that folder over too. "As you can see Diego Ruiz's death was ruled accidental."

Cora places the folder between the two of them and opens it. "I don't understand. If the death was accidental how did she get convicted for murder?"

"Carla confessed to strangling her son."

"Why would she confess?"

"The police questioned her for nearly thirty hours without a break. Until she finally gave in and confessed. No food, no water, no restroom break. According to the form she filled out to have her case considered by the Freedom Project, the police pushed her around, bullied her, and called her names. She felt like she didn't have a choice. She's in the country illegally. She doesn't speak the English very well. They threatened to deport her entire family. She was alone and completely at their mercy. What would you do?"

She nods. "I see your point. Is there any way for her to recant her confession?"

"The Freedom Project has relationships with a couple of experts on false confessions. I've already sent out a copy of the police video to them. I'm hoping they can give us some insight. Here's the video." I give her a DVD copy. "In it you'll see how tired Carla looks. Her clothes are disheveled. There's a bruise near her right eye. Who knows what all they did to her, what they said."

"What do you need from us?" This is the first time Nolan's spoken.

His voice is deeper, rougher than I expected. I look at him—really look at him—for the first time. As the lead investigator on the case I'm going to be spending a lot of time with him. I should've been paying better attention. On the surface he's a placid lake. There's a quietness to him that makes me wonder if he's as deep as he seems or as dumb as a box of rocks. Either way I envy his calm. Drawn up tight and strung out so thin, I sometimes vibrate inside like a plucked string. There is no stillness in me. I'm like a bee flitting from flower to flower never landing for very long.

His seemingly tranquil nature intrigues me. I press him for more, leaning closer to ask, "What do you mean?"

"It seems like you've got everything sorted out with the experts. I'm just wondering what you need a private investigation agency for?"

Cora doesn't say a word as she turns her attention from Nolan back to me.

"A couple of things," I say. "I've been able to locate one witness, an eight year old boy, who can testify that when he and Diego were kids, Diego liked to wrap the elastic cord of the bed sheet that strangled him around his throat and pretend he was Spiderman. I want to see if we can find Inez Torres, the neighbor who often babysat Diego. Filipe, that's the eight year old, said that she chastised Diego for putting the cord around his neck more than once. They can corroborate Carla's version of events.

"I also need you to find Carla's defense attorney, John Martin. He disappeared shortly after her conviction. I'd really like to see his notes and paperwork on the case if they still exist."

"What do you mean *disappeared*?" Cora asks.

"As in vanished off the face of the earth. His family filed a missing persons report a little more than a month after the trial."

"Do you suspect foul play?"

"I don't know what to make of it. The timing of it... I want to know if he really disappeared or if he relocated and didn't tell anyone. And if he *did* relocate, why?"

"Maybe he went into witness protection." Nolan meant it as a joke, but his quip is a possibility I hadn't considered. But then why would a defense attorney go into protective custody?

Cora turns to Nolan. "That's a thread we'll definitely have to follow. There's no way the Federal Marshalls would tell us if he was in witness protection, but we can try to see if there was something in his background or in one of his cases that might cause that to happen."

"A court-appointed defense attorney isn't likely to have the kind of cases that would warrant protective custody," I say. "Even if he did, there's attorney client privilege. He couldn't testify using any information he received during his defense of a client."

"He probably ran off with a mistress or something." Nolan shrugs. "Or he's dead."

I'm not sure I like his flippant attitude. "If he was dead there would be a death certificate."

"Not if he was murdered."

I can't say the thought hadn't crossed my mind, but the question is *why*? "Why would someone murder a low level public defender? There's nothing in his background that warrants it."

"Not even his personal background? Maybe he had an affair with a married woman with a vindictive husband. Maybe he had a gambling debt he couldn't repay. Maybe he fleeced a client and they exacted revenge." Nolan jerks a shoulder. "Or maybe he drove off a cliff and died somewhere too dense to see the wreckage from the road. He could've given up his life and gone native. I knew a guy who did that. He walked out on his family and into the forest and never came back. There are a million possibilities here."

"And we'll exhaust them all," Cora says, blinking back her surprise at Nolan.

Maybe those still waters run deeper than he lets on even to his coworkers. Intriguing.

"I have an appointment to visit Carla tomorrow. I'd like you to go with me," I tell Nolan. "We can ask her about her attorney and about her neighbor. She might have information she doesn't realize she possesses."

"Tomorrow?" I can see in his head he's rearranging his weekend plans.

"I know it's Saturday—"

"No. It's okay. No problem. What time?"

"It's a long drive. How about I pick you up around eight tomorrow morning?"

"Can we stop for coffee before we hit the road?"

"Sure."

His smile is brief, but flashy, catching me off guard. "Give me your number and I'll text you my address."

He enters it into his cell as I rattle it off. A few seconds later my phone pings with his text. An odd thrill runs through me. I don't give my number out easily. Especially not to strange, attractive men, but a part of me wanted him to have it. That same part also hopes he'll use it for more than business, which is absurd. I don't mix business with personal. Not anymore.

Which is why I've turned Kurt down the last three times he called to get together. As much as my body craved to have him over me, pounding into me I just couldn't give in. I shouldn't have given into him at all, it went against everything in me, but there was something intriguing about having a relationship that didn't go any deeper than the sexual. In the months since our last hook up something changed for me. While I enjoyed the sex it left me feeling strangely dissatisfied.

My attraction to Nolan is a new song in the old refrain. My pattern. Hooking up with a guy I have no business getting together with or any intention of taking it to a deeper level. Not that Nolan's showed an ounce of interest in me. If anything I get the impression I bore him. I almost smile at the thought. That's good. A guy like him has to have a girlfriend anyway. So probably all of my insecure internal ramblings are for nothing.

"Thanks," I tell him, keying his name into my phone.

Cora rises. "I'm going to go make copies of the coroner's report. Do you want me to make any extras?"

"Actually, yes. I'd like a copy for myself that I can bring home with me at night."

"Can you make an extra copy for me too?" Nolan asks.

His request surprises me. Some of my astonishment must show on my face because he tilts his head and smiles at me. He waits until Cora leaves with the file, then leans across the table toward me.

"I can't be a workaholic too?"

"Are you?"

"Yeah. Sometimes. When it's important."

"What plans do you have to cancel to go to the prison with me tomorrow? Because I know you had something going on."

He leans back in his seat one brow raised. "Ms. Garcia are you asking me if I have a date tomorrow?"

"No," I blurt out. "Of course not." But that's exactly the information I was stupidly angling for.

"I have plans to go fishing tomorrow with some guy friends. I can go next time they go out. No biggie."

"You don't have to explain to me—"

"Not that you would ask, but I don't have a girlfriend. So I have lots of empty nights to go over coroner reports and do some side work on the case. I'm guessing you have a similar situation?"

"I don't fish, but yes. Lots of empty nights."

That smile again. Short-lived and showy. It's quite devastating. I pull my gaze from him and fix it on the papers in front of me. Carla stares back at me. She's the reason I'm here and I'd better start remembering it.

"This case is important to you."

I raise my gaze. "They're all important to me."

"But this one's special. You get this determined look on your face and a little line right here." He motions between his eyebrows with a finger. "Your lips kind of press together and your nostrils get bigger. I can almost hear the wheels turning in your head."

"My nostrils don't *get bigger*."

"Flair. Whatever. I'm right though, aren't I? What is it about this case that gets your motor running? Why is it so personal for you?"

"It's not—"

"Ms. Garcia, don't bullshit a bullshitter."

"I'm not."

He glances down at the duplicate file in front of him. "She kind of looks like you. Is she family?"

"What? All Mexican's look the same to you?"

"Whoa. You don't know me well enough to insult me."

He slams the folder closed and clasps his hands on top of it. "Never mind. Forget I asked."

I let out a sigh. I really need to learn how to be less defensive. "She does look a little bit like my cousin, Alicia."

He doesn't say anything just stares steadily at me.

"Carla and I share some things in our pasts. That's all I feel comfortable telling you. It's really none of your business."

"I should've known it would be a complicated answer. You're not exactly an uncomplicated woman."

"What does *that* mean?"

"It means you're interesting." He mumbles something that sounds suspiciously like *and hot as hell* as Cora comes back into the room. That smile makes a sudden, fleeting reappearance.

My stomach does a slow roll low in my belly.

"Here's your original." Cora hands me a folder, then another. "And your copy." She gives a file to Nolan and keeps the fourth for herself. "I have another appointment that's just arrived. Are you two okay in here?"

"We're fine." Nolan gives her the same smile he just gave me and I feel like an idiot, thinking I was special. "We'll come up with a game plan for tomorrow and I'll shoot you an email tomorrow night with a recap of our prison visit."

"Sounds good." Cora turns to me with her hand out. "It was nice meeting you, Lila. We'll work very hard for Carla. I guarantee it."

I shake her hand. "Nice meeting you too. I look forward to seeing what your team comes up with." When she's gone I turn back to Nolan to find him watching me. "What?"

"You know I'm pretty much her *team*, right?"

"Well I do now."

"Don't sound so disappointed. I think we're going to do great things together."

The way he says it makes me think of all the *great things* we could do together. I really need to find a new pattern and stop lusting after men I can emotionally distance myself from. Men like Nolan Perry.

3

NOLAN

I lean against the low wall out in front of my apartment complex waiting for Lila to pick me up. I'm surprisingly nervous about today. It's not a date, but apparently my body didn't get the memo because I'm sweating buckets in the cool winter air. A line trickles down my back and I rub at the base of my spine to keep it from rolling right on down into my ass crack. This happens every time. I'm a sexy, smooth, mother effing beast when I meet a woman I really like. Right. I'm an idiot. Once again I'm attracted to a woman I have no business getting the hots for.

But damn she's pretty.

The longer I sat in that conference room with her the more she charmed me. By the end of the meeting she made me totally forget about my insane, going-nowhere crush on Cora. I even tried to flirt with her. But like usual my lame attempts were wasted on a woman who has absolutely no interest in me. Like zero. I may as well have been putting the moves on the chair next to me. Every time she brushed me off I liked her a little bit more.

There must be something seriously wrong with me.

She pulls up in what my dad would call a reliable sedan. The kind of car he gets for my mom. It doesn't fit what I'd pictured Lila driving and yet it does. No nonsense. Dependable. Stable. That's her. I wonder what she'd look like in my truck. She'd probably take one look at my jacked up truck and make some comment about how I was compensating for something. I like big trucks with maxed out rims and big, fat tires. Sitting up high above the rest of traffic with my wrist slung over the top of the steering wheel, gives me an indescribably high. I bought one of my mom's cast-off cars for surveillance to help me blend in, but it's boring to drive.

I climb in the passenger seat and look over at Lila. She's got tight jeans on with boots and a sweater that is doing amazing things for her tits. Damn. I hadn't realized how stacked she was. Her long black hair is down. Double damn. It's shiny and thick and I have to shove my hand under my thigh to keep from reaching over to touch it. She smells good too. Spicy. Sexy. Mouthwatering. I didn't notice that yesterday. I want to lean over and nuzzle her neck just under her ear where the scent will probably be strongest.

This is going to be a long ass car ride.

"Hey," I say, thankful it didn't come out as an embarrassing squeak, and praying my deodorant is doing its job.

"Hey." She gives me a cursory once over and I can't tell a damn thing from her expression. "I passed a Starbucks a block or so back. That okay?"

"Sure."

She waits until I've buckled my seatbelt before checking her mirror and pulling back out onto the street. I direct her to Starbucks and we place our individual orders. She gets one of those sweet coffee drinks with about twelve kinds of syrups pumped into it and sauces zigzagged up the side of the cup. It's topped with whipped cream and sprinkles. Just looking at it makes the roof of my mouth itch. I get my usual Café Americano and we're back on the road again. I point her toward the freeway and join the scant few folks who didn't get to sleep in on a Saturday.

Her radio's tuned to some classical music station. Not too loud. Between that and the hum of the tires on the road I'm glad we stopped for coffee or else I'd be nodding off. I stayed up late last night pouring over Carla's case and making a list of questions I want to ask her. I secretly hope all of my work will impress Lila. Dumb, huh?

"Have you met Carla before?" I ask, needing the conversation to keep myself awake.

"No. This will be the first time. I spoke to her on the phone right after I got assigned her case, but we didn't get into any more than the barest introductions." There's a pause. "She cried."

Lila's profile is partially obscured by her hair, but the slight tremor on the word *cried* lets me know how affected she was by that one, brief phone call. It's clear this case has some kind of special meaning for her. If I can crack what that is I might have a shot at cracking the mystery that is Lila. World-class poker players have nothing on her. She's stone-faced and placid as calm water. Is she really that composed or is it a well-honed façade?

"I hope we find a way to get her released. The sooner the better. She really got screwed over by the system."

She flickers a glance my direction like something I said surprised her. "Yeah. She did."

"I made an appointment at four o'clock today with Debbie Martin, the defense attorney's wife. She's still living in their house. I'm hoping she'll let us go through his home office. There might be a duplicate copy of the work he did on Carla's case. Or maybe some notes or something. I hope that's okay. I wasn't sure if you had plans..."

"You could've texted and asked. But no, I don't."

"I wasn't sure of the protocol here." God I sound lame. Like a giant doofus.

"If it's about the case you can text me anytime, okay?"

I nod which is dumb because her eyes are on the road so she can't see me. She looks over at me again a little longer this time. I wish she'd turn the AC on. It's freakin' hot in here. Every time I inhale I take her in scent, which is damn distracting. Her hands rest lightly on the wheel at ten and two just like she was probably taught in driver's ed. She checks her mirrors at regular intervals and signals every lane change. She's the poster child for proper driving. A rule follower to the max.

She's short so her seat is pulled all the way forward, practically cramming her up against the wheel. Her breasts brush it every time she looks over her shoulder to make a lane change. I wonder if it's the friction that made her nipples hard or something else. It sure as heck isn't the temperature in here. *Is it getting hotter?* I could swear the heat just went up a couple of degrees. I rub my sweaty palms on my jeans. She notices the movement.

"Do you mind if I crack the window?" I ask.

She hits the buttons and both of our windows go down a couple inches.

"Thanks."

"Sure."

I resist the urge to sniff myself because I know she didn't roll hers down because she's hot. Damn. I probably stink. We ride in silence for a while. The cool air is helping. I can't smell her as much anymore and I finally stop sweating like beast. To refocus my mind I take out the list of questions I have for Carla. One of the biggest is what was she doing when her son died? Why didn't she notice he had the elastic cord around his neck and was slowly suffocating to death?

I'm not sure how to present the question without accusation. Because there's a big truckload of blame to lay at her feet. She was the adult in charge. She should've noticed *something*. At least the silence. Kids are loud. I know that from spending five minutes with my cousin's kids at Christmas. What was she doing that she didn't realize that her kid was unusually quiet? Why did it take her so long to reach him that the paramedics couldn't revive him either at the scene or in route to the hospital? The doctors didn't have any better luck. They called his death shortly after he arrived at the hospital.

Diego died in the same small, crappy apartment in the next room from where his mother supposedly was. It was too early for him to have been in bed. Why was he in that room alone with the door closed? It just doesn't add up for me. How do I get answers to my questions without sounding like one of the cops who coerced her into confessing? And how do I do it in front of Lila? Especially given how close she seems to be to this case.

Maybe I'll get lucky and Lila will ask them for me. Ha. I wish.

"Are those your notes on the case?"

I look up to find Lila glancing back and forth between the road and the notebook resting on my thighs. I know she's trying to get a peek at my notes, but the thought that she's interested in anything in and around my lap has me shifting in my seat.

"Ah, yeah," I say.

"Tell me about them."

"They're questions really. That I was thinking about asking Carla."

She makes a motion with one of her hands, taking it off the wheel momentarily, that invites me to elaborate. Here goes nothing.

"I was wondering what Carla was doing when Diego died." There. It's out. I wait for what comes next—censure, anger, annoyance. I just don't know.

"I have the same question myself. Since Carla didn't testify at trial no one asked her that."

I relax a little in my seat. "Why was Diego in a closed room alone? It was too late for a nap and too early for bed. Not that I know much about kids, but nine o'clock in the morning seems like a strange time to put a kid down. Why didn't she check on him until it was too late to save him?"

She nods, her lips pressed into a grim line. "Yeah. I had the same thoughts."

"Any guesses?"

"One or two, but I'd prefer to hear it from Carla."

I want to ask her what her guesses are, but if she were going to share she already would've.

She gives my notes another look. "What other questions do you have?"

"I was wondering why her kid wasn't in school. I mean, aren't most four year olds in preschool or something?"

"That's a very privileged thing to say."

"What does *that* mean?"

"It means that most immigrants don't make enough to pay for preschool. They're too busy trying to feed their kids."

"You're twisting my words, making me sound like a racist."

"Which is exactly the kind of thing a racist says."

I shift toward her in my seat. *Is she serious?* "Are you serious? Is that what you assume about me from the what? two hours we've known each other?"

"No. I got it from the racist thing you just said."

"I was in no way being a racist. Ignorant of immigrant issues, yes. But not a racist." Now I'm getting hot for a whole *other* reason. "You've got a chip on your shoulder the size of Texas, you know that? Don't project your issues onto me. You don't know anything about me."

"*My* issues?"

"*Your* issues. Maybe you're the racist here."

She jerks the wheel changing lanes so suddenly I have to grip the door handle to keep from tipping over into her lap. We swerve across the three lanes to the shoulder where she brings the car to an abrupt stop, making my seatbelt tighten as I jerk forward then back in my seat.

"What the hell was that?" I demand.

"Where do you get off calling *me* a racist?"

"Where do *you* get off calling *me* a racist?"

She twists in her seat. Air puffs in and out between her lips as her chest rises and falls, making her breasts swell up and down. Her cheeks are red and her dark eyes narrow at me. Whoa is she hot.

"Don't say racist things if you don't want to be called a racist," she grinds out.

"I'll take my licks when I deserve them, but you're way out of line here. I don't know who screwed you over or how, but don't take it out on me. It was an honest, if ignorant, question. We're not going to get anywhere on this case if you turn on me every time I say something stupid. Because I can guarantee that I'm going to say *a lot* of stupid things by the time we're done here."

Her lips part in surprise. A truck honks its horn at us as

it passes. Several beats go by with us glaring at each other. We're close enough that I can smell the sweet coffee drink on her breath and see myself in her dark, reflective eyes. There's a lot going on behind them. *What is she thinking?*

I don't have to wait long to find out.

"You're honest." A corner of her lips tilts up. "I like that."

"Are we good now?"

"Good enough." She sits back in her seat and pulls the car back onto the freeway.

I have no idea what just happened or why, but I think I passed some kind of test with her. Which is pretty dang ironic since I've never been very good at tests. Especially given by a woman I'm interested in.

Hmm. Okay. I'm *interested* interested in her. Weird. I'm not sure I even *like* her. Especially after what just happened. She might be slightly insane. Which is probably *why* I'm attracted to her. I've been known to date women who are somewhat unstable. It's a thing with me. Which is why I haven't dated much lately.

My last girlfriend showed up at my apartment and asked if her boyfriend could stay at my place while he visited her because she lived with her parents and they still thought she was a virgin. Yeah. That's right. My girlfriend's *boyfriend*. She stopped being my girlfriend the second I slammed my front door in their faces. Unbalanced. Unpredictable. Unsuitable. Unattainable. Unyeilding. And all of the other *un* adjectives. The more *un-y* they are the more I seem to like them. Lila may as well be wearing a big giant UN on her forehead.

Man she's pretty though.

A short time later we pull up the prison and park. Lila gets out of the car without a word, goes around to the trunk, and opens it. I follow her not knowing what else to do.

"Empty your pockets and put everything inside," she

says as she powers off her phone. "We can't take anything into the prison so we may as well leave everything here. Shut your phone off so it doesn't ring and announce to would-be thieves that there's something more than the spare in here."

I do as she says, digging everything out of my pockets. I'm in the process of turning my phone off when something moves out of the corner of my eye.

"Plan on getting lucky some time today?" Lila twirls a condom between her fingers, flashing it back and forth.

I snatch it out of her hand. "A scout is always prepared." I drop it back into the pile with the rest of my stuff and slam the trunk closed.

"*Why did you do that*?"

"Do what?"

"The car key is in the trunk. How are we going to get out of here?"

"Call Triple—shit! Our cell phones."

She drops her head back and stares up at the sky. "What did I do? What could I possibly have done to deserve this?"

"It was an accident. And who leaves the keys to the car *in the trunk*?"

She glares at me. "The person with the keyless remote in her purse. That's who."

"I'm sure there's a phone we can use to call roadside assistance."

"That would be fine except they usually want the card number when you call. Mine's in my purse in the trunk. Where's yours?"

I close my eyes and lower my head. "In my wallet. In the trunk."

"Yup."

I mentioned that I'm kind of a fuck up, didn't I?

4

LILA

I felt really bad about the stupid fight I had with Nolan on the way out to the prison right up until he locked the keys in the trunk of the car. I'm kind of sensitive to subversive racism. The overt stuff I can handle. It's the double-meaning comments, the subtle injustice of being treated slightly differently that drives me nuts. It happens so down low that most people don't even know it's happening.

Like the time when my grocery store had a vodka tasting. The sign clearly indicated that they would card everyone who tasted. I was standing close by trying to choose a wine for a dinner party. A blond woman came up for a taste. The woman giving out the samples was very chatty with her. Then a black woman who was clearly older than the blond woman approached the table. The sample lady carded the black woman. She never carded the white woman. See what I mean? Subtle. Subversive. But there all the same.

That's the kind of discrimination I can't abide. It's what keeps minorities like me—like Carla—on the other side of the line. Most people will probably think I'm being overly sensitive, looking for something that's just not there. But it's there. It's *always* there.

I know Nolan didn't mean his comment the way I took it. He's not a bad guy. A little goofy. Maybe a little absent-minded. I can tell he wants to be helpful. He's driven in a way he doesn't have to be. After all, there's no money in this case for him. He's not getting paid a cent to be here with me today or for any of the work he'll do. I need to remember that and stop being so hard on him. He doesn't deserve it. It doesn't hurt that he's earnest and cute. Not really my type physically, but there's something about him that seems to light a fire in me. Maybe that's why I've been such a bitch to him. Distance. That's what I'm trying to get here. Distance and perspective.

I sigh inwardly and vow to not be so rigid and quick to draw the wrong conclusions with him. It's not really his fault about the key in the trunk either. I embarrassed him. What was that thing he said about it? Oh, yeah.

"You were a boy scout?" I ask, trying not to check out his ass as he bends over to see if there's anyway he can open the trunk.

"Mmm. Eagle Scout."

"So you know how to do stuff like start a fire and pitch a tent."

He glances up at me and I realize the double meaning in my words. My whole face goes hot.

"I didn't mean... I mean you can do survival stuff," I stammer.

"Yeah." He straightens, leaning a hand on the trunk. "If we're ever stranded in the woods I gotchya. What I don't have is a way to open the car."

"If we can borrow a phone I can see if my sister can drive up with the spare key."

"You don't have that service where they can unlock your car by satellite, do you?"

"No. I didn't want to pay extra for that."

He nods. "I'm sorry I got us stranded here."

"I'm sorry I teased you about the condom."

"I carry it more out of habit than a necessity. Especially lately."

It's the second time he's mentioned being unattached since I met him. I'm not sure what to make of it except I'm happier about the reminder than I should be. He's interested and not being very subtle about it.

"I know what you mean," I say quietly.

"Yeah?"

I nod. My gaze catches on his lips, which are unexpectedly fuller than most guy's. There's a pull between us, an invisible thread that seems to connect us. I can feel it getting tighter and shorter as he leans in. Or is that me? I put a hand on his chest to steady myself. Beneath my hand his body is hot, far hotter than the weather would explain. But I'm not thinking about anything except how close he is now. He smells like a man in an earthy, essential way.

I look up into his eyes. He's watching, waiting, drawing me in without moving an inch. His focus shifts to my mouth and fixes there. And then he leans down, moving so slowly it seems to take forever for our lips to meet. They brush together once, twice. A pause. He shifts closer and comes at me again this time with more purpose. His mouth is hot on mine. I tease the seam of his lips and taste coffee. His body is flush against me, but his hands stay where they are. Mine snake around his neck and pull him in.

It's like he suddenly woke up and realized we were kissing because without warning his arms are around me. One hand plunges into my hair. His other arm bands around my waist, hauling me up fully against him. I groan into his mouth at the feel of him. He tilts his head, taking the kiss deeper. Oh, man it's good. There's nothing but him and me and the way our bodies press together in all the right places. The kiss winds down slowly from an all out assault to barely there brushes. We part and stare in shock at each other.

Where did *that* come from?

It was like the rumbling of a freight train in the distance and then all of a sudden it was barreling toward me and I was too slow to get out of the way. Then it hit and all I could do was hurtle along with it. There was no stopping it. I had to give over to it and see where it would take me. Like an out of body experience.

"Wow," he whispers.

"Uhnn." Is all I can manage. I can't put two coherent thoughts together let alone organize them enough to articulate.

"That was...*wow*."

A car pulls in next to us and it's like an alarm goes off inside me. I startle. *What am I doing?* Carla's inside that prison waiting for us and we're out here making out like we don't have anything else to do but scratch an itch.

"We shouldn't have... I mean it was... But we shouldn't have." I make a back and forth motion between us. "You know."

"Yeah. I know. You're right. We shouldn't." He studiously stares at a point beyond my shoulder. "Maybe we should go inside. Try to find a phone we can use. Talk to Carla." He stares at my mouth like he wants to fall into my face and pick up where we left off. "Definitely *not* kiss again."

"Absolutely." I put a hand up like I'm gong to hold him back, then remember that was how this whole thing started in the first place. I fist my hand and drop it to my side. "We should *absolutely* not do that again."

"That would be bad."

"Very, very bad."

"Okay." He sucks in a breath and takes a step back. "Okay." He gestures for me to go ahead of him. "After you."

"Right." I force myself to turn on my heel and walk toward the prison entrance.

He's checking out my ass. I can almost feel his gaze like a touch, a light pressure followed by a rush of heat up my spine...and elsewhere. A couple steps later he falls in next to me. His hands are shoved deep into his front pockets like he has to corral them so they don't wander where he doesn't want them to go. I'm trying to sort out what exactly happened back there and what it means going forward. I don't have time to start something new. I don't *want* to start something new.

We enter the building. I go to the window to see if it's possible to use their phone while Nolan veers off in another direction. A flash of irritation goes through me, but I breathe through it and politely ask the guard behind the window if we could borrow his phone. He asks for my ID, which is in the trunk.

He shrugs. "Sorry. Nothing I can do."

Great. I thank him and turn around to see where Nolan's wandered off to in time to see him approaching with a guy in some kind of uniform.

"This is Ted," he says. "That's his tow truck in the parking lot. He says he can get your car doors open no problem, right Ted?"

"For twenty bucks."

"Our wa—" I start.

Nolan cuts in. "No problem."

"Follow me out to my truck," Ted says.

I give Nolan a *what was that?* look as we head back out to the parking lot.

He leans down next to my ear, making all of the fine hairs on my neck rise. "Better not to mention we don't actually have the money right now."

"Oh. Right," I say a little too breathlessly.

In no time Ted pops the door locks. I immediately open the trunk and retrieve my purse. Nolan pulls a twenty out of his wallet and hands it to Ted at the same time I do.

"No," Nolan says, pushing my hand away. "It's my fault. I'll pay."

Ted takes the money from Nolan and goes back inside the prison. The first thing I do is take the key fob out of my purse and slip it into my pocket along with my ID. We head back into the prison in silence. I can tell that Nolan still feels bad about the trunk incident. We check in with the guard behind the window and take a seat to wait.

"All's well that ends well," I offer, trying to smooth things over and get them back to where they were pre kiss.

"That *was* a lucky break," he agrees, but there's still something troubling him.

"I'm not mad. I mean, I was, but I'm not anymore."

He gives half a nod and turns away to watch the TV playing quietly near the corner of the ceiling. I fold my arms and look the other direction at the other TV hanging on the opposite side of the room. We stay that way until they call our names to go in and see Carla. The screening process while not quick is efficient and we're soon entering the visitor room. We take an empty table and wait for Carla. Nolan's been quiet the whole time. I shouldn't care what he thinks. We're just coworkers after all, but his sudden change of mood throws me off.

"Is something wrong?" I ask.

"No." He doesn't look at me, giving all of his attention to the door Carla will walk through.

"Why are you quiet all of a sudden then?"

"I'm thinking."

"About what?"

His gaze stays on the door. "About how I want to kiss you again."

A small atomic bomb goes off in my chest and I have to swallow before I can answer. "I thought we agreed that would be a bad idea."

"It's a horrible idea."

"Then stop thinking about it."

"I can't." He turns to me. "Can you?"

"This isn't the time to talk about this."

"I'll take that as a *no*."

"That doesn't change anything."

"Actually," he says with a hint of a smirk. "That changes a whole lot of things."

"I don't—" Carla comes through the door cutting me off, which is good. I didn't like the direction the conversation was headed. "There she is." She has no idea what I look like because we've never met so I wave to get her attention.

She eases into the chair across from us. "Lila Garcia?"

"Yes," I speak to her in Spanish like I did on the telephone so she'll feel more comfortable. "It's nice to finally meet you. This is Nolan Perry. He's helping me with your case."

"*Mucho gusto* Carla," he says with a really bad accent. I give him points for the effort.

"Nice to meet you too," Carla responds in Spanish. "What do you do?"

Nolan looks to me. It seems as though we've reached his limit for the language.

"He's a private investigator," I answer for him. "He's going to help us locate your neighbor Inez Torres. Any idea on where we might be able to find her?"

"Inez had family in Jalisco just outside of Guadalajara. She talked about moving back there. She has a sister who lives there. But I don't really know. It's been a long time. She could've passed."

"I couldn't find any record of her death so I'm assuming she's still alive. Any other ideas where she might go? Somewhere in the states maybe?"

"She only talked about going back to Mexico. She was older, close to my mother's age. You know how they reminisce about home." Her gaze strays to Nolan then back to me. "He's really a private investigator?"

"Yes. Why?"

"Seems kind of young...and cute. Not like the PI's on TV."

I laugh and Nolan smiles like he's in on the joke, making me wonder if he can understand what we're saying. Better to change the subject. "We're also trying to find your attorney John Martin. His wife filed a missing person report shortly after your trial. He just disappeared."

"Disappeared? I don't understand."

"Was there anything unusual about him? Anything he might have said or you might have overheard that might help us find him?"

"It's not liked we talked a lot and we didn't talk at all after the trial. He told me what to do and I did it. I didn't get to ask a whole lot of questions." She leans in and lowers her voice. "I've been studying about the law. He didn't do a good job on my case. He let them prosecute me when there was no crime. He didn't call any witnesses on my behalf. It was like he wanted to lose my case."

"Did he give you anything or show you anything that might help?"

"No. Nothing. That asshole was worse than no lawyer at all."

Nolan interrupts. "Did you ask her the questions we talked about in the car?"

"Not yet," I tell him. Then to Carla, "We have to ask you some tough questions. Please be as honest as you can. There's no judgment. We need all of the information you can give us to help you."

She glances over at Nolan who is patiently listening even if he doesn't understand everything we're saying. "What do you want to know?"

"Why was Diego left alone so long in that bedroom? Why didn't you check on him sooner?"

Wrapping her arms around herself, she sits back in her seat. Her gaze slinks away to somewhere on the floor to her left. I can feel Nolan's stare on the side of my face. I can't look at him. All of my attention is fixed on Carla. I have an idea of what her answer might be from talking to some of her acquaintances. I wouldn't ask, but this *will* come up if we can get her case before a judge. She'll have to answer this question and more just as difficult as this one.

"I was behind on the rent," she starts, her words halting and forced. "I needed more time to come up with the money. If I let my landlord do whatever he wanted he'd give me more time, sometimes take it off my rent."

"You mean sex?"

She nods.

"How long was Diego alone that day?"

"An hour. Maybe a little more. I wanted to go check on him, but..."

"I understand." I need to get her off this subject that's causing her so much pain. I know her shame. The guilt...it must be unbearable. If only she'd checked in on him... I shut down that thought and redirect the conversation. "Tell me about Diego. What was he like?"

Her gaze swings back to me and it's like someone turned on a light inside her. "Sweet. So sweet. And good. He was the best. I miss him. So much."

"I hear he liked superheroes."

"Mmm, yes. Spiderman was his favorite. He liked to pretend—" She breaks off and I can see her visibly gather herself to continue. "He made a cape with the old bed sheet. I tried to throw it away, but he had such a fit. I didn't think...I never imagined. He didn't have very many toys. So I gave in. I wish I'd thrown it away."

"It's not your fault. It was an accident."

"A stupid accident." She picks at something on her arm. "Will I have to talk about what I was doing that day?"

"Probably. But I'll be right there with you."

"Will you do something for me?"

"Sure. What?"

"Will you take some flowers to his grave. Maybe take a picture of it for me. I don't know where he is. My parents wouldn't tell me. They blame me for what happened. Maybe they're right."

"They're not right. There's no one to blame here."

She doesn't say anything, absorbed in her own tortured thoughts.

Again I hate to ask, but... "What was the name of your old landlord?"

"Hector Rodriguez."

I go for another redirect. "Did your lawyer ever have anyone with him when he came to see you in prison?"

She looks up at the ceiling like she's thinking. "There was this man once... He poked his head in the room to say something to Mr. Martin. He didn't see me at first. When he finally did he left right away. I knew him."

"From where? Who was he?"

She has the same expression she had when I asked her what she was doing when Diego died and she won't look at me all of a sudden.

"Carla? Who was he?"

"I don't know his name."

"What do you know about him?"

"I knew him like I knew my landlord."

"You had sex with him?"

She nods.

"For money?"

She nods again.

"Did Mr. Martin use the man's name or say anything that might give you an idea who the man was to Mr. Martin?"

"No, but I think Mr. Martin worked for him."

"What makes you say that?"

"It was how they talked to each other. The man did all the asking and Mr. Martin did all the answering. I didn't understand very much English back then—not as much as I do now—so I don't know what they were talking about."

"Can you describe him for me?"

"White. Brown hair. Blue eyes. He had a tattoo on his chest, the word *sacrifice*, and one on his left calf of a dagger with a ribbon wrapped around it with words."

"How did you meet him?"

"He drove up and I got in his car. He came back a few

more times almost like a regular. Then Diego died and I didn't work anymore."

"Where did he take you when you got in his car?"

"I told him where to go. Suede, my handler, had this motel for us to take our customers."

"How many times did you see him?"

She shrugs one shoulder. "Six. Eight times. I don't know. Maybe more. He wanted to get together and didn't want to track me down. I had a phone number I gave out for that. Suede took care of my appointments. We met at the same motel every time."

"What was the name of the motel?"

"The Lucky Inn on Second Avenue. Downtown."

We talk for a full hour. All the while Nolan sits patiently, smiling reassuringly at Carla whenever she glances at him. I don't learn anything new, but I do learn quite a bit about Carla as a person and as a mother. She loved her son. His death devastated her. She's more confused than angry about being convicted for his death. I'm not sure I'd feel the same as her. I'm so angry *for* her there's no doubt in my mind that I'd be blind with rage if I was in her place.

We say goodbye and as I reach the door to leave I look back to find her watching us. She looks so lost and alone I want to go to her and hug her but that's not allowed. I have to remember the warning they gave us in law school to not get attached to our clients or too invested in the outcome of their cases.

But as Carla holds up a hand in goodbye before turning to go back to her cell I have a hard time separating myself from her. *She is me and I am her* is a chant in my head as I walk out of the prison a free woman.

5

NOLAN

Lila fills me in on her conversation with Carla. I take notes, jotting down names and places. Her tone is flat, her eyes on the road. She rests her elbow on the car door and rubs at her forehead as though she has a headache. I wish the Lila who argued with me and accused me of being a racist would come back. I don't much like her, but she's imminently more tolerable this this subdued, sad version of Lila. The visit caused her pain. She's right. There are things she's experienced that I will never know. Things she and Carla have both been through that are foreign to me.

We don't talk about the kiss. We especially don't talk about what we think about it or why it happened. There's a third passenger in the car, hanging its arms over our shoulders, trying to get us to acknowledge it—the improbable attraction between us. I know she can feel it. I'm not even sure she likes me, but she's thinking about that kiss. Maybe not as obsessively as I am. But she's thinking about it and that will have to be enough for now.

Glancing down at the notes I made of the meeting, I'm

struck by how much work there is to do. We have to track down the neighbor, Carla's landlord, her attorney, and a mysterious man who paid to have sex with her. It was hard for Lila to tell me about what Carla did to support herself and her son. I think she thinks I'll be judgmental about it. I'll admit that there was a moment or two where I had a hard time not thinking badly about Carla for screwing her landlord while her child suffocated to death in the next room. I'm still having trouble with that. I think Lila is too although she would never admit it.

Now I understand why they put Carla on suicide watch when she was arrested. I imagine she blames herself for Diego's death. She was *right there* in the next room. The what if's must have nearly broken her. They probably still do. I don't know how she deals with it on top of the loss of her child. Pain is etched into her features, making her look older than twenty-three. She lost everything that day. Her son and her whole family. Lila told me that Carla's parents haven't spoken to her since Diego died. I can't imagine what that must be like.

My family is small but we're tight. I glance at Lila and wonder if she's close to her family. I want to learn more about her. What makes her tick. What her likes and dislikes are. What gets her hot. What makes her sigh. What makes her beg for *more*.

I glance out the window, trying to put the brakes on those thoughts. This isn't the time or the place. The only consolation is that she's just as messed up about that kiss as I am. What she'll do about it is a total unknown. I'd better back off...for now. Better to give her some room. This case is messing with her head. She's gone from the calm, cool, and collected woman in charge I met in the office to the pissed off, chip-on-her-shoulder woman on the defense I met on the car ride out to the prison to the hotter-than-the-California-desert woman turned on by my kiss to the contemplative, saddened woman identifying with her client I'm faced with now.

"Do you want me to reschedule with Mrs. Martin?" I ask, trying to coax her out of her funk.

"No. I don't want her to change her mind about helping us."

"I doubt it. She thinks we're going to help her find her missing husband. She doesn't know the real reason we're coming to see her."

She whips her head my direction. "*What?*"

"I wasn't sure how cooperative she'd be if I told her we thought her husband was an incompetent hack who caused an innocent woman to go to prison for a crime she didn't commit."

"What exactly did you tell her?"

"I told her that I was a PI, working with the police on cold cases. You're my assistant by the way."

"I'm your— Why?"

"I thought I covered that with the whole can't-tell-her-that-her-husband-screwed-up explanation."

"Do you lie often in your line of work?"

"Almost constantly. This might shock you, but people generally don't want to talk to PIs. We're not like cops where people feel compelled to spill their guts. So sometimes we have to improvise. This is me improvising and getting us info we might not get any other way."

"Any legitimate way you mean."

"Yeah. Pretty much."

"It's that easy for you to lie?"

"No. It's not easy, but it's necessary. It's taken me a while to get used to it. I'm not all that sure I'm very good at it."

"You have a point about the wife," she concedes. "She definitely wouldn't let us near her husband's files if she thought we were going to discredit him."

"I was thinking of subtly suggesting that her husband's disappearance might be linked to one of his cases, hoping she'll open his files to us. If there are any files. It's been long enough since he disappeared that his office files are probably in storage somewhere. His law office would never let us look through them. I'm betting everything that he kept a second set at home."

"The files I keep at home are a limited version of my office files, but there might be enough in there to give us some clue as to why he didn't put up his best defense. Before Carla's trial he had a pretty good record as a public defender."

"The wife also might know who the mystery man was who used to pay Carla for sex." I gesture toward the freeway exit. "Get off here and turn left."

"Good point. She'd know his coworkers." She eases the car off the freeway, stops at the light, and turns toward me with a slight smile. "Why can't *you* be *my* assistant?"

"Because I'm the PI." I considered her for a moment. "Is it going to be tough for you to let me be in charge for a while?"

"Maybe."

I laugh. "I didn't have an issue with you being in charge back at the office or driving us today or with Carla. Does that make me more evolved than you?"

"Probably." The light changes and I get her profile again as she makes the turn. "I prefer being in control."

"Noted."

"That's not what I meant."

"What's not what you meant?"

"You took that to mean sexually."

"I took it to mean in every situation. In bed, out of bed. In the car, out of the car. In the office, out of the office. I have no problem with you being in charge by the way."

"Stop it."

"Make a right at the next light."

"I mean it. This thing, this whatever you think it is between us isn't a thing."

"So you admit there's something between us."

She makes an exasperated sound at the back of her throat. "I'm not doing this."

"Just because we're attracted to each other doesn't mean we have to act on it. I think you're right." I turn my head to look out the window like I'm bored when I'm really trying not to smile. "We should ignore it. Pretend there's nothing there. That kiss was a one off never to happen again."

I can feel her gaze on me. Taking a slow breath in for composure, I turn to look at her. There's a puzzled crease between her brows as we wait at another light. She studies me with the concentration of a scientist examining a specimen. I don't fit her mold for me. Good. I'm glad we're both at a loss as to how to deal with each other. I'd hate to be the only one struggling here. I also think she's right to a certain extent. I have a lot to prove with this case, a lot to make up for. Trying to get into the pants of a lawyer from the Freedom Project would probably be a really bad way to prove I'm a professional.

Not that she's not worth the effort. I just can't afford to give into the temptation that is her gorgeous, curvy body and beautiful face. But *damn*. What I'm giving up for my career.

"I'm glad you agree." But she doesn't sound like she

agrees. She sounds like she wishes I'd try to talk her into another kiss. Or three. Or something beyond kissing.

"Make a left where that white car is."

We ride the rest of the way in silence broken only by the directions I give her.

John Martin's house looks like every other house on the block only more run down. Like its occupants went on vacation for a month or two. The lawn is mostly dead except for the nearly knee-high weeds here and there. The screen door hangs loosely from its frame at a slight angle. There are two cars parked in the driveway. As we walk past them I notice one of them is covered in dust. Probably Mr. Martin's car. A trail of faded ceramic gnomes runs along the walk. The last one's been decapitated, the head totally gone.

I ring the bell, scanning the neighborhood. "We might want to talk to some of the neighbors," I whisper to Lila. "They might give us more info than the Mrs. You never know. Nosey neighbors can be a PI's best friend."

A woman answers the door. She's younger than I expected. More attractive too. But then I'm not really sure exactly what I expected.

"Hello, Mrs. Martin," I say. "I'm Nolan Perry from Nash Security and Investigations and this is my assistant Lila Garcia."

She holds the door open for us. "Come in."

The inside of the house is in much better shape than the outside. Everything's clean and tidy. The air smells like fresh baked cookies.

"Can I get you two anything to drink," Mrs. Martin asks. "I made some cookies. Chocolate chip."

Lila's stomach rumbles followed closely by mine and I realize that we never stopped to eat lunch.

"They smell wonderful," Lila says. "I'd love some cookies and milk if you have it."

"That actually sounds amazing," I tell her. "I'd love some too. Thank you, Mrs. Martin."

She laughs. "You sound like my kids. Please have a seat and call me Debbie." She waves toward the living room sofa. "I'll be right back."

Lila sits on the couch, but I roam the room, getting a feel for how the Martins lived. There's a neat little row of photographs on the mantel. Family vacation pictures from before Martin disappeared I'd guess since he's in them. There are two children—a boy and a girl. The four of them pose together in one frame. Another is of Mr. and Mrs. Martin alone, their arms around each other. This was clearly a happy family. Not the kind of family a man willingly leaves.

My mind circles back to the conversation I had with Cora and Lila about what might have happened to Martin. He's either dead or is unable in some other way to return to his life. I hope we find him for a whole set of new reasons. One of which is approaching us now.

Mrs. Martin—Debbie—returns with a tray filled with a plate of cookies and three glasses of milk. She sets it on the coffee table. I take a seat next to Lila in time to be handed a napkin and a small plate. Debbie sits in a chair to my left.

"Thank you," I say. "I was just admiring your family photos. That was Yellowstone, wasn't it?"

She looks wistfully at the mantel. "Yes. We took that trip just before John disappeared."

"How exactly did he *disappear*?"

Debbie examines a cookie like she's going to take a bite before laying it back down on the plate in her lap. "He left for work one day and just didn't come home. I called him in the afternoon, but he didn't answer. He'd do that if he was with a client or in the courtroom so I didn't think anything about it. Then when he didn't come home around the time he usually did I called him a second time. He didn't answer that call either. I didn't start to panic until a few hours later when he hadn't called or returned any of my texts. I knew something was wrong.

"I called the police and filed a missing persons report right away. They found his car parked where he usually parks at work, but no one in the office saw him come in. Somewhere between the parking lot and the office he vanished. I'm hoping you coming here today means that the police are looking into his disappearance again. Since the trail grew cold it seems like they gave up trying to find him."

"We'll do our best," I tell her. "Had he gotten any unusual phone calls in the days before his disappearance?"

"No. Not that I noticed."

"Did the police find his cell phone?"

"No. They tried to see if they could catch its signal, but the phone seems to have vanished with John. Don't you have all of this information from the police?"

"Some, but it doesn't hurt to go over it again with you. You knew him better than anyone. What was his mood in the days before he went missing? Did there seem to be anything bothering him?"

"No. Not that I noticed. Just the usual stresses."

"Did he have any visitors or change his schedule in anyway?"

"No. Everything was exactly as it always had been until the day he vanished."

I thought about this next question during the ride to the Martin house and just how I could phrase it to accomplish what we are really here to do. "Did he ever talk to you about any of his cases? Were there any that might have bothered him more than the others?"

"He talked to me about them in general terms. Mostly about his frustrations with a judge or opposing counsel. No specifics about the cases themselves. He believed deeply in privilege and had very high ethical standards for himself and those he worked with. It was one of the things I really loved about him, his devotion to his clients."

Beside me Lila chokes on her cookie and starts coughing.

I give her a couple of thumps on the back. "Are you okay?"

She nods and takes a sip of milk.

I turn back to Debbie when I'm sure Lila's okay. "Did he keep a home office?"

"Yes." She gestures over her shoulder. "Down the hall."

"Would you mind if we had a look?"

"The police already went through it."

"There might be something they overlooked in their initial investigation. You never know."

"I haven't touched it since..." She gives the hall a troubled look. "I suppose a fresh set of eyes couldn't hurt."

I have to put a hand on Lila's lower leg where Debbie can't see so she doesn't bolt up off the couch. "We'll be respectful of his space. We don't want to disturb anything just have a look around."

Debbie rises without a word and goes down the hall. Lila and I exchange a look in which I try to warn her to have patience and let me continue to lead. She looks up at the ceiling like she's searching for that patience and then nods her head in agreement. We follow Debbie to a closed door at the end of the hall.

"I haven't touched it," she says. "Not even to dust. I just can't bring myself to go in there."

"We understand." Lila rests a hand on Debbie's shoulder. "Thank you for letting us have a look around."

Debbie pulls a wad of keys out of her pocket, selects one, and unlocks the door. "I've got some things to do in the kitchen." She tears up a little. "Let me know when you're finished." She darts back down the hall without a backward glance.

Lila eyes the door like it's the entrance to a tomb.

"At least she won't know if we moved anything since she never goes in there," I say.

She gives me a look.

"*What*?"

"I know you're right and there's a bigger picture here, but there's something about what you just said that just isn't right."

"If you're doubting my sincerity just know that it's not with John Martin. It's with Carla. I'm not callous. I'm a realist. I feel bad for Debbie, but I don't give three shits about her worthless husband."

Turning the knob, I go into the room without waiting for her response. Just like the car, the entire room is covered in a fine layer of dust. Not only has Debbie not been in this room since Martin disappeared, her kids haven't either. There's a desk at the far end of the room facing the door. Behind it is a series of file cabinets. Martin was a pig. Candy and fast food wrappers clutter the desktop and overflow the trashcan. He must have chucked his soda bottles as he emptied them across the room because there's a pile of them in the corner.

"I'll be surprised if there aren't any rats or cockroaches in here," Lila whispers as she closes the door behind us with a shudder. "The rest of the house is so *clean*."

"Yeah, it's strange. You'd think she would've kept up with the trash. She wasn't joking that she never comes in here. I can't see her leaving this room like this if she knew how bad it was."

"Definitely not."

I immediately move to the file cabinets. They aren't labeled. I slip on a pair of latex gloves and try a few of the drawers, but they're all locked. I glance back at Lila. She's surveying the room like she doesn't know what to do.

"Lock the door, will you? Just in case." I pull out my set of lock picks and examine them, trying to decide which to try first.

"What are those," she asks in a stage whisper.

"Lock picks." I gesture toward the door. "Would you? I don't want to get caught by one of the kids or Debbie if she suddenly decides she wants to watch us."

"But won't it be weird if she tries the door and it's locked?"

"It'll be a lot less weird than walking in on me picking these locks."

Nolan clearly has no problem crossing lines I'm not comfortable with. I hesitate, wondering if I'm this person. If I'm someone who will do *anything* —including breaking the law—for my client. Nolan waits for me to decide. He's impatient, but not with me. He seems to know himself and is totally fine with bending the rules for a good cause.

How can he be so confident? Maybe because he's done this before and knows he'll do it again. It's part of his job— the lying and the law breaking. It's not part of mine. I've spent my whole life following the rules and trying not to stand out. This would be a huge change of character for me. Is this who I want to be?

And then I think of Carla and the look on her face as she went back to her cell. She's depending on me. I can't choke when things get hard. I have to live up to that trust even if it means doing something I'm not comfortable with. My hand moves toward the door. I watch it as though it's not mine. It's a traitor's hand. I flinch at the click of the lock. It's unusually loud in the quiet, dusty room.

When I look back at Nolan he's watching me with a knowing half smile. In the dim light filtering in through the half closed blinds he doesn't look as confident as I originally thought. Could what he does for his job bother him on some level? Is he just as conflicted as I am about what we're doing? As soon as I have the thought the look on his face changes to determination as he pulls a slim tool from the pouch in his hand and turns to the file cabinets.

"Why don't you take a look at the desk," he says over his shoulder.

The pop of the lock and the subsequent sliding of the file drawer makes me glance back at the door sure that Debbie must've heard the noise. After a moment or two I realize that no one is coming in to catch us.

"If you'd be more comfortable hanging out with Debbie or in the car, I'd understand."

"No. No. It's okay." I move toward the desk, curling my lip at the filth. "I just wish I had a pair of gloves."

He reaches into his pocket and pulls out a wad of something. "Here. I always carry two pairs."

It's then that I realize he's already wearing what look like surgical gloves. The wrongness of what we're doing washes over me again. I force myself to take the gloves and struggle to put them on. Nolan is already back flipping through the files by the time I manage get the gloves on. I want to look over his shoulder and at the same time I know that would be a step too far past my law-breaking threshold.

I eye the desk again. Disgusting. There are dried bits of food and liquids all over everything as though he ate every meal at this desk for years and never cleaned up. I lift a stack of folders and leaf through them. None of them have Carla's name or anything related to her case on them so I put them back careful match them up again with the blank spot in the dust. A tablet of paper rests next to his computer keyboard. I flip the pages that are folded back forward so I can look through them.

Behind me, Nolan closes a file drawer and opens a new one. I turn my attention back to the tablet. Martin's handwriting is as messy as his workspace. On the fourth page in I'm able to decipher a word that looks like 'Ruiz', Carla's last name.

"I think I've got something here," I tell Nolan.

"Take a picture with your phone and move on. We don't have a lot of time here."

I snap pics of the page and several more after that, then fold the pages back the way they were and put the tablet back. There's another scrap of paper with Diego's name on it half waded up. I smooth it out and take a picture of it before crumpling it up again. The interior of the desk yields absolutely nothing except an old fashioned phone book the kind my parents use to keep our relatives address and phone numbers in. I photograph every page, having no idea if any of it is even relevant to what we're looking for.

"What about the computer?" I ask.

He looks up from the file his taking pictures of. "Jiggle the mouse. See if it comes to life."

I do as he says and am shocked that the screen lights up. There's no password to get into it. I minimize the Word doc he had open for a summation he was writing for another case and check out the desktop, looking for something with Carla's name on it.

Nolan bumps my hip. I look down to find him holding out a thumb drive to me. "Download anything that looks important. Start with his emails if you can."

Another threshold to cross. I try not to think about it as I take the flash drive, at the same time ignoring how prepared for stealing Nolan is. Armed with the little gadget I turn back to the computer. There's an Outlook icon on the desktop. I click it and am shocked that it's not password protected. I make note to firm up my own security. I bet Nolan could help me with that.

I type Carla's name into the search box first for his incoming mail, then his outgoing mail and trash folder. As quick as I can I highlight everything and send a copy of it all to the thumb drive. I close out of that program and send the file marked 'Ruiz' on the desktop to the flash drive without even opening it. We're running out of time. I can almost hear a clock counting down the time until Debbie comes in and catches us.

There's another folder with a number instead of a name. I send that and just about everything else to the USB drive without even knowing if it's relevant. When I'm done I pull the stick out and bring the summation back up again. I blow on the dust on a stack of books next to the computer so it scatters across the keyboard, disguising the fact that the computer was tampered with.

"Nice," Nolan says in approval. "Good thinking."

I'm not proud that I thought to cover my tracks. Quite the opposite.

"If you're done there take some pictures of the room— close ups of things and the whole room in general."

I do as he says and take a picture of the whole desk. I go around the room snapping things here and there. I have no idea what's important and what's not. I'm getting a really icked out feeling the longer we're in here and it's not just because of the filth. It's almost like we're being watched. I wrap my arms around me on a shiver.

"Are you all right?" he asks.

"I don't know. I feel weird. Like someone's watching us."

His head comes up from the drawer he was looking through. He closes it and starts to wander the room, checking out objects here and there. He pulls out a flashlight and switches it on to examine the ceiling vent, then moves on to the bust of President Kennedy in the corner.

"Son of a bitch," he whispers. Lifting the bust from its resting place, he flips it over. "Hello there." He reaches into the neck and pulls out a small black box with a wire and small circular thing attached. "Gotchya." He lifts a small chip from the box and puts it in his pocket. From his other pocket he pulls a similar card and inserts it into the box, then puts the whole contraption back inside the bust the way he found it and sets it back on the pedestal. He keeps his hand over JFK's eyes.

He looks up at me and whispers. "Good work. Always follow your instincts. Can you get the door? Time to go."

He's so calm it's almost spooky. I have no idea what happened other than we were indeed being watched and possibly recorded. I'm totally on board with getting the hell out of here. I unlock the door and check down the hall.

"All clear," I whisper.

He slides his hand off the eyes of the bust, staying just out of range of the camera and slips out the door after me. I pull my gloves off like he's doing. He takes both pairs and stuffs them in his pocket.

"Let's go find Debbie and say goodbye."

We get to the end of the hall just as Debbie comes out of the kitchen toward us. An explosion of panic goes off inside me. Was she the one watching us look through her husband's office? Or was the timing just coincidental? If it wasn't her, who was it?

"We just got a call about another case and have to go," Nolan tells her smoothly. He holds his hand out to her.

"Thank you for letting have a look around your husband's office."

"Did you find anything useful?" she asks.

"We'll be in touch if we have any news about your husband." He grips my arm and tows me toward the door.

"Thank you for the milk and cookies," I manage to mumble. I'm so freaked out I'm shaking.

Nolan's hand moves up my arm to my back as we go down the front walk. I look over my and Nolan's shoulders to find Debbie standing in the doorway, frowning after us.

"Damn it," Nolan spits out as he opens the car door for me.

"What the hell happened back there?"

"We almost got fucked. And not in a good way. Are you okay?"

He wraps his arms around me and rubs up and down my back. I curl into his embrace, tucking my arms between us. I like the way his arms feel around me way too much, but I'm past caring about keeping him at a distance right now. There are more important things going on. I look back at the house, but the door is now closed and Debbie is gone.

"The good thing is that the camera wasn't on a live feed." He tightens his embrace and I snuggle deeper into it. "We should be okay. I think."

"What do you mean *you think*?"

"I've got the SD card. Hey, you're okay." He kisses the top of my head. "I've got you."

"We shouldn't have gone into that office. It was wrong."

"It's what I do."

"I don't like what you do."

"Sometimes I don't like it either. Especially when I screw up. Damn it. I should've checked for cameras when we first went into the room. I hope it was the only one."

I groan. "Don't say that."

"It probably was the only one." He looks up and down the street. "We need to get out of here. Give me your keys."

I hand them over and he helps me into the car. It doesn't occur to me until we've pulled away from the curb that I did indeed let him take charge and it doesn't feel weird or frightening. It feels...comfortable. Safe. I don't look too hard at that or at how reassuring it is to have him next to me in the car right now. He handles my car with ease and competence.

"Do you have the USB cable for your phone?" he asks.

His question confuses me for a second and then I remember the photos I took. "Yeah."

He takes an unfamiliar series of turns and I realize he's taking me to his apartment. Of course. I drove. He'll probably upload the pictures from my phone and send me on my way. That's good. The way I'm feeling I'm not so sure it's a good idea that we're alone. This is what I wanted. So why do I suddenly feel abandoned?

"Are you hungry? Do you want to grab some food?"

He glances at me sharply. I don't know where his head was at, but my questions seem to throw him.

"I'm hungry and I want to know what's on the SD card you pulled from the camera," I explain.

Some of my anxiety about being alone must've come through my voice because he takes my hand, prying it away from the other one where it was all twisted up.

He gives it a squeeze. "Yeah. Debbie's cookies aren't sitting real well with me either. How about In N Out?"

The familiar red and yellow sign is lit up in the distance.

"Sounds good."

He maneuvers the car into the right lane and turns into the drive thru. We give our order to the employee going car to car to make the long line go faster and he punches it into the tablet he's holding. Nolan eases the car forward and rolls the window back up.

"You okay? I know you weren't very comfortable with what we did back there."

"*Not comfortable* is putting it mildly. I've never ever broken the law before."

"Never? Not even once?"

"No. Not even a traffic ticket."

"You're kidding."

I shake my head. "I'm not."

"Wow. I don't think I've ever met anyone who was such a straight arrow."

"You say that like it's a bad thing."

"Don't get me wrong. I think it's cool. I've just never met anyone who hasn't messed up at least once." He shifts in his seat, propping his elbow on the door and rubbing his chin. "What I do must seem really bad to you. Are you looking at me differently now?"

"A little. Yes."

"And not in a good way."

I shake my head again.

"Damn. I'd say I'm sorry, but I'm likely to do something that skates the line between legal and illegal again. Probably more than once before we're through here. Are you going to be okay with that? Cause if not then maybe we should think about you not coming with me while I'm investigating this case."

"I don't know. I'm not really sure I'm okay with what *I* did today. I stole from a man. I looked through his things."

"Technically you didn't steal. Neither of us did. We copied things and took photos, but we didn't take anything. Debbie let us into that office. There was no breaking and entering. And I did replace the SD card in the camera with a blank one so again technically nothing was taken. Just switched out."

"That is a mighty thin line you walk."

"I can live with it. Can you?"

"I don't know. I'm struggling with it. I know what you're saying is true. Everything is there exactly like it was before we walked in except for the SD card. *Technically.* I've never had to add a qualifier like that to anything I've ever done. It feels weird."

"Maybe we should concentrate on what each of us do. Separately. We can meet up later and compare notes."

He's giving me an out. The thing is I'm not sure I want it. This case is my responsibility. *Carla's* my responsibility. Not that Nolan wouldn't give me all of the information he discovers, it would just be second hand. I'm not sure I'm comfortable with that either. The control freak in me doesn't like that idea at all.

I can't have it both ways. I either have to let Nolan do his job separately from me like he said or I go with him and maybe do things that redefine my morality. Which to choose?

"I was planning on going to that motel tomorrow," he says, cutting into my thoughts. "Maybe talk to some of the local girls to see if they remember Carla. It's been a while so it's doubtful. Prostitutes don't have long lives. That's probably something you shouldn't do with me since I plan to pick them up like I'm a john and it would be odd to have another woman in the car with me. You could visit Diego's grave like you promised Carla."

A test. To see if I can handle giving him free reign. I know he's right. I shouldn't go with him to that motel tomorrow. This is going to be really hard. I had no idea when I decided to take this case that it would make me examine who I was as a person.

"Okay," I say. "We can meet up later and go over everything."

"It'll probably be late by the time I get back. Why don't we meet up Monday after work?"

"What about everything we found today?"

"We'll start on it tonight and see where it takes us. If we need to we can meet up again tomorrow afternoon."

"Why not in the morning?"

He gets a funny shy smile. "It's Sunday. I go to mass at nine."

"You go to church?"

"What? Are you surprised that someone with seemingly no moral compass would be religious?"

"No. Yes. I don't know. Wow. This really highlights how little we know about each other."

"I would've pegged you for a fellow Catholic."

"My strong moral character comes more from living most of my life as an illegal immigrant than from catechism and Sunday school."

He gives me a long, considering look, but he doesn't ask what most people would ask—are you still in the country illegally.

"My family and I got our documentation when I was fifteen." I don't tell him how or why. I'm ashamed to. It's not a pretty story. It's not a happy ending.

I cried when our paperwork finally came through. Not because I was glad, but because it didn't matter who I was or how hard I had worked. It wasn't my good grades in school, my part time job after school or the volunteer work I did at the local Boys and Girls Club that changed my status from undocumented immigrant to documented immigrant—it was my rape.

Nothing I did or could ever do would have the same power over my family's fate as my rape has. That's an incredibly sad thing to contemplate. The days after receiving our paperwork were darker for me than the days and months after my assault. I didn't share that with my family. I didn't want to take away their joy. Our lives changed. We didn't have to live in fear anymore. For that I'm grateful.

Since then I've made fighting for the rights of the undocumented my mission. I understand them. I *am* them. Carla and I are more alike than we are different.

"That's great he says. Why don't we go to mass together tomorrow so you can see the other side of me." He winks. "I'm not totally morally corrupt you know."

I know. And I'm more than who I used to be or what happened to me. I should cut Nolan a break. He's not a bad guy and he got us into Martin's office. Something I wouldn't have been able to do. I owe him an apology.

We pull up to the window to pay. I give Nolan money for my half of the bill. A few minutes later we're headed back to his apartment with steaming bags filled with burgers and fries. He unlocks his front door and I'm struck again by how harshly and wrongly I've judged him based on what little I know of him.

The apartment is neat and clean. Not as tidy and Debbie's house, but it's definitely cleaner than my apartment. Dread washes hot over me followed by panic. Pushing my secret shame away, I force myself to look around his apartment. His furniture isn't fancy. It's serviceable and comfortable. I guess that's all a guy really needs. He watches me, no doubt trying to gauge my reaction.

"Nice place," I say.

He gives a half laugh. "That's high praise coming from you. Come and sit at the table. I'll get us some plates."

"Am I really that harsh?"

"You're that particular."

I watch him move around his kitchen like he spends a lot of time in there. The image of him in an apron and not much else flashes in my mind and I sit down hard in a chair at the table. This day has really screwed with my head. He's screwed with my head. I can't pin him down. Just when I think I've got him all figured out he does or says something that throws everything out the window. I can't find a compartment in my brain to slot him neatly into.

And that could be a very dangerous thing for my resistance.

7

NOLAN

"What wine goes with cheeseburgers?" I ask Lila. She looks like she could really use a drink. This day really shook her. I've never met anyone like her. I want to say she's naïve, but she's not. She's world weary in a way I never will be. Where that comes from I don't know. She grew up undocumented. There's a whole story there, an entire unpublished novel I'd imagine. I can't ask her about it. I have a feeling it's not something she talks a lot about.

We seem to have turned some kind of corner. She's not outright rejecting me like she was before. Maybe it was the shared experience of going through Martin's things. She thinks we have very different thoughts and feelings about the experience. They're not as different as she wants to believe. *We're* not as different. I've gotten used to what I do, but I'm not entirely comfortable with it. It's what I do, not who I am. I think that's the major difference between us. I can separate the two. She can't. That's going to make it difficult for her to see past what I do to who I am.

She looks up at me and I can still see the war going on

behind her beautiful eyes. "Red, I think, since we're eating beef."

"Red it is." I pull a bottle from my wine fridge, open it, and pour us each a glass. I set hers next to her plate and join her at the table.

She takes a big sip. Bigger than I imagine she normally would. "Mmm, that's good." She downs another gulp.

We dig into our food each of us absorbed in our thoughts. Something's bothering me and I can't quite put my finger on it.

I do a mental finger snap. Carla.

"You didn't seem surprised when Carla told you she was a prostitute," I say, circling back to our interview with her.

"Not really. I've seen it before. People do what they have to do to survive."

"So you can you separate who Carla is from what she did to support herself and Diego?"

"It's not like she had much of a choice being undocumented. Plus with her back ground..." She lets the thought trail off, closing down her expression.

"What do you mean *her background*?"

"She had Diego when she was fifteen. There's no father listed on his birth certificate." She raises her brows like I'm supposed to infer something from that information.

"What are you saying?" I know I sound dense, but she's back to talking in riddles.

"Diego was the result of rape."

"Man. She hasn't had it easy, has she? Welcome to America. Jesus." I take a couple gulps of wine.

"No, she hasn't."

"I feel like I should apologize as a man and as an American, but that's stupid."

"It's sweet, but unnecessary."

"If you can separate who Carla is from what she did, then why can't you do it with me?"

She tilts her head slightly and frowns at me. "That's not the same."

"It is actually. Very much the same."

"You can get another type of job. You don't have to do what you do."

"I know this may seem strange to you, but I *like* what I do. I'm proud to be a private investigator. I'm prouder still when I get to help out on cases like Carla's. It's the reason I became a private investigator instead of a cop. It's the reason I applied for a job at Nash Security and Investigations. I wanted the chance to help free people who were wrongly convicted." I take a sip of wine, contemplating the events that led me to be sitting here with her now. "Just like you. I may not identify with Carla in the same ways that you do, but I know what it's like to make mistakes, to feel like the world is working against you."

"When has the world ever worked against you?"

"Every damn day it feels like sometimes. I don't know what it looks like from the outside, but the truth is I've worked hard to get where I am. Nothing's ever been handed to me. I have to try and try again. I fail. A lot. That's not something I'm proud of, but it's the truth. I screw up. Like today with the trunk and the camera. I should've checked for surveillance devices before we started searching that office. That's a mistake I won't make again."

"Maybe it's not so much the world working against you as it is you working against yourself."

"That's a fair summation. My point is that things aren't always cut and dry. People aren't what they seem like on the surface. There's more to me and you too than it looks like from the outside. That's all I'm saying. And if you can over-look Carla's faults, why can't you overlook mine?"

"You really care about what I think of you?"

More than I should. "Why not? We're friends or working toward it. We have crazy chemistry. Who knows where that will lead if we decide to follow it. We're going to be spending a lot of time together. And I'm...I'm going to shut up now." *Before I dig myself in any deeper with my shovel of desperation. Idiot. Talk about working against yourself.*

She twists the stem of her wine glass, then drinks the remainder of its contents. I refill her glass—her third—as she starts talking, her manner a lot more relaxed than it was when we first walked in.

"You go to church. You took on Carla's case with nearly the same enthusiasm as I did. You seem to have a good sense of right and wrong. At the same time you do things that ride the line, but somehow manage to stay barely legal, which tells me that you have morals that are important to you. You're hot and you kiss like you took a master class in making out. And your apartment..."

"What about my apartment?"

"It's cleaner than mine."

"Can we go back to the kissing part?"

"What I'm saying is I don't have a bad impression of you." She sets her wine glass down after a drink and I notice it's half empty. "I might even like you."

I sit back in my chair stunned. "Well, shit. I hope that's not the wine talking."

"It probably is and I probably shouldn't have any more if I'm going to drive home." She pushes her glass away from her.

"You could always spend the night."

"You're riding the line again, buddy."

"Right. Okay. Shutting up now." I stand and clear away the dishes and trash.

Behind me I hear something that sounds suspiciously like *And you have a nice ass too*. But there's no way Lila would ever say something like that, is there? The wine must be affecting me too. I grab the bottle off the table and stuff the cork back in it. I rinse our wine glasses and put them in the dishwasher, then grab a couple of bottles of water out of the fridge. The last thing I want is one or both of us getting drunk and doing something we might regret later.

"Follow me back to my office," I tell her. "And bring your phone and charge cord." It's time I got my head back on business and try not to think about how she said I'm a good kisser. Although that was my favorite part.

She casually peels off her high-heeled boots and grabs her purse. She's much smaller without them than I'd anticipated. I'm not a big guy, but I'm suddenly conscious of how much larger I am than her. It's weird. I never thought a woman being so petite could be a turn on, but with her it totally is. But then nearly everything about her does it for me. Like how she took off her shoes and made herself comfortable in my apartment. That has to mean something, right?

She follows me down the hall to my home office. I'm a bit of a geek when it comes to computers, but even more so when it comes to surveillance equipment—spy cams, bugs, computer and mobile phone spyware, GPS trackers, and bug detection equipment. That's why I'm so upset with myself that I didn't bring my hidden camera and bug detector. Another lesson learned—keep one on me at all times.

Behind me Lila gasps. I turn to look at her. Her eyes are wide as she takes in the room with its shelves and shelves of equipment. I try to see the room as she might.

Some of the pieces blink and whir while they carry out their various tasks. Most are new, but some are old technology like the CB radio and a PC that only accepts floppy disks.

Some guys are into computer games, some cars. I'm into electronics—how they work, what they can do, and how I can use them. I've been fascinated with computers and electronic devices since I was a kid. In fact, my parents' old VCR sits on a lower shelf, a tape hanging out the front of ALF, that old show about an alien stranded on earth who hides out with a family and tries to eat their cat. It's a favorite of mine. I'm kind of a geek and I've just let the pretty lawyer lady see how big a dork I really am.

I focus on her and her reaction, which seems to be hovering somewhere between awe, confusion, and shock. She doesn't know it, but when we entered my apartment we triggered the hidden cameras throughout much like the one we found in Martin's office. Fortunately that screen is currently off. She walks the room, checking everything out. Holding my breath, I wait to see what she'll say when she's done.

"This is...*awesome*. How long have you been collecting?"

I let out the breath I was holding. This is a good response. The one I was hoping for.

"Since I was a kid. I've traded up as technology advanced, but I still like some of the old machines like the two different kinds of VCRs, the cassette deck, and the reel-to-reel tape recorder. You never know when you'll come across old film reels or cassette tapes and you'll need something to play them on."

"My parents still play records. They insist the sound is better than CDs."

"They're right to a certain extent."

She glances around again. "This is really cool. You surprise me."

"In a good way I hope."

"This time, yes. Absolutely."

I clear my throat, trying to dislodge the lump that's suddenly formed. "Your phone and cord?"

"Oh, yeah. Here." She starts to put them in my hand.

"If it's password protected I'll need you to key it in."

I look away when she punches in her code. She hands it to me and I plug it into the USB port on my computer. This machine is my baby, my most prized piece of equipment. I built the PC myself to the specifications I wanted. I login in and click on the icon to upload her photos. I could upload everything on it into my computer and she probably wouldn't know it. But that's a line I would never cross.

"Pull up that chair," I tell her, motioning to the office chair across the room that I use with my Mac computer. Yes, I have both a Mac and a PC. "And bring it over so we can look at the photos together."

When her phone is finished I plug mine in and upload the pictures of the files that I took. I had no idea if any of it will help us or not. Lila will know more about them than I do. There was a lot of legalese I didn't understand. I just photographed everything I could find with either her or Diego's name on it. I even shot the file Martin had with his own name on the tab.

Lila drags the chair over and sits, taking a long drink from her water bottle. She dabs her mouth with the back of her hand. "Are those the pictures you took of the files?"

"Yeah. I'm glad you're here. You can help me decipher it. There was one in particular..." I scroll through until I find the one I want to show her. "This one." I lean back so she can get closer to the screen.

Her eyes narrow. "*No*. It can't be."

"Is it what I think it is?"

"*Holy shit.* Why didn't he file it? Can you print it out? Just the first three pages are fine. I want to see what his argument was."

I do as she asks. In seconds the printer is done and I had her the sheets of paper.

She scans the pages, flipping through them a couple of times. "His argument was solid. He probably would've won. *Why didn't he file it?* I don't understand. This is a motion to dismiss the case against Carla. He sites the coroner's report declaring Diego's death an accident and the judge's misapplication of the burden of proof in Filipe Nuñez's competency hearing as a witness in the case as well as his denial to hear the testimony of an expert who would've shown that Filipe's recollection of Diego wrapping the cord around his own neck was credible and consistent with what Carla said in her initial statement to the police."

"In English?"

"It means that the when the judge declared Filipe unfit to testify because of his age that he put the burden of proof on the defense to *disprove* the charges against Carla rather than putting the burden on the prosecution to *prove* the charges. He totally ignored the principle of *innocent until proven guilty*, the very foundation of our justice system."

She shakes the papers. "Again, why didn't he file this? He was right. Why did he choose to be incompetent and let the trial go on? Why did he let his client get convicted for a crime when he could disprove the entire basis of the prosecution's case with the coroner's report? There was no crime. There never should've been a trial let alone a conviction. *Why?* I just don't get it."

"Doesn't this give us what *we* need to free Carla?"

"Oh, yes. But I want to know what made him not file this motion. There must be *some* reason. I want to be really sure here. We need all of our ducks in a row. We may only get one shot at reversing her conviction and I don't want to waste it going in with only part of the information. What else did you find in his files?"

"He had a file on himself. Let me see if I can find... Ah. Here." I'm glad I took a picture of the file tab before photographing the contents inside so I know what goes where.

"Bank statements," Lila says. "I wonder if Debbie knows about this account."

"Huh, not likely. Look at the charges."

"What do you mean? He could've bought anything from Two 2 Tango or Leah Unlimited."

"Actually those are spank-by-the-minute websites."

She turns to look at me at the same time I look at her and I suddenly realize how close we are. Closer than we were in the car. I can smell the mixture of wine and cheese-burger on her breath mingled with her perfume. The combination is like some strange aphrodisiac that has me semi-hard in an instant. Or maybe it's just having her near that makes my whole body hot.

"Spank by the *what*?" Her words are breathy or else it's me projecting because the way she says *spank* sets off flares inside me.

"Spank-by-the-minute. You know, those sites where you watch someone get themself off while you get yourself off."

Her lips part on a soft *oh* and I imagine all sorts of things involving her mouth. "How do you know this?"

"I did some webcam work for Leah Unlimited. They wanted cameras the customer could control with simple keystrokes—zooming, switching camera angles, and so on.

They gave me a list of other websites to ah, visit to get an idea of what the competition was doing so they could do something different."

"And one of the other websites you *had* to visit was Two 2 Tango?"

"Yes."

"For *research*." She makes air quotes on the word research.

I can't help the smile that creases my cheeks. "They paid me a lot of money to do it too. I still do some contract work for them from time to time."

"So you have to check their site to make sure it's working properly."

"Are you asking me to show you the website?"

"I just can't imagine John Martin doing...that."

"There's nothing wrong with it. It's perfectly safe. The safest sex available."

I pull my gaze from hers and use my backdoor access code to enter the site. The screen fills with smaller screens or rooms of men and women in various stages of arousal. We're immediately surrounded by the sound of their panting, moans, and dirty talk. Lila's gaze is glued to the screen, her eyes wide.

"Which room do you want to enter?" I ask her, my attention fully on *her*.

"Is there a..." She licks her lips. "Is there a way to see which room Martin entered?"

"No. They don't give me access to their billing department. But, if I had to guess..." I choose a box at random because they're all pretty much the same and click on it.

The screen is suddenly full of a young blond woman dressed like a schoolgirl. Her skirt is hiked up around her waist and her blouse gaps open. She's not wearing any underwear. I watch Lila as she watches the girl thrust a huge black dildo in and out of herself while twisting her nipples and crying out. The camera zooms in on her face, then out to focus on the way her breasts jiggle.

"Are you doing that?" Lila asks, her voice wispy and soft.

"Controlling the cameras?"

"Yeah."

"No. The customer paying to watch her is."

"Do you... Is this...the kind of thing *you* like?"

"I'm not into voyeurism, no."

I lean a little closer, drawn to her by the charged air around us. The schoolgirl's moans get louder and louder until she climaxes. Lila licks her lips again, her eyes wide on the image before her. In that moment I'm overcome with the desire to find out what Lila sounds like when *she* comes and what I could do to her to make her to scream my name the way the girl on the screen is crying out for some guy named Josh.

"I'd rather have the real thing," I whisper hoarsely. "To touch and *taste*. Right in front of me."

8

LILA

The girl on the screen writhes and moans, pinching her nipples and plunging the huge phallus in and out of her. I can't look away. I've never seen anything like it. I had no idea such a thing even existed. Nolan watches me watch the girl. He doesn't touch me or say anything, he just observes. Having him beside me as the girl nears orgasm does something to me. My nipples are hard, pressing against the cups of my bra. I want to take my breasts in my hands and do what the girl is doing, pinching and tugging her nipples.

I rock my hips forward, pressing my clit against the seat of the chair, trying to get some relief. It's not so much what's happening in front of me it's what's happening between Nolan and me. Maybe it's the wine. Maybe it's my limited experiences. Or maybe it really is the girl rolling around on her bed. I don't know. All I know is that I want Nolan to touch me. The longer he doesn't the more I want him to.

Can he feel electricity bowing and arcing between us? Is it affecting him the way it's affecting me? Is it the girl or is it me or a combination of both?

"Do you…" I stammer. "Is this…the kind of thing *you* like?"

"I'm not into voyeurism, no."

The girl's back arches and she screams out for some guy named Josh. I'm wet between my legs. I press harder into the chair seat sure I'll leave a wet spot behind, but I don't care. I feel like that girl on the screen needing something, but it doesn't come.

"I'd rather have the *real* thing." He's suddenly closer, his voice a rasp that rubs between my legs. "To touch and *taste. Right* in front of me."

I bite my lip to keep from moaning.

"Lila." My name is a whispered caress against my ear. "Do *you* like watching?"

I open my mouth to deny it, but all that comes out is a gasp. The girl on the screen pulls the dildo out of her and licks it. The sound she makes is less convincing than any of the others she's made. This part of the fantasy isn't hers.

"Turn it off."

He does as I ask, bringing the bank statement back up on the screen. I'm on edge. I want—no need—him to touch me and yet I don't think I could handle it if he did.

"I shouldn't have showed you that," he says. "I'm sorry."

I turn to look at him. His eyes are a metallic brown like brass or copper. Mesmerizing. He's looking at me with a mixture of concern and desire as though he's not sure which he should be feeling.

I tilt toward him without really thinking about it. "I *asked* you to show me."

"I know you did, but… Are you okay?"

"I'm fine." I want that to be true, but it's not. It's *so* not.

He brushes the back of his knuckles across my cheek. His gaze is everywhere on my face, bouncing between my eyes and lips and where he's caressing me. I want him to kiss me. I can tell he wants the same thing, but something's holding him back. Is it something I'm doing or not doing?

"You're really beautiful." His whispered compliment seems to have surprised him somehow. He drops his hand and sits back in his chair.

"Thank you."

He clears his throat. "It's late and it's been a long day."

"I... Yeah. Jeez. Wow. I didn't realize it was so late." I have no idea what time it is, but it's clear he wants me to leave.

I grab my phone and start to stand. My legs are a little wobbly from the wine and the emotional overload of the day, making me tip to one side. I grab his shoulder to stabilize myself. It's strong and steady under my hand.

He catches me by the arm. "Are you okay to drive?"

"I'm just tired." I move away, out of his hold.

"Are you sure? Maybe you should stay..." His offer isn't very convincing.

"I really should go."

"What time do you want to meet up tomorrow and where?"

"Tomorrow?"

"To go over the rest of the stuff we found at Martin's." He tilts his head, concern on his face and in his voice. "Are you sure you're all right?"

Something inside me snaps. The edge I've been walking all day lists to one side and I feel myself falling into uncharted territory and I realize I'm about to do something I've never done. Oddly I'm not scared. I'm not nervous. I'm determined.

"You know what?" I say, taking a step toward him. "No. I'm not okay."

"What's—"

I grab him by the front of the shirt and the back of his head and press my lips to his. His body jolts in a stunned jerk, then his arms wrap around me, dragging me tight against him. He angles his head, taking the kiss deeper. For a split second I'm too shocked to react and then I fist his hair tighter. He makes a low noise in the back of his throat and rocks his pelvis against me. He's hard and hungry as though he's been waiting forever to get me in just this position. His arousal sends mine into overdrive.

His hand is in my hair, his other arm wrapped tight around my waist, holding me to him from mouth to thighs. He tugs on my hair, tipping my head back, and goes for my neck with bites and licks that make me moan and grind against him. I've never wanted anyone the way I want him right now. Reaching between us I get my first feel of him. The sound he makes in my ear slices me with shards of desire from where his mouth is to where I'm wet and throbbing with need.

He palms my breast. There's nothing hesitant about his touch as he circles my nipples with his thumb over my sweater. It's not enough. I want his hands on my skin and mine on his. I push back so that his hold on me loosens and drag my sweater over my head. I get a split second to see the look on his face before I dive for him again. He comes at me like he's starved, his hands everywhere. I get my hands under his shirt. He's all lean muscle and hot, hard flesh.

He yanks his shirt off and tosses it. Something crashes on the other side of the room, but he doesn't seem to notice. He stares at me. His gaze is a match strike to my already out of control emotions. Hooking my arm around his neck, I reach for him, pulling him down to me. His kisses turn dirty. Each one is a lick to my clit, which is pulsing to the hard hammer of my heart. I want it like this. Hard. Fast. Nasty.

My bra is gone in a second, replaced by his hands. I twist against him. It takes me a moment—because he constantly distracts me—to get his pants open. His breath puffs hot on my neck as I stroke him. He makes an incoherent, strangled sound. I like it and the effect I have on him. He shoves his hand in my pants, finally touching me where I most want to be touched. His fingers slide through my slickness. My grip on him loosens. I push against his hand, practically riding it.

His mouth is hot and urgent on mine as he backs me out of the room. We hit the hallway wall and he turns us. Walking backward, he pulls me into another room. I get a vague sense of the space when he tears his mouth from mine and lifts me, spinning us so that I land on a bed. He comes down on top of me. Kissing his way down, he latches onto my breast. I clutch his head. My hips buck against the hard ridge pressing between my legs.

He's a madman, shoving at my pants as his mouth wrecks me. I twist under him. I want him inside me. *Now*.

"Yes," he rasps, tugging harder on my pants.

Oh, god did I say that out loud?

"They're stuck," he mumbles against my breast.

It takes me a moment to realize he means my pants. My tight pants. Damn it. I pull my leg up to try to get at the hem to pull on it. The angle change throws him off to one side of me. I struggle to jerk my jeans over my foot, but my arms aren't long enough. He suddenly realizes my battle because he leverages off of me and grabs my calf. His eyes never leave mine as he strips off my jeans. Then he's on me again. Slower this time, but somehow just as fevered. I wrap my legs around him.

He feels so good. So damn good. I don't know what I could've been thinking considering starting things up with Kurt again. It was never like this with him. Or anyone else.

Sex hasn't exactly been easy for me. Not that I have hang ups. I've worked hard to get to where I can enjoy sex. It's just that I think too much and those thoughts get in the way of me having an orgasm sometimes. Why can't I just absorb myself in the sensations and stay engaged? Why can't I be like the uninhibited woman on the website? What's *wrong* with me?

Those thoughts have a cooling effect. Where I was thrashing under him a moment ago I'm now still and barely responsive.

Nolan notices and leans on one elbow to look down at me. "Hey." He brushes the hair back from my face. "Where'd you go?"

I open my mouth to answer, but everything I could or would say feels wrong. This isn't the time to have this talk. I don't *want* to have this talk. I want to go back to the place in my head where I was nothing but sensation and need. Pushing all of those thoughts aside, I bring him down for a kiss, trying to get back to where we were before. I give it my best effort, but it's not the same. It's forced and fake.

He stays with me for a second, then breaks it off. "What's wrong? Is it something I did?"

"No. God. No. It's... Will you just keep kissing me?" I put his hand on my bare breast. "And do some of this and that down there." I motion toward my crotch. "I'll catch up."

"I don't want you to *catch up*. I want you with me."

I let out a frustrated breath and look away, blinking back tears. I hate when I get like this. "I will be. Just keep going."

He moves his hand from my breast to my cheek. "Was it too much too fast?"

"It wasn't fast enough."

"I don't know what that means."

"It means that I don't want to think. I just want to feel. Touch me. Come on."

"You have no idea how much I want to do that, but it feels like I'm forcing myself on you and that's something I'd never do."

Turning my head to the side, I put my hand over my eyes. Why do I have to complicate things all the time? Why can't I be *normal*?

"Would it help if we watched that website again?"

His question startles me. I pull my hand off my eyes and look at him. *Would* it help?

"I don't know," I answer honestly.

"You want to try or do you want to forget it for tonight?"

Pushing him back, I sit up. "I think we should probably just forget it."

"Okay." He's trying to hide his disappointment, which makes me feel worse.

"Maybe we should try the website."

His laugh is short and filled with a combination of disbelief that this is even happening and, surprisingly, some real humor. "I really don't want you to have to try that hard to get it up for me. If it's not happening, it's not happening."

"I'm sorry."

"It's just a timing thing. It's been a long day. You're tired."

"You're sweet to think up those excuses."

I look down at myself. I'm naked except for my underwear, which are not exactly sexy. It wasn't like I planned to have sex when I put them on this morning. Suddenly I feel overexposed and vulnerable. I cross my arms over my chest. Nolan sits up next to me and puts his arm around me. He still has his unzipped pants on. I can see the outline of his hard on though his boxers. It's a nice hard on. I would've liked to have done more than just touch it.

"I'm not that sweet. A part of me is kicking myself for not doing what you told me to do. I could be inside you *right now*."

My nipples harden beneath my palms and my clit throbs at his words. I concentrate hard on resisting the urge to press a hand between my legs. "*God*. Don't talk like that."

"Sorry." He sounds contrite, pulling his arm from around me. "Let me get the rest of your clothes."

He gets up and leaves before I could tell him that what he said didn't disgust me. It got me hot. But now I'm too embarrassed to correct him. God. What's wrong with me? Watching that girl get off and Nolan's dirty talk does it for me, but I don't know how to tell him that. He comes back with my sweater and bra in one hand and his shirt in the other. I get the full view of his bare torso and it's...*damn*. This guy works out. I'm glad to have my sweater to cover the rolls on my stomach and my thick thighs. I'm not exactly skinny or even trim. I don't work out.

"I'll be in the other room," he says and leaves again without the explanation I feel like I owe him.

I'm pretty sure I'm the first girl to get cold feet right in the middle of things with him. Now everything is going to be awkward between us. I clasp my bra and adjust my breasts in the cups. They're too big for how short I am, making me look like I don't have a waist. Not like that girl on the website. I hop off the bed and finish dressing in record time. I need to get out of here. The longer I stay the more my embarrassment skyrockets. I'm so humiliated. I don't know how I'm going to face him or how we can work together after what just happened.

I give the rumpled bedspread a regretful glance. I bet it would've been really good with him. I was totally into it until right before I let the thoughts creep in. He's waiting out there for me. What do I say to him? Sorry I got you all hot and bothered, then got weird on you? *Ugh!* I frustrate myself. I can only imagine how he feels.

Taking a deep breath, I head down the hall. Nolan is standing behind the kitchen bar washing our wine glasses. I spy my purse on the coffee table and grab it on my way to the door. I'm outside and half way down the walk when he catches up to me.

"Hey. Are you all right?"

"*God* I really wish you'd stop asking me that."

"Let me at least walk you to your car."

"I'm fine. I've got it."

"But you don't have your keys." He dangles them in front of me.

I grab them. "Thanks. I'll see you tomorrow."

"*Lila.*"

I stop at the tone in his voice.

He positions himself in front of me. "Don't make it weird, okay?"

"Too late."

"It's not too late. Come here." He holds his arms open to me.

I want to dive into them and have him tell me everything's okay. But it's not. My cheeks burn with humiliation and I can't look him in the eye. He puts his arms around me and rubs my back. I stay stiff, my arms wrapped around me.

"I like you," he mumbles against my temple. "I want to get to know you better. That can take as long as it needs to. Okay?"

I nod, liking the way his stubble catches in my hair and the way his arms feel around me. I like him too. He releases me, but leaves one arm across my shoulders as we walk to my car. I lean back against the driver door intending to say something, anything, but he presses his lips to mine, sealing in any words that might've tumbled out. He backs away. I can't see his expression in the darkness, but there's a reluctance to his movements as he brushes my cheek with his knuckles, then purposefully strides away. I climb in the car and start it. As I drive past his apartment I notice he's standing on the porch, watching me. He turns to go inside as I pass.

I want to pound my forehead on the steering wheel and burst into tears. Instead I force myself to drive carefully and calmly home.

9

NOLAN

I have no idea what happened between Lila and me. I keep going over and over it in my head. She was with me right up until it looked like things were really going to go down and then she sort of shut off. Was it something I did or *didn't* do? First times can be tricky, but everything between us seemed to just flow. I can't say I've ever had that experience before. Usually it's a lot of blind groping and getting it wrong until you figure out what works between you. There was none of that with Lila. *Everything* seemed to work between us.

So where did it go wrong?

When she told me to just keep going that she'd catch up I had to really control my reaction. I didn't want her to lie there and endure it and I can't believe she would think that was what I would want. No guy wants that. Except selfish assholes. I'm a lot of things, but I'm not a selfish asshole. I want a woman to be with me. Hell, I *love* it when a woman takes the initiative like Lila did last night. Total turn on.

I replayed the video of us in my office about eight times trying to figure out where things went wrong, but everything was fine. It was in the bedroom that things got weird and I don't have a camera in there. Well, that wasn't the *only* reason I replayed the tape. It was damn hot. And if I used it to relieve myself of some pent up energy that was okay, totally normal and above board. Especially since I deleted it as soon as I finished. Being able to watch myself with Lila while remembering what she felt like was seriously the most intense thing I've ever done. Porn has it's place don't get me wrong. But that tape of Lila and me? Better than *any* porno *ever*. I was sorry to delete it, but it was the right thing to do.

If Lila ever found out about the video and what I did while watching it I'm pretty sure that would be the last time I'd get to see her naked. And oh man, the thought of never getting to touch her again...torture. Pure torture.

Whatever it was that freaked her out we should probably talk about. I would've tested the subject further last night, but I had a feeling that would only make things worse. So I let it slide. I seriously doubt she'll be the one to broach the subject so I'll have to figure out a time and a way to bring it up without making things worse between us.

As I pull up outside the Lucky Inn motel where Carla worked as a prostitute, I wonder what Lila's doing. We're supposed to meet up at my apartment after lunch to continue going over the things we found in Martin's office. I did some digging after Lila left and found out some interesting things about John S. Martin Esquire. I can't wait to share them with her. But first I have to try to find a needle in a haystack at the Lucky Inn.

And what an aptly named place it was too. In the five minutes I've been sitting out front I counted eight different sets of prostitutes and johns going in and out of the rooms. The rooms seemed to be shared by the girls because two of the rooms had one set of people come out and a completely different set go in not two minutes later. The Lucky Inn is a typical two story motel with an open second floor balcony and room doors that face the parking lot, making it really easy to watch people come and go (no pun intended).

A couple of guys stand around outside. Not together though. One hangs out on the second floor balcony and the other leans against the crumbling stucco wall at the bottom of the stairwell on the ground floor near the snack machine. Guards, if I have to guess. Whoever runs their prostitution ring out of here has a slick operation going that's for sure. The Lucky Inn is definitely a No-Tell-Motel and I have a feeling a guy wandering around asking unwanted questions about a former prostitute and her johns would not be welcome. I hate to disappoint Lila but there is no way I'm getting out of my car to start knocking on doors or even go up to the office to make inquires. I'm pretty sure the goon guards would be on me faster than the people coming and going (pun intended).

I snap a few photos of the motel and the guys standing around. The one on the bottom floor takes notice and heads my direction. I start my car and peel away from the curb.

I like my teeth exactly were they are thank you very much.

I feel like I need something to give Lila so I drive to the crappy apartment complex where Carla lived with her son. It looks a lot like the motel, but with the apartment doors facing a center courtyard instead of the street. Spying the rental office sign, I get out of my car and head toward it. What are the odds, Hector Rodriguez, the asshole landlord who extorted sex for rent from Carla is still here? I have to try anyway. Maybe the new landlord can tell me where I can find Rodriguez if he's no longer in charge.

The office smells like coffee, cigarettes, ass, and some kind of air fresher that clearly isn't working hard enough. An older woman with shoe polish black hair sits behind a scarred desk reading a Spanish language newspaper. For the millionth time I wonder why I took four years of French in high school instead of Spanish. I have yet to even visit France, but in Southern California I'd use Spanish every day if I could speak it. Right now I blend in about as well as the horrible print of the woman's blouse blends with the shocking wallpaper behind her. Not a good thing for a PI.

She squints up at me as I close the door. "*¿Puedo ayudarle?*"

See? *Every* damn day I'd use it.

"*No hablo Español*," I respond.

She sets her paper down and rapid fires more Spanish at me, no doubt cursing me out. I stand there and take it until she winds down, then picks up her newspaper again, shakes it out, and puts it between us. I'm ignored.

"Do you know where I can find Hector Rodriguez?" I ask.

"*No se.*"

I wish I'd brought Lila with me. "I really need to talk to Hector Rodriguez," I say slower.

She tilts the paper down and rattles off more Spanish. I understand one word *policia*—police.

I shake my head. "No policia."

"Then what the fuck are you doing here looking for my asshole ex-husband, white boy?"

The switch in her is jarring. Her English has no accent at all.

I produce my business card. For some reason people who don't like the police don't mind spilling everything to a private investigator. I hope that's true of the woman glaring at me.

"My name is Nolan Perry." I hand her the card. "I work for Nash Security and Investigations. I'm here on behalf of my client Carla Ruiz. I understand your ex-husband was the landlord here when she and her son, Diego, lived here."

"*Pobrecito chico.*" Mumbling some more in Spanish, she closes her eyes and crosses herself, then looks up at me. "Such a tragedy. I'm Margarita Rodriguez. What do you want to know about the *pendejo* who gave me gonorrhea? I'll tell you whatever you want."

Neighbors and furious exes—a PI's best friend.

"According to Carla, Hector was ah, *with* her the morning Diego died."

"You mean screwing her in place of rent. Don't be delicate. It's the reason he's my *ex*-husband. Do you know how much money I lost because he couldn't keep it in his pants? Tens of thousands. That's a lot of damn money. He's supposed to be paying it back, but the *cabróne* hasn't had a job since I kicked his lazy ass out. Or so he says."

"Do you know where I can find him?"

"Shacked up with some *flaca* crack whore in Chollas View last I heard. If she was smart she should've kicked his ass like I did. Hang on. I'll get you the address." She riffles through the things on her desk and then pulls out a scrap of paper. "I'll make you a copy." Without leaving her seat she turns to the copier. "Here you go." She hands me a warm sheet of paper with an address and phone number scrawled on it.

"Thanks. I appreciate it."

"Is that the if-I-need-a-favor-you'd-do-it kind of appreciation?"

"Depends on the favor."

"I heard Hector's aunt somebody died and he inherited some money. I want it."

"I could get you the info faster if you have his social security number."

"As a matter of fact..." She digs around her desk again and comes up with another scratch piece of paper, makes a copy, and gives it to me. "Here you go."

"Thanks."

"If you can find out he has a job or any other hidden money, will you let me know?"

"You wouldn't happen to have the contact info for a past resident here, would you?"

"Tit for tat. I like you, white boy. Who are we talking about?"

"Inez Torres. She used to babysit for Carla sometimes."

"Inez is that worthless *pendejo's* cousin. We stayed good friends after she found out he was screwing everybody in the complex. She's loyal that one. Of course I know where she is. Hang on." She searches her desk again, locates another scrap of paper, copies it, and hands the copy to me.

Never in a million years would I have thought there was anything remotely useful on that mess of a desk of hers. Boy was I wrong.

"Thanks, Margarita. Should I call you here or at another number if I find out any info on Hector?"

She goes through the mess on her desk again, writes something on the business card she finds, then hands it to me. "My cell." She runs gaze over me like she's making some kind of judgment call about me. "You have a wife or girl-friend, white boy?"

The image of Lila's beautiful face comes into my mind. "Maybe."

"Huh. I've seen that look before. Want but can't have.

She's lucky this girl that you want. If she doesn't come around you call me. I have a daughter in college. Pretty. Smart. You'd make beautiful babies."

"I'll keep that in mind. Thanks, Margarita."

"Any time, white boy. You get me that *cabróne's* money."

"I'll do my best."

I head out into the mid day sun and check the time. Just after twelve. I'm supposed to meet Lila at one. I plug Inez's address into my phone. It's not far from here. I debate whether or not I should go on my own or wait to go with Lila. I'd better wait. Inez is a potential witness. This is Lila's area of expertize. She'll be glad I was able to find her so easily and it sounds like she might be amenable to helping Carla.

On the way home I think about how it's going to be to see Lila after last night. I asked her to not make things weird. I just hope *I* can do what I asked of her. I feel like we need to talk about what happened and what almost happened. At the same time I'm freaking out about it. What if she thinks it's a mistake? What if she's so embarrassed that she totally shuts down any chance we might have to see where our attraction might lead? What if she just totally pretends *nothing* ever happened?

That last thought is the one that bothers me the most. I can deal with any of the other possibilities, but her pretending there's nothing between us, that nothing major happened...no can do. If I have to I'll resurrect the video of us in my office out of my computer trash can and show it to her. No one viewing that tape could ever think there's no connection at all between us.

10

LILA

I'm running late...again.

I hate being late, but this time I did it on purpose. I lay awake half the night reliving everything that happened before and after I freaked out. *Before* is definitely my favorite. The after is what made me lose sleep and procrastinate leaving the house. I had to remind myself that Carla needs me. Any embarrassment I might feel is nothing compared to what she went through and is going through. I can deal with Nolan.

I think. Maybe.

What I can't wrap my head around is what he might say. Is he going to pretend nothing happened, try to pry why I freaked out of me or is he going to tell me it was all a mistake and nothing should ever happen between us again. I'm not sure which I'm dreading the most and which I really want to happen. And right there is why I was up all night.

I used some of my insomniac time to locate Diego's grave. It took a while, but I managed to do it. Fortunately it wasn't far from my house. I stopped along the way and bought several different kinds of Spiderman balloons. The clerk asked me if they were for my son. I told her they were for my nephew. For some reason I couldn't tell her they were for a dead little boy and that I'm taking them to his grave for his mother who is in prison convicted for murdering him. There was no reason to ruin her day with that kind of horrific reality. So I lied and said I was in town for a surprise visit with my sister and her family.

I don't know why I did that. I despise lying. Watching Nolan lie to Debbie Martin as though he did it everyday—and maybe he does, I don't know—showed me a side of him I didn't particularly like. Is he rubbing off on me? In the short time since I've known him has being around him changed me and not in a good way? Normally it takes months of dating for me to get to the point I got with Nolan in a matter of days. That can't be good, right? The people in your life should bring out the best in you not influence you into behavior you find shocking and abhorrent.

And yet... I *liked* doing bad things with him. What does that say about me as a person that I would throw out all of my principles for a man who lies, breaks into people locked file cabinets, shows me porn, and talks dirty in bed? What does it say about *me* that I got off on those things, that I want to watch *more* porn with Nolan while he gets me naked and says nasty things? What does it say about our differences that he went to church this morning and I didn't? Who's the degenerate here, him or me?

I pull up in front of his apartment and cut the engine. Here it is. The moment of truth. Should I bring up last night right away and set some boundaries for how things will be going forward? Or should I let *him* bring it up to get a feeling of where he's at about it?

As I get out of my car and go up the walk, I decide that I'm a coward and that I want to wait to see if he brings it up or not and what he says about it. There. Settled. Except it's not. Now I'm dreading what he might say.

Pressing the doorbell, I give myself a pep talk. *You can do this. It's no big deal. These things happen. You're both adults.*

He opens the door wearing jeans and a t-shirt that molds his body. His feet are bare. So dang sexy.

"Hey. Come on in." He holds the door open for me. "Have you eaten?" He keeps talking without waiting for my response. "I just got back and haven't had the chance to yet. What do you like? I've got a stack of take out menus or I could whip up some sandwiches or something. Unless you're gluten intolerant. Oh wait you ate cheeseburgers so I guess—"

I cut him off by grabbing the back of his head and slamming my lips against his. For some reason his nervousness totally took mine away and replaced it with a boldness I didn't know was in me. I release him and we stare at each other, chests heaving, eyes blazing. He opens his mouth like he's going to say something, but I stop him with another kiss. I don't want to talk. He seems to get the message and the next thing I know I'm backed up against the door with one of his hands on my breast and the other clamped firmly on my behind.

I grind against the growing ridge in his jeans. It's not enough. Wrapping a leg around him, I open my legs wider. He presses me into the door practically dry humping me toward orgasm. This is what I crave from him. Mindlessness. Just need and want and taking and giving. His mouth is driving me crazy. He doesn't give me any time to think. My shirt is shoved up along with my bra. His hands are magic on my bare flesh. I moan into his mouth. He's a little rough and I like it.

He replaces a hand with his mouth, sucking on my

nipple, drawing it deep into his mouth. I grip the back of his head and hold him to me. Hands skate down, bunching up my skirt. He makes a low noise in his throat when he finds me wet. His fingers slip into the waistband of my underwear and he comes at me with everything he's got, stroking my clit and working my breasts. I'm going to come. Clutching his head tighter, I dig my nails into his shoulder. Almost...almost...

"Oh, god!" I cry out.

He takes me down slowly with little kisses and light strokes. He doesn't stop touching me. I don't know how he does it, but he takes me up again. Panting and clutching at him, I want it. I *crave* it. I need him inside me. I reach for him, but he's already bare and rolling a condom on. He lifts me roughly. The door is hard against my back and he's hard against my front. I wrap my legs around his waist.

"*Fuck* me," I gasp against his neck not recognizing my voice. "*Hard.*"

"*God*, yes."

I feel him right there. He thrusts deep, banging me against the door, but I don't care. I'm full of him and it's not enough.

"*Harder.*"

He redoubles his efforts, crashing into me over and over. He sinks his teeth into the side of my neck, making my hand fist in his hair. Oh, *god* it feels *so* good. The harsh sounds of our breathing fill the room along with the heavy scent of sex. He adjusts me slightly and hits some magical spot inside me. Crying out, I clutch him tighter. His thrusts are relentless. Hard. *So hard.* And deep. Lunging at me over and over again, he doesn't give me time to think. There is only sensation.

My whole body tenses and I come, screaming his name.

He grips my hips, his fingers digging into my flesh as he reaches climax. His hot breath on my neck sends goose bumps throughout my body. He pulses inside me and I can't think about anything. My mind is an absolute blank. I'm wrapped so tightly around him that I have to force my arms and legs to relax.

He lifts his head and brushes the hair out of my face, giving me a soft smile. "Hi."

"Hi."

He kisses me gently, with purpose. It's not like any of the other kisses he's given me. There's something sweet about the way he looks at me and how he lightly strokes my hair. I'm caught by what I see in his eyes. I can't help but smile shyly back at him. Somehow this moment feels more intimate than what we shared a few moments ago. I don't know what to say to him. Maybe if I knew what he was thinking...

He looks down to where we're still joined. I can't see his expression. I look too. The sight of him inside me does something strange to me and I reflexively clench around him. His groan is unexpected. He liked it. I make a note to try it to do it again. If there is a next time. I watch in fascination as he grips the base of his shaft and the condom and pulls slowly out like he's reluctant to leave me. I can't remember being with a guy who didn't withdraw right away to get rid of the condom.

He sets me back on my feet and makes an attempt to right my panties and skirt. There's care and tenderness in his touch. I keep my gaze on his face, hoping it will give me clue as to what happens next. All of the worrying I did was a waste. I should've been thinking about this moment. The *after*.

He straightens and gives me a kiss. "I'm going to go take

care of this." He gestures toward the condom still wrapped around him. "Have a seat. I'll be right back."

I watch him go, thinking this would be a really good time to just take off and not have to deal with what comes next. But I'm kind of curious about it. What does this mean? Should it mean anything? Is this a one off or are we going to be doing this on a regular basis? I'm not sure of what I want. It feels like I should want *something* from him. Most women would want some kind of commitment, wouldn't they? Or at least an assurance that they are the only one. It's funny, but I don't feel like I need any thing from him. Maybe this was just an itch we both needed to scratch.

He comes back all tucked in and heads straight for me. I realize I'm still up against the door, staring blankly at him. Like I'm frozen in place, afraid to move. But that's ridiculous, isn't it?

"Are you all right?" He caresses my face. "You look a little pale. Was I too rough?"

"No," I manage to croak out. "I'm okay."

I want to tell him he was *exactly* rough enough and that I've never had sex like that before. Now I know what it feels like to be *fucked*. Because that wasn't plain ordinary sex. It went *way* beyond that to something you'd see in a movie or read about in a book. Something fantastical and unachievable. But I can't say any of that to him without sounding ridiculous. He's clearly more experienced than me. This was probably just another bout of rigorous sex for him. Nothing out of the ordinary.

I concentrate on fixing my skirt, trying to ignore the delicious ache between my legs. With every moment I get flashes of him pounding into me that mingle with the soreness until I want to grab him and feel him between my legs again.

"You sure?" he asks. "You seem a little wobbly."

"Are we going to do that again?"

"Well... I don't know. Do *you* want to do it again?"

"Do you?"

His lips part like he's going to say something. I fist his shirt and haul him toward me. He claps a hand over my mouth to stop me from kissing him again.

"Yes," he says in a hurry, laughing. "I want to do it as many times as you'll let me." He takes his hand away.

"I'm going to let you as many times as you want to."

"Well. Okay then. That might be a lot."

"I'm okay with *a lot*."

"Okay." He's staring at me with a kind of surprised awe. "All right. Good to know."

"Okay."

"I'm starving."

"Me too."

We order food. While we wait for the delivery, Nolan tells me what he found out this morning about Carla's neighbor and landlord. I keep expecting things to get awkward, but they don't. We seem to be back where we were before the sex.

"I'll call and make an appointment to meet with them," I tell him. "I'm not sure how forthcoming Hector is going to be or even if he'll agree to see me."

"If he does I'll go with you to meet with him. I don't want you going alone."

"Why?"

"He's a predator. What he did to Carla amounts to rape. I'd prefer it if you didn't go near him at all."

"That's not really your choice to make."

"You're right. It's not. But will you please not see him without me?"

I nod. The truth is I'd feel more comfortable if Nolan went with me. Not because I'm afraid, but because I'm not sure how *I'll* react. Carla was victimized over and over. Hector is just one of the people who took advantage of her and abused her. Just the thought of being in the same room with that man sets of me off.

"Thank you," he says. "We still have the rest of the stuff from Martin's office to go through. Do you want me to bring my laptop out here or work in my office?"

"Your office is fine."

"Go on in. I'll take care of the trash."

I wander down the hall, studiously avoiding his bedroom where everything crashed and burned, and go into his office. This room with all of its humming machines is somehow soothing to me. Odd. I've always thought of computers and other electronics as necessary, but what Nolan's built here is more than that. It feels alive, like a forest of machines that breath and think.

A couple of the screens are dark, but there's one that draws my attention. The views change every few moments, rotating between the front door, living room, kitchen, and this room. I watch Nolan stuff our fast food containers in the trash, then it cuts to the hallway, then to a view somewhere above me. I raise my gaze, but I don't see the camera. He's got his whole place wired except his bedroom and bathroom. Does that mean he has video of us in here last night and of us up against the door earlier?

"Oh, shit." He brushes past me and switches the screen off. "I have a lot of equipment in here and surveillance is kind of a hobby with me in case you haven't noticed. I film all the time. Security. I'm kind of a geek about it." He keeps rambling and I let him. "Sorry," he finishes a few moments later.

"Are you recording us right now?"

"Yes. It's always recording."

"What about us at the front door?"

"That too."

"And us in here last night?"

"I deleted that."

"After you watched it."

A guilty blush stains his cheeks. "Yeah."

"What did you think when you watched it?"

"I ah, didn't really...that is...we weren't in here that long."

"How many times did you watch it?"

He hesitates. "Several."

"Why?"

"I ah, enjoyed it."

"You got yourself off to it."

"Yeah." If it's possible he gets even redder.

Nodding, I try to think of what we must've looked like. "Was it...hot?"

"Very."

"Can you undelete it? I want to see it. And the front door too."

"You're not pissed?"

I shake my head. Surprisingly, I'm not. I know he didn't tape us on purpose and I believe him when he said that he deleted the first video. I'm curious to see what we look like, what *I* look like. The feeling of getting caught doing something naughty and dangerous comes over me. I like it. *A lot.* Nolan's woken a side in me that I didn't know I had. I side I'm anxious/scared/curious/excited to explore.

11

NOLAN

"Hang on a second," I tell Lila.

I can't believe she's not pissed about the video. There's a look in her eyes that makes me think watching herself on film *excites* her. Repressed, rigid Lila has a kinky side. I saw a glimpse of it last night when she watched that girl get herself off. And then again when she grabbed me and kissed me and begged me to fuck her. That word coming out of her mouth was so damn sexy. It totally set me off. I had no idea she could be so fierce and *hot* for it.

I go to my bedroom and grab a couple more condoms. If this is going to go the way I think it's going to go I want to be prepared. When I return I find Lila standing exactly where I left her except she's not looking at the screen. She's looking at me and the way she's looking at me makes me nearly trip over my own feet. I try to act cool like this kind of thing happens everyday for me when the truth is it *never* happens. Not like this anyway.

First of all, I never show my office to anyone. A woman has never set foot in here before Lila. Second of all, I've never taped myself with a partner and I've certainly never watched myself with one. And third, I don't think I've ever been with anyone as hot as Lila. Seriously. She smokes from head to toe and she has no idea, which just makes her all the more *interesting*. Not just interesting, but *enticing*. When I'm around her I feel like a dog scenting a bone with my mouth open and my tongue hanging out. Do you know how difficult it is to act and sound cool when you're practically panting all the time?

"Play the tape from last night first," she says.

"Okay."

I sit at my desk and click on the waste paper basket at the bottom of the screen. Even though I deleted the tape I didn't empty the trash expunging it permanently. I can't help but think I did that on purpose like some kind of unconscious premonition. But that's dumb. How could I possibly know Lila would want to watch it? The real reason is I wanted to give myself the option of watching it again. I'm not ashamed to admit that. I'm a dude. That's a dude thing to do.

I locate the file and click on it. Last night I trimmed it so that it starts right as we do—from when Lila grabbed me and kissed me. *God*, it's even hotter watching it a with Lila than without her. When she pulls off her sweater and I get a look at her for the first time... Man I wish the camera would've been on my face so I could see the glazed shocked look on my face. But then I'd be looking at myself and not at her. I really think I was given eyes just so I could look at her. She's beautiful almost otherworldly so. Like something so beautiful *can't* be from this world.

I can almost feel the weight of her breasts cupped in my hands. I'm so caught by our images on camera that I nearly forgot that Lila is there until she makes a sound somewhere between a gasp and a groan. Then I can't look away from her. I wonder if she's watching herself or me or the both of us together.

"Is there sound?" Her voice gives away nothing.

In answer I raise the volume until the room is filled with the sounds of us. We watch another few minutes until I walked her backwards out of the room and the video ends. The silence that follows is filled with so many unspoken thoughts and un-acted upon feelings that I'm afraid to move. I don't want to influence what happens next.

"Now the front door," she commands.

I gladly obey, needing *something* to focus on. It takes me a while to find the moment when I opened the door to her earlier. I skip ahead in segments, not wanting to watch us have sex in reverse. I finally find it and hit play. This tape is much more surreal than the first one. I haven't seen it before so the moment when she grabs me and kisses me throws me off guard. The angle again is on her with my back to the camera.

"Turn it up," Lila says, her request as forceful as the way she kissed me.

The sound isn't as clear as the office because the room is bigger, but there's no mistaking her demand for me to *fuck* her. My already hard dick somehow gets harder. She's all fire in the video. There's no doubt she wants—no needs— me. I'm rough with her. I wince at the way her body slams into the door over and over. She clings to me, her face contorted, her mouth open. I can still feel the slide of her on my dick as I pulled in and out. She comes and the sound she makes wraps around me like a warm fist. Beside me Lila is silent. If her knuckles weren't white where she clutches the edge of the desk I would think the scene playing out in front of her is having no effect on her.

Afterward, when I kissed her softly, her expression changed from surprised to confused. I didn't notice that at the time. Now I wonder about it and the way she didn't move when I left her to get rid of the condom. She stayed against the door as though she was glued to it. I ask her if she's okay in the video, if I was too rough. She says no, but everything about her says otherwise.

And then she asks me if we're going to have sex again. I really wish I could see the look on my face because what she said next was so shocking that I'm sure I'm staring at her all bug-eyed and uncool. Then again maybe not. At least I sound cool and she sounds...she sounds... I'm not sure how she sounds. Not confident, but not unconfident. Intrigued. That's the word. I didn't notice it at the time, but it's almost as though she's studying the results of some kind of experiment and deciding if it's worth exploring further.

I'm not sure how I feel about that so I stop the recording right before she tells me that she's going to let me have sex with her as many times as I want to. A chill races through me. At the time I thought it meant that she wanted it— wanted me—as much as I wanted her, but now I'm not so sure. Was it a pity fuck? A make up for her calling it off last night? Something she felt obligated to do?

Everything I'd been feeling since we had sex now feels fake and false. Like I cheated on a test and got an A on it but it wasn't really my achievement. I want to—no I need to— watch the video again, but I can't do that with her standing here. If I could replay what she says after I come back from the bathroom over again and watch her face more closely maybe I can get some kind of clue as to what's really going on here. Because I'm not sure she'd tell me if I asked.

"Are you going to delete them?" she asks.

I should. It would be the gentlemanly thing to do, but I find I can't lie to her. "No."

"Why? So you can get off on them again?"

"No." I close the window of the recording and pull up the bank statements we got from Martin's office. "We need to finish going through these and the rest of the stuff we got. We have a case to work, remember?"

For a moment she doesn't say anything. She stares at me, her head tilted to one side as though trying to read my thoughts. "Is something wrong? Did I do something wrong?"

Maybe she can read my mind. "I don't know. Is there?"

"What do you mean?"

"Nothing. Why don't you pull up that chair and we'll see what else Martin might have been hiding?"

She hesitates and then does as I said. I'm not usually this freaked out and confused after being with a woman. There's always some level of uneasiness when things are new, but never this level of awkwardness. Maybe I'm just being stupid and reading too much into her reactions. I've never seen a replay of myself with a woman. Maybe this is all normal. She's got to be feeling some anxiety about it too. Past agreeing that we want to have sex again, we haven't talked about anything beyond that.

Normally that's not a discussion I'm really interesting in having, but there are unusual circumstances here. We're thrown together for the duration, working closely together on Carla's case. The forced proximity accelerated things in an unnatural way. Maybe it's time to slow it down and start over. Focusing on the case will give us both room to breathe even though we're within touching distance.

"Let's see what other perversions await us on the bank statement," I say, scrolling through the pages.

Page after page it's more of the same. Martin had a serious live porn habit.

"That's a lot of money flowing into and out of that account," Lila says thoughtfully. "Where did it come from?"

"He couldn't have made it being a public defender?"

"Not hardly, no."

"We can't pull up his tax or banking records, but maybe there's something more in his files or on his computer that will tell us where the money was coming from. But right now..." I plug the SD card from the camera into my computer. "I want to see why Martin had his office under surveillance."

I click the icon for the card to open it. The camera must be motion activated because the video starts when the door is already half open. John Martin comes into the room and closes the door behind him. Not just closes, he locks it. Odd. He immediately goes behind his desk and drops to his knees, then disappears under it.

"What is he doing?" Lila asks, leaning closer to the screen.

"Maybe there's a hidden compartment or he's got something taped underneath the desk. I wish we'd had time to check it out." I wish I'd *thought* to check it out. Another live and learn moment for me that comes too late.

Martin pops back up, shoves a hand in his pants pocket, then immediately goes to the bookcase to the left of the desk and drops to his knees again. He starts pulling books off the third shelf without any concern about where they fall. When the shelf is empty he reaches into it. It's not apparent what he's doing at that angle until he sets a piece of wood from the back of the bookcase on the floor.

"A secret compartment," I say. "What are you hiding Martin?"

On screen, Martin reaches into his pocket and pulls something small out.

"A key?" Lila asks.

"Looks like."

Martin crouches lower, the hand he had in his pocket reaching into the back of the bookcase. He makes a motion like he's opening a door, then pockets the key again. Leaning down, he stretches a hand into the bookcase and pulls out a box. He lifts the lid and looks inside. It's hard to tell, but it looks like he's relieved. Then he replaces the lid and puts the box back. He goes through the whole process backwards until the key is back under the desk again.

"What was in that box?" Lila asks.

"I wish I knew. Did you see the look of relief on his face when he lifted the lid?"

"Yeah, whatever is in that box he wants kept hidden or safe."

Martin unlocks his office door and leaves. The video ends a few moments after the door closes behind him. Definitely motion detection. The door opens again after an indeterminate time. Debbie Martin appears in the frame as she closes the door and locks it behind her.

"I thought she said she never went in her husband's office," Lila says.

"Well, she's a liar."

"But why lie? What does it matter if she goes in there or not?"

"I think we're about to find out."

Debbie heads straight for the bust of JFK and the camera.

"Well, son of a bitch," I breathe. "*She* installed the camera."

Debbie fiddles with it then the picture goes black. It

doesn't come back on again until Debbie replaces the bust. As soon as it's in place Debbie leaves.

"Dang it," Lila says. "Whatever she did during the blackout will forever remain a mystery."

"Not necessarily." I rewind the tape to where Debbie first walks into the room. "Pay attention to the floor in front of the bookcase." I forward the tape to where Debbie reactivates the camera and then pause the video. I touch the screen. "See that spot there?" That wasn't there when she came into the room, but it's there when she leaves. I don't know if she dropped something or something fell off of her onto the floor or not, but she definitely went for the box hidden at the back of the bookcase."

"So she didn't trust her husband. Interesting. I wonder if he ever found out that she was on to him."

"Maybe we'll find out."

I start the video again. It continues to where Debbie leaves the room, then goes black. The door opens again. Could be hours or days later. There's no time or date stamp on the video so there's no telling when all of this occurred and how far apart.

Martin's back. This time he doesn't lock the door after he closes it. He goes to his desk and sits down. He works on his computer for what feels like forever. The video is in real time. I fast forward a bit to where he gets up from his desk and goes to the bookcase. He selects a book from the top shelf. As he starts to turn away he pauses, then bends down. He picks up whatever it was that Debbie dropped on the floor. His gaze immediately goes to the door. In an instant he's up, the book falls to the floor. He locks the door, then goes to the desk and ducks down behind it just like the first time. He rushes to the bookcase and shoves the books off the shelf. His movements are hurried and panicky.

Lila and I instinctively lean toward the screen. Martin pulls the box out and lifts the lid. He sits back on his heel, a staggered look on his face. The box falls from his hand. He covers his face with his hands and rocks back and forth. Whatever was in that box is gone and Debbie Martin has it.

12

LILA

"Is there any way to enhance the video, maybe zoom in to see if we can get a glimpse of what was in the box?" I ask Nolan.

I can't believe what we just saw on the video and I can't believe I felt sorry for Debbie Martin. She seemed like *such* a sweet lady. What was in the box and why did they both want it so much? Does it have anything to do with Carla's case or is it something just between a husband and a wife? I wonder if Debbie knew about her husband's porn problem and if Martin's dalliances ever stepped off the computer screen and into real life. While interesting, in a titillating way, we might be following a bogus lead here.

"I'll see what I can do," Nolan says, ejecting the SD card from his laptop. "I'll work on the other computer while you go through the files you copied from Martin's computer." We do some chair shuffling and then he inserts the thumb drive into the laptop in front of me. "Let me know if you find anything interesting."

He's cool now, all business, like when I first met him. He said nothing was wrong, but I don't believe him. Does he regret having sex? He seemed fine right up until we viewed the video. Did he think I was weird to want to watch the video of us? He watched it without me and he said he planned on viewing it again. It was only fair that I got to see it too, right? After all I was in it.

Maybe it embarrassed him. I mentally replay the video in my head and I can't see how he could have anything to feel awkward about. Unless he has some hidden hang up. If I knew him better I might be able to figure out where things went wrong, but I don't. And right there might be where the problem lies. I don't really know him at all. This might be his MO—love 'em and leave 'em, don't get attached and don't get tied down. That's fine if that's the case. I'm not looking for a boyfriend.

But I would like to have sex with him again. I'd also like to record the sex and watch it either with him or on my own. That admission is *so* not like me. Reliving the moments when I was free for what feels like the first time in my life, struck me in a way I have a hard time putting into words let along comprehending. I don't know what it is about this man or this apartment or whatever it is that's changed that makes me feel less like me, but I like it. I like it a lot. That should scare me more than it does. Not being scared should scare me more than it does. This whole situation should have me running the other direction.

Perhaps if I just tell him outright that I don't expect this to become a relationship he can get past whatever it is that's bothering him.

That's a good idea. I'll just lay all of my cards on the table, so to speak, and let him know I'm only in it for the experience and nothing more.

"Nolan?"

"Yeah?" His answer is distant and preoccupied.

"About what happened earlier...the sex."

"What about it?" He doesn't take his attention off the screen in front of him.

"I don't want you to think that I expect anything from you whether we do it again or not."

"Okay."

"So does that mean you want to do it again or you don't want to do it again?"

He lets out a humorless laugh. "Oh, we're going to do it again."

"All right. Good. Glad that's settled." I turn to the computer in front of me.

"And we're going to film it. From all angels."

For a moment I can't speak. It's like he read the thoughts I'd stuffed into the far corners of my mind, too ashamed to admit them. "I'd like that."

"When I finish doing what I can to the video here I'll set up the cameras in my bedroom."

My heart drops a beat as though my body stopped working for a split second to fully absorb his words. I force myself to focus on the task I'm supposed to be doing. Thinking about Carla helps. She's the reason I'm here. We have to figure out what happened to her lawyer and why he didn't file that motion to dismiss and if there's anything we've missed that could trip us up when we file a post conviction motion for a new trial. I really want to nail this the first time out and not have it go on to appeals. That would only prolong Carla's suffering.

I open the thumb drive and glance through the files I uploaded from Martin's computer. I hold off on the emails for now and open the file marked with Carla's last name. It opens to another window with a bunch of files in it. These files are not numbered sequentially and don't disclose anything about their contents. I right click on the first one and click on 'get info'. This folder was created less than a month before Carla's trial.

I open it only to find another window with more files. At least these are labeled in a way that makes sense. There's the coroner's report, a transcript of Carla's confession, depositions, Martin's notes, and other elements of her defense. I already have a copy of the coroner's report, but something makes me click to open it.

It's empty. Nothing's there. Strange. I X out of there and click on the transcript of Carla's confession. It immediately opens to the text record created by the transcriber like it should. I click out of that file and open the folder marked 'notes', which brings up another set of folders. I go through all of those and they're all normal.

I try the coroner's report again thinking I must've missed something. Nope. Blank. So odd.

"Hey, Nolan. I found something weird here. Or maybe it's not and I'm giving Martin more credit than he deserves."

"What is it?"

"An empty folder where the coroner's report should be."

"I couldn't enhance the video enough to figure out what was in the box anyway. Let me see." He changes seats with me.

I lean over his shoulder to watch. He does some kind of wizardry on the keys, bringing up black windows with white font. He clicks around some more and then reopens the coroner's report to reveal a folder hidden within the folder.

"Private folder," he murmurs, then does some more computer magic. "Password protected." He manages to get it open.

"It's gibberish."

"Not necessarily." He starts copying and pasting lines of

text into a new document. After a few moments he looks up and me and laughs. "He gets an E for effort, but an F for originality. He hid a message in transposition cypher within html code."

At my confused look he clarifies. "He wrote a bunch of words backwards and tried to hide it within html code, trying to make it look like it was part of the code. Except even a beginning programmer could figure this out. More than likely he did it to confuse someone who doesn't know html code and wouldn't know if there were any extra characters randomly thrown in."

"What does it say?"

He types the words in the correct letter order, slowly revealing the message. "I think it's an email."

"How can you tell? There's no email address."

"It's too short and informal. The format is more like an email than a letter." He finishes typing the message and reads it out loud. "Got it. Meet you Sunday at three at the usual. Don't forget to adjust your witness list accordingly. I'm counting on you."

"What does that mean? Was there any signature, email address or other identifying information in the code?"

"Nothing. The rest is standard html coding."

"Coding for what?"

"Let's convert it to text and see." He does some more magic and up pops what looks like the home page for the San Diego County District Attorney. "What the... This can't be right."

He goes onto the Internet and pulls up the website for the district attorney's office and clicks on the 'About DA Clifford G. Billits' tab. Sure enough it matches the page with the exception of the website banner at the top and the website navigation widget on the side.

Nolan sits back in his chair. "Whoa."

"I think the words you're looking for are *holy shit*."

"Does this mean what I think it means?"

"That the DA wrote this email to Martin? I think so. Why else would he put the email in the middle of the coding for the DA's 'about me' page?"

"I wish I could hack into Billits's email and find out, but that's a line I'm not willing to cross. Don't look so surprised," Nolan says, sounding genuinely affronted. "I do have my moral limits."

"I know you do. The look on my face was me reacting to my own thoughts, which for a moment actually entertained the idea." I press my fingers into my eyes. "I don't know what's come over me lately."

"Must be my influence."

"It is, but not in the way you think. I just... I don't know. I'm surprised at myself. I didn't know I had this side."

"A wild side?" he asks with a sly tilt to his mouth.

"An inappropriate side, a bending of the truth and the law side, a risk taking side. None of that is me. Or at least I never thought it could be me. I don't know what's happening to me."

"Maybe it was there all along waiting to come out and you've suppressed it all these years."

"I don't know. Maybe."

"You *like* it."

I sigh. "I do. And I can't believe that either."

"If I do something here or..." He makes a sweeping motion, indicating the office in general, then gestures toward the rest of the apartment "...*elsewhere* that you're not comfortable with let me know."

I shake my head. "You're fine. It's me."

"I get it now."

"Get what?"

"Your reactions. When we watched the video I got the feeling that there was something wrong about the way that went down for you. That maybe it was... I don't know...an experiment and that maybe you weren't all that comfortable with what happened or perhaps you regretted it. Or that maybe you were using me."

"*Using you?*"

It's his turn to shake his head. "Never mind. It doesn't matter now."

"No. Tell me what you mean."

"That you were slumming it for the experience."

I honestly don't know what to say to him. His words repeat over and over in my head. *Slumming it for the experience.* I'm not sure which of us should be more insulted by that statement—him or me. My emotions war with each other each, making their case to be heard. I don't know whether to laugh at the ridiculousness of the statement or be furious with him for thinking so little of me and of what we shared. I don't know how it was for him—I mean, I thought I did, although *clearly* I didn't—but it was pretty cataclysmic for me.

It obviously wasn't for him.

"And you were willing to let me *slum it* again for the experience?" I ask, incredulity coloring my tone. "Are you acting out some sort of penance or something? Was it that terrible for you or are you that desperate to get laid?"

"No. No. Nothing like that. Shit. I shouldn't have said anything. It was just a thought. A stupid, insecure thought that I should've kept to myself. It has absolutely nothing to do with you."

"Huh. Cause I'm pretty sure it was about nothing *but* me."

"Just forget that I said it, okay? I'm an idiot."

"You'll get no argument from me."

"It wasn't terrible," he says after a long pause. "Far from it. It was fucking *amazing*."

"It was?"

"Wasn't it?"

"Yeah. It was."

"Okay then. So we're okay?"

"I honestly don't know." And I don't. "I'm still a little confused by your choice of words."

"They're a reflection on me not on you. I think you're incredible."

"You do?"

He gives me a sweet, slightly lopsided smile. "Yeah. I do."

"In that case, yes, we're okay."

"Good because I was looking forward to setting up those cameras later." He takes my hand and tugs me close.

My whole face goes hot and some other places too. "Me too."

"Yeah?"

"Yeah." I lean down and kiss him.

He tries to pull me into his lap, but I resist. If we get caught up all the time we'll never figure this case out. I tell him that and he reluctantly releases me. My attention goes to the computer screen and DA Billits's photo. I met him once shortly after finishing law school. He seemed like a nice man. But first impressions can be deceiving.

White with brown hair and blue eyes Billits matches Carla's description of the man who paid to have sex with her and popped his head into the room while she was talking to Martin. I can't help but think that brief visit was no coincidence. That maybe Billits wanted Carla to see him and to know that he was pulling the strings. This explains so, so much about what happened with Carla's case.

"Can you print me out that photo of DA Billits?" I ask Nolan. "I want to show it to Carla the next time I see her. He might be her mystery man."

Nolan loses his smile. "Double *holy shit*."

My thoughts exactly.

13

NOLAN

"He certainly fits the description," I tell Lila. "But then the description is vague enough to fit my cousin Joe, my friend Dominic, and half the guys I went to school with. If *my* eyes were blue it would describe me."

"Yes, but remember the tattoos? She said he had one on his chest and another on his left calf. She described them in detail."

"Gotchya. I bet if I surfed the web long enough I could maybe find a photo of our friend the DA here on the Internet with shorts on and no shirt. He might not have posted a pic of himself, but maybe a friend or relative did." I give Lila her chair back, dropping a kiss on her forehead. "Keep going through the stuff you found on Martin's computer. See if anything else weird pops up while I work on this. Good catch by the way."

"I'm going to go through the rest of this with a fine tooth comb, but you might want to check for anymore hidden files when I'm done just in case."

"Download everything onto that computer then give me the thumb drive and I'll go through it on this one."

"You got it."

I get to work scouring the Interwebs for photos of the DA, using variations of his name, his wife's name, and their kids' names. Someone really needs to talk to the DA's teenagers about setting social media accounts to private. The stuff they post is shocking and I work for an online porn company. Don't they know that the Internet is forever?

It doesn't take long before I come across vacation photos from the Billits's trip to Cancun three summers ago. There's a shot of him playing volleyball with his sons and daughter, but he's wearing a tank top and the shots are mostly from the waist up. I scroll through until I find a shot of him kissing his wife on a lounge chair. They're both lying on their stomachs, but Billits's left calf is just visible in the side shot. And there right where Carla described it is a tattoo of a jagged knife with a banner wrapped three times around it. There's some wording that if I just... There. *Death before dishonor*.

I'm shaking as I take a screen shot, documenting where the image came from. I glance over at Lila. She's concentrating on the screen in front of her. I'm almost afraid to go on with my search. We just inadvertently stepped in the big, giant pile of shit. If this is the guy... A part of me doesn't want to believe it's him. Especially after going through all of the pictures of Billits and his happy, happy family.

I force myself to close the photo and continue the search. And it's there on Billits's sister-in-law's Facebook page that I find a photo of him at a pool party. He's smiling and holding a beer, his arm slung around his oldest son's shoulders. And right across his left pec—over his heart—is the word *sacrifice* in bold letters.

Cold splashes over me. This is our guy. This is the guy who paid to have sex with Carla. This is the guy who likely fixed it so she'd be convicted for murder. This is the guy we're up against. I have a feeling once he finds out what we're doing and that we're onto him, this investigation is going to take a turn that could be disastrous for us all, but Lila in particular. In her line of work she's going to come up against this guy and his office in defense of her clients. He's bound to have friends in high places, friends like judges who would see no problem implementing the good old boys network to squash a no name bug like Lila. I bet when she took this case on she had no idea it could jeopardize everything she's worked so hard for.

I screen shot the photo and bring up the other pic so that they're side by side. There's no doubt this is the man Carla described. We'd have to show her the photos to be sure. I take a moment to find photos of men about the DA's age and coloring and save those as well, putting together a photo array that Lila can show Carla. I then crop the tattoos from copied screen shots and then print those all out too.

Now I have to break the news to Lila. She looks so calm reading through the files from Martin's computer. I'm sorry I opened my mouth earlier about my doubts. I shouldn't have said that stuff to her. It's not her fault I'm an insecure jackass. I'm not entirely sure what's going on between us other than we both want it to continue. Right now that will have to be enough and I'll have to bite down on my tongue to keep from saying something stupid again and screwing it up.

I can't even manage to not fuck up the best sex of my life. You'd think that would be a no brainer, but apparently not for me. I need to stop questioning her motives for wanting to continue this thing between us and just enjoy it for however long it lasts. Speaking of...

I sneak out of the office, grab the two extra cameras out of the hall closet, and go into my bedroom. Where to put them? Glancing around the room, I calculate the best angles. If I had more I'd set them all up. I can't believe I'm actually looking forward to this. Voyeurism has never been my thing. Working for the sex websites is the perfect side job for me because I'm not tempted to sample the merchandise. But this is different. This is Lila. And watching Lila come is almost—okay not even close—as good as being inside her when she comes. An experience I very much want to have again.

If I don't manage to fuck it up.

The cameras are a quick install since there's no need to hide them. I set them to activate with motion and head back to the office where I find Lila leafing through the photos I printed.

She looks up at me with wide, dark eyes. "It's him isn't it?"

"Yeah."

"Ah, damn. *Damn it*. I have to report this."

"To who?"

"The police."

"What exactly are you going to report? What's the crime besides prostitution, which will only come back on Carla?"

She looks down at the pictures. "I *will* have to report it. If we can definitively connect the DA to Martin and show that he influenced Carla's defense."

"What would happen to him? Realistically?"

"Realistically? Probably not much—sanctions, maybe ejection from the California Bar Association—unless we can prove he had something to do with Martin's disappearance."

"Martin could've disappeared himself. People do it all

the time. He had a lot of secrets, a wife who was spying on him and took whatever was in the box he was hiding, money coming from who knows where, and he was a public defender who was in the pocket of the DA. He had a truck-load of reasons to vanish. I wouldn't be surprised if he was on an island somewhere telling barely legal women how to touch themselves while he jacks off."

"If you were to disappear, how would you do it?"

"Some might start with a new identity, but that's too obvious and not as easy as it sounds. Although with Martin's occupation he probably came across a lot of people who could help him in that regard. Establishing himself with a new identity wouldn't be easy. He could get a bank account, but wouldn't have a credit history to rent an apartment or set up utilities or buy a car."

"Then he has to be using a different identity."

"Not necessarily." I lean against the doorframe, cross my arms and rub my chin, really getting into this. "He'd need access to his money. Unless he set up a new identity before he tapped into whatever it was that was funding his porn habit—and the fact that he had a bank account in his own name proves he didn't think that far ahead—he'd have needed his ID to get his money out of the account.

"I think... Of *course*." I come off the doorframe and go to the computer Lila was working on. "I want to see his bank statements again." I pull them up and scroll through looking for the one weird charge. "There." I point it out on the screen. "Goddamn this guy is an idiot." I jump back over to my computer.

"What? What is it?"

"The only out of place charge on the account."

"A book store? He could've bought anything there."

"Maybe. But here's the thing, Martin's not smart enough

to have disappeared on his own. He had help. The trails he left all over the place prove that."

"What kind of help?"

I do some not-exactly-legal maneuvering on the Internet and hack into Martin's online account with the bookstore. And there in his order history is the help Martin got—How to Vanish Without a Trace for Numbskulls.

"*Idiot*," I say out loud. "He violated the first rule of How to Vanish Without a Trace for Numbskulls—*buy the book with cash*."

"You're kidding me. There's a Numbskull book for how to disappear?"

"There's a Numbskull book for just about everything, including how to give a woman an orgasm. Which I've read by the way."

"Clearly. So you think Martin used the book to disappear?"

"Yeah. I think that's exactly what he did. The only other option is that he's dead."

"But we'd know if he was dead. There'd be a death certificate and the police—" She gasps. "You mean *murdered*."

"That's a possibility, but it's a distant second. The police haven't come across anything so far that leads to his having been murdered. Hang on. I'll be right back." I go out to the living room and pull my copy of How to Vanish Without a Trace for Numbskulls and bring it back with me to the office.

I flip through the book to a section I'd highlighted. "Here." I tap the page. "Disinformation. Leaving behind a trail so wide and tangled that it would take forever to sort out. That's why we found the bank statements in his office. He *needed* them to be found. It's part of his disappearing act.

I bet if we pull his credit report we'll find that he applied for utilities and a place to live in another state. Maybe even a couple of different cities. But none of them will be for where he actually is. Disinformation. It's brilliant. Except that we have access to the road map he used, which means we know that all of the clues he left are really dead ends."

"So how does that help us find him?"

"We'll have to hope he slipped up somewhere. I'm betting it's the online porn sites. That level of addiction will be hard for him to break. He might think he's clever using different services than he used on that bank account, but I have no doubt he's regularly visiting those sites. We just have to figure out which one or ones."

"You said you couldn't access their billing records."

"I can't. It's on a different server than the cameras. But I can access user names. Using his bank statements I can try to recreate his pattern—the days and times he's most likely to be online and for how long. From that I can look at the user names online during those times. You'd be surprised how many times people use the same user name over and over."

"That sounds tedious."

"It would be, but I think I have a program I can adapt and run to help me find him."

She sighs. "Well, at least I now know why Martin didn't file the motion to dismiss the charges. The DA stopped it. But how?"

"The money. I bet if we dig around enough we'll find that Billits funded—either purposefully or accidentally— Martin's disappearance."

"That makes sense. No one would think to look for a tie between the two of them. After all, what could they have in common? Martin disappears and no one's the wiser to their plot. Carla's in jail. She didn't say anything about their possible connection during her trial and, by nature, she's not someone who would rock their carefully crafted boat. She was the perfect victim. They both got something out of her conviction—Billits covered his paying-for-prostitutes tracks—if that was what this is really about—and Martin got his chance to disappear."

"You bring up good points. What is Billits's motive for wanting Carla convicted? She's a poor, illegal immigrant prostitute. How could she possibly hurt him? Anyone would believe him over her. He exposed himself to her by walking into that meeting between her and Martin. Why? All he had to do was not open that door. I can't believe it was an accident unless Martin set him up. That I could believe. Maybe that was how the extortion started. And why did Martin want to disappear? There has to be more to it than a nosey wife."

"Reminds me of that movie *Strangers on a Train*. Two unlikely people meet and plot murder for each other. But in this case it's a plot to convict a young woman who lost her son."

I snap my fingers. "That's it. That's exactly it. We've been trying to figure out the why of Martin going along with Billits and assuming it had to do with money, that Billits paid Martin to throw Carla's trial. But what if it wasn't? What if Billits did something for Martin in return and the money has nothing to do with any of this? I bet if we track down the source of the money it won't have come from Billits."

"I see where you're going with this and it makes a lot more sense than trying to make it all about the money. The question then is what did Billits do for Martin and how do we figure out what it is?"

"We need to dig deeper into both Martin's and Billits's backgrounds. There's a connection there. I can feel it."

"Let me see what I can find out from the legal side of their lives. I can discreetly inquire about them from friends and from a couple of courthouse clerks I know and trust. They know all of the good dirt on the attorneys—who's sleeping with who, who's having an affair, who has a gambling problem and so on. It's a regular hive of gossip and intrigue."

"Be careful," I tell her. "Billits went through a lot of trouble to get Carla convicted. He's hiding something there. Something worth potentially destroying his career over. In fact, if you can keep it quiet that we're working on Carla's case that will give us more room to move around. I don't want him tipped off before we have what we need on him."

"I'll talk to the Freedom Project director about not putting Carla's case up on the website, but everyone in the office knows I'm working the case. There's no way to contain that without tipping our hand."

"Good point. Maybe we should engage in some disinformation of our own in that regard."

"I like the way you think." She smiles really big and something sharp and pointy stabs me in the chest. This woman is going to twist me up. I can already tell. And I'm going to like it.

"Maybe I can let it be known that Carla isn't being cooperative," she continues. "Which she isn't. There's more going on here than she's telling us and I'm not entirely sure I believe her story about this mystery man walking in on her meeting. She leaked just enough information to get us curious, but not enough to really know what's going on here and how, exactly, Billits fits into all of this.

"I can also spread it around that you're hitting a brick

wall where Martin is concerned, that you're difficult to work with and I'm thinking of finding a new PI to take over the case."

"Ouch." I clutch at my heart. "But I like it. Dissension among the ranks. It'll make it seem as though the case is stalled. We could maybe even throw in a public fight for a few key people to witness."

"I like the way you think." She places a hand on my chest and slides it up until she's fisting my hair in her hand. "You're very good at what you do."

Her compliment catches me off guard. *Very good* isn't how I'd describe my bumbling investigative skills. And then I realize she's not talking about my PI work when she puts her other hand between my legs and cups me. I let out an inarticulate noise more out of shock than excitement although excitement quickly catches up, as I start to get hard against her palm. She pulls me down for a kiss. I like her aggressiveness and the way she takes charge. I'm all for letting her lead. Before I know it she's got my pants open and is stroking me.

I've hardly moved since she started touching me, but all of a sudden its like I've been plugged in and I tear at her clothes. I want her naked. All the way bare this time, arching her back as I work over her. Or riding me, with her breasts bouncing around as she drives herself up and down, while I grip her hips. Or on her hands and knees, her ass thrust up in the air as take her from behind, watching my dick disappear inside her. She swipes her thumb in my precum and I groan into her mouth.

I'm way too far ahead of her. I need her as hot—no hotter—for me than I am for her. I want her to beg me to fuck her just like she did last time. She's got my dick in one hand and my balls in the other and I can't seem to work her bra. The damn thing is stuck or... *Fuck*. Is she getting to her knees?

Oh, my god she is.

Baseball. My Aunt Nancy. Her hot breath over me. HTML. The feel of her mouth around me. Santa Claus. Her tongue swirling around my head. That TV show with the detective and the writer... I slide my hand into her hair, urging her to suck me deeper, harder. The sound she makes when she takes me into the back of her throat. *Goddamn*. Email I need to answer. My mom's meatloaf. Her wet finger circles my asshole.

No, she's not.

She pushes in, hooking her finger just right. My knees buckle and I have to grip the edge of the desk to stay upright. She strokes inside me and somehow takes me even deeper into her mouth. My fingers tense in her hair.

"Coming," I manage to warn her a split second before I'm pouring into her mouth.

Trembling, I grip her head and the desk harder, groaning as I look down at the way her lips wrap around me. She looks up at me and winks as she slides her finger out of my ass and her mouth off my dick. She wipes the back of her hand across her mouth. As she stands I realize she's still fully dressed. I have to rectify that. Her shirt is first, then her bra. She watches me with wide, expectant eyes. It's time to put that bragging I did earlier to the test. I yank her skirt and underwear off her at the same time. Finally. She's finally naked and I have to take a moment to drink her in.

She's curvy, round in all the right places. I lick my lips trying to draw enough spit to say something, but there are no words in my head. Instead I lead her to one of the office chairs. Her gaze flickers to it nervously for a second before I push her down into it. Then I'm shucking my clothes as fast as I can get them off. It's my turn to go to my knees in front of her. I part her thick thighs and get a look at her. She's already wet, her little landing strip of hair glistens. I lick my lips again in expectation. I can feel her watching me, her arousal quickly melting like it did last night. I have to do something to get her back with me.

I grab one of the handles underneath the chair and pull, dropping the back of the chair down. She gasps and reaches out for the arms of the chair to keep from falling out of it. She's laid out now. Her breasts fall to the sides. I push her knees farther apart. She lifts her head and I catch the gleam of excitement in her eyes.

"*Suck me*," she demands.

There is nothing else for me to do but obey.

14

LILA

Nolan kneels between my spread thighs, gazing down at my pussy. He licks his lips again like he's in for a treat. I hope he's really good at this because I have yet to meet a man who truly is. Most of them do it out of a sense of obligation or else they have no idea how a woman's anatomy really works. There's lots of pointless licking and sucking in the wrong places, while thrusting their fingers. They moan like they're enjoying it and I always know they're faking it. They're just hoping to get it over with as soon as possible so they can get to the part where I suck them off in return.

Nolan slides his palms up the inside of my thighs. His gaze is firmly fixed on my pussy and he looks like a man on a mission. I have to watch. Shoving my hand under my head to keep it up, I have the perfect view down my body. Great. My breasts have slid into my armpits. From this angle my stomach has more rolls than planes. My thighs spread across the chair's seat making them look twice as wide. But Nolan doesn't seem to notice any of that. He's totally and completely focused between my legs where he's using his fingers to separate my folds like this is a physical examination or something.

I squirm and his gaze flickers up to mine. Gauging my reaction, he strokes his thumb lightly across my clit. My internal muscles contract, making my hips flex slightly. He smiles as though he's just discovered something extraordinary. I'm in trouble here I suddenly realize. This guy might actually know what he's doing. Without taking his eyes off me he lowers his head. I'm sure he's just going to dive in and go to town, but he doesn't. He drops kisses up my inner thigh, beginning about half way up. First one leg then the other. He nuzzles between my thighs and my pussy. There's nothing rushed about his movements. He watches my reactions, focusing on what makes me gasp. Teasing me, he takes his time, as though he's just playing, he's not really going to eat me out.

He licks and kisses the sides, building the sensations one on top of the other. His finger joins the fun, entering me partially before withdrawing in a steady rhythm. I'm swept away on a sea of pleasure and can't keep my head up anymore. The anticipation grows the longer he takes to get to my clit. My legs tremble. I want to push his head down and ride his face. Fisting his hair, I try to urge him to get on with it, but he ignores me and continues the same slow torturous movements. I silently beg him to give me what I need.

Just when I think I'm going to die if he doesn't do it, he flicks my clit with his tongue in a constant pulse. My back arches and my body tenses. The need to come rides me hard. It's next level, but still not enough. I'm close. So close. I open my mouth to beg him. Before I can get the words out he does something with his fingers and his tongue strokes me so strong and steady I break. Screaming, I grip his hair harder and come all over his face. I grind up into him, trying to extend my orgasm.

He strokes two fingers into me in a *come here* movement. His tongue continues its assault. I'm practically ripping his hair out and the arm off the chair. Another wave of pleasure hits me harder than the last. I lose it all over again, crying out a second time. I lift my head to find him still watching me. I shake my head for him to stop. He doesn't. I can't take any more, but I don't push him away. He keeps up with the same steady rhythm. Fingers and mouth. Watching, always watching. It's like he's taken a master class on getting me off. It builds again. Not as sharp, but just as high. I thrash in the chair, wanting to come and scared of it at the same time.

My voice is hoarse. I can hardly catch my breath. And still he keeps going. That same steady, pulsing beat. Unaltered. Unrelenting. Unending. His gaze dares me like it's a competition. I want to close my eyes and shut him out, but I can't look away. It's too intense, this intimacy. I feel it taking me over, pulling me under. He's doing this to me. He's making me feel too much. I hate what he's doing. Yet I can't get enough. I need him to make me come. I need him right where he is. I need—

Jackknifing in the chair, I scream his name when I come. I push him away with my hands and feet. I can't take it anymore. Finally. Relief. Sagging back in the chair, I go completely limp. It's only then I can close my eyes. My whole body throbs in time with my pulse, the hardest beat between my legs. My nipples are hard, sensitive peaks. I'm hypersensitive and exhausted yet this is the most alive I've ever felt. I didn't know it could be like this. I've had orgasms, but nothing like the ones he just gave me.

Feeling like I should say something to him, I open my eyes. He's still on his knees at my feet, jerking on his dick with the hand he had inside me. It's so wet I can hear a squelching noise as he strokes up and down. It's my turn to watch him come. He stares at me like a man watching a porno. His roaming gaze is a touch my body responds to. With a low groan, he drops his head back and comes all over his hand. The cum runs down his fingers as he milks out the last drops. And still his eyes never leave me.

A smug, satisfied smile creases his face as he lifts his head. He knows he's ruined me for all other men. I want to know how he learned that and yet I don't. For some reason the thought of him working some other woman over like that bothers me more than I want to admit. He grabs his shirt and uses it to clean himself up. I still can't move. Seeing him get himself off after getting me off has to be the most erotic thing I've ever witnessed.

He puts his hands on my knees and leverages himself up until he's over me. He tugs me closer for an open mouthed kiss. There's no shyness in him about tasting me after I'd had him in my mouth and he'd had his mouth on me. If anything it only makes the kiss hotter. It's unabashed and direct, a claiming of sorts. My wet pussy slides against his stomach as I arch up to met him, fusing our torsos together. Our bodies reek of sex and carnality. The whole room smells like an orgy. I never want to leave.

Our hands tangle in each other's hair, trying to draw ever closer. It doesn't feel like we could ever be close enough. Our skin creates too much distance between us. I'm drained. Totally spent. But he still manages to stir something in me that could quickly get out of control. I want him inside me next time, I decide. I want him over me, then behind me.

As the kiss winds down, I'm shocked at the plans I've made for us. This wasn't supposed to go that far. In my head it was a fling. I was sure I'd grow bored once the novelty had worn off. The thing is, I *like* the novelty. The novelty is at the core of it all. He's awoken something in me I hadn't realized existed. By the look he's giving me I can tell he feels the same. It's the dirty, the downright necessary-ness of what's between us that sits at the heart of everything that's happening.

And that's not something that can be denied.

We can try and we probably will. I know I will because it scares me. *He* scares me. This wasn't supposed to happen. It was a simple itch I scratched. A walk on the wild side. It was supposed to be like the men who watch those girls on screen. Not real. A fantasy. I was supposed to be a voyeur. Stepping outside of my world for just a moment, keeping one foot in as an anchor so I don't get lost. But I'm already lost. I want him again. He's awoken a thirst in me that only he can quench.

I want his hands and mouth on me. I want to be naked, rolling around in damp cum stained sheets with him. I want the scent of our sex to always fill my nostrils. I want to claw and scratch and scream and shout and break the bed. I want to yell for him to stop and not mean it. I want to be sore, so sore I can hardly walk and every time I sit down I replay how I got that way in my head to the point where I have to put my hands in my panties to assuage the never ending need for him.

As though hearing my thoughts, he lifts me out of the chair. I wrap my legs around his waist and my arms around his neck. I'll go wherever he takes me as long as he fucks me again. And again. And again.

He takes us to the bathroom and starts the shower. A part of me doesn't want to wash off. I want to stay sticky and sweaty. And another part of me wants to be clean just so we can get dirty all over again.

He lowers me to the floor. There's something lost and panicked about the way he's looking at me, like I might bolt and he won't be able to stop me. I kiss him, not wanting to see the doubts he has about me. They're the same doubts I have about myself. I'm not an all in kind of woman. I have too many outside things pulling at me. If I think about them they'll ruin this moment and take away what will happen next just like they did that first night. I have to make sure I don't think. I have to convince him not to let me think, to keep me in the physical because the mental is not a place I should be allowed to linger.

He breaks the kiss and draws me into the steamy shower. I'm immediately pulled against him. His mouth comes down on mine, but the tone is different. It's slow and lazy. His touch is light and constant. He runs his hands all over me as though he's learning the landscape. I've never been touched with this much care and interest. He wants to know me. I find myself wanting to know him in the same way. Mimicking his movements, I explore him. He's hairier on his lower body than his upper body. He doesn't have much chest hair, but the happy trail leading from his belly button to his cock is dense and so sexy I spend a long time running my fingers over it curiously.

"You're not what I expected," he whispers against my ear.

"What did you expect?"

"Honestly?"

I nod. He's holding me so close no water can get between us.

"A cold bitch."

I pull back to look at him.

"Sorry, but it's true. You were very...bristly." He laughs at the face I make. "You accused me of being a racist."

"Everybody's a racist."

"I'm not going to respond to that while I've got you naked. I have too many plans."

"What plans?"

"I like surprising you." He grabs the bottle of shower gel and pours some into his hand. "Now, dirty girl, let me wash you."

He goes back to caressing my body the way he did before only now his hands are a lot slicker. The slip and slide of his touch lulls me into a seductive trance. He could do just about anything to me right now and I'd let him. I don't know how he's doing it, luring me into giving over more of myself than I ever intended. But I don't care. I've never felt like this. He's like a drug and I'm a willing addict, holding my arm out to mainline more. That's all I want—*more*.

He rotates me, putting me under the showerhead. The water slushes over me. It's hot, but not as hot as his gaze. It never leaves me. I don't think I've ever been the center of anyone's attention like this. That's part of his temptation. I don't know whether he's doing it on purpose or not, but it works on me.

We get out of the shower and towel off. He leads me to his bedroom. Expectation rises inside me. What is he going to do to me next? He directs me to get into bed and he climbs in beside me. His arms go around me and he pulls me in close. I wait for him to make a move, but he seems content to leave things the way they are. He's hard so I know he's ready. Why isn't he doing anything? Maybe he's waiting for me. He seems to like it when I initiate things.

I'm just about to let my hands do some wandering when he says something that makes my whole body tense.

"Will you spend the night with me?" When I don't respond he angles back to look at me. "It's a simple question, Lila."

I sit up and pull the sheet around me. It *should* be a simple question. I can see how he might expect that. At this point in the relationship most guys do.

"I don't do that."

"What? Spend the night?"

"Yeah."

"With anyone or just me?"

"With anyone."

He shifts, sitting up against the pillows. "Can I ask why?"

"I'd rather you didn't." I glance at the clock. "It's getting late and I'm hungry. If we're done here then I think I'll go home." I start to climb out of bed, but he grabs my wrist and stops me.

"*If we're done here*? What's that supposed to mean?"

"If we're not going to have sex."

I can't get a read on the look on his face. It's a combination amused, confused, and angry and I don't know what it means.

"Wow. I knew you were going to be a tough nut to crack, but not this tough. So I'm what to you then?"

"What do you mean?"

"I mean what are we doing here? Is it just fucking for you?"

"Well, yeah. What else could it be?"

"Exploring a possible relationship?"

"Okay. I can see we're done here. Thanks for everything, but I think it's probably best if we go back to just being colleagues." I try to tug my hand free. He tightens his grip.

"We're not done. I have a whole list of things I haven't gotten to do to you yet and I intend on getting to every single one more than once before we're through. If we're ever through."

"What do you mean *if we're ever through*?"

"It's a *really* long list."

"Wh-what's on it?" I can't hide my excitement.

He flips me onto my back. In a second he's on top of me. Hard, hot, and angry. "I'm not going to tell you. You're going to have to stick around to find out."

"A hint."

"No."

"I don't see any point to this."

"Do I have to tie you to my bed to get you to give us a try?" His smile is all teeth at my soft gasp. "*Oh*, you'd like that, wouldn't you?"

I shake my head. But there's nothing I'd like more.

He captures my wrists and pulls my arms over my head. "*Don't move*," he orders. "I mean it."

My heart's beating so hard and fast I can't do anything else but obey. He goes to his closet. I get a nice view of his backside. Gripping the iron headboard, I wait for him to come back. This is another thing I didn't know I'd be into. I'm shocked that there's no shame in that admission. I want to let him do things to me that no one else has ever done.

He comes back to bed with a wad of neckties in his hands. I can't stop staring at them. What is he going to do with them? What is he going to do to me? He takes my wrist and knots a tie around it, then attaches the other end to the headboard. He does the same with my other arm. I'm sweating and practically panting by the time he secures my legs to the footboard. He stands at the foot of the bed looking at me. A trickle of wetness leaks out between my legs. My breasts ache for him to touch. I like being at his mercy. I like not knowing what's going to come next.

"You're going to spend the night," he pronounces.

I shake my head.

He quickly tamps down the flash of disappointment that crosses his face. He clears his throat. "I'm going to convince you."

"You can try."

He studies me for a long moment, drawing out my anticipation. "What do you want me to do to you first?" he asks.

"My breasts. Touch them. Suck them."

"What will you give me in return?"

"Whatever you want."

"*Whatever* I want?"

"Yes." My voice is soft with expectation.

He vaults over the foot rail, making me bounce when he hits the mattress. Crawling on his hands and knees, he comes over me. He lowers his head and takes my nipple in his mouth. I arch up, pulling on my bindings. He fills his hands with me and takes his time sucking and caressing my sensitive flesh. Straining toward him, I buck and writhe. I love what he's doing but I need more.

"Touch me between my legs," I beg.

He pulls his mouth off me and licks a path to my ear. "No." His voice is soft but firm.

"*Please*."

"You promised me whatever I want."

"What do you want?"

"I want to know why you don't want to spend the night with me."

"I'm here now."

"Only because of the sex. Which we're not going to get to if you don't answer my question."

I open my mouth to speak, but only a moan comes out as he pulls my nipple deep into his mouth.

"The truth, Lila," he says around my nipple, creating a shockwave that moves from where his mouth is straight to my pussy.

"I can't."

"Why can't you?" He licks around my areola and I close my eyes in ecstasy.

"I-I just can't."

"That's not an answer," he growls. "Are you married?" There's real anger and jealousy in his tone. "*Answer me.*"

"No. I'm not married."

"Living with someone? Engaged? What?"

"None of those. I'm not with anyone."

"Then what's the problem?"

"Untie me."

"I'll only untie you if you tell me you don't want this." He slides his fingers across my clit and I moan. "But if it's so you don't have to answer my question then I'm not going to untie you."

He strums my clit a few more times. The ties bite into my wrists as I twist and strain. The sting only enhances my pleasure.

"*Please*, Nolan."

"I'll make you come." He easily finds my rhythm again. "I'll make you come any way you want. But first you have to answer me. The real answer or else I'll get you close over and over and stop before you come."

"Yes." I nod in desperation. "Do that."

"*Lila.*" His voice is soft with disappointment. He stops touching me and looks down at me with a combination of pity and sadness. "Why?"

"Because you wouldn't understand," I practically yell, pulling frantically on my restraints. "You wouldn't understand."

"What wouldn't I understand?"

"Untie me!"

"No."

"Untie me." I try to bite at the tie on my right wrist but I can't quite reach it.

"Lila."

He's trying to reason with me. There is no rhyme or reason to all of the things that are wrong with me. Tears threaten to leak from the corners of my eyes not because I'm physically hurt, but because he's awoken the thing that I keep locked down tight.

"Lila." Leaning over me, he takes my head in his hands. "What is it?"

"I can't," I gasp out. "I can't. You wouldn't understand."

"*Lila.*" The way he keeps repeating my name cracks something inside me. "Lila." He strokes the hair back from my face. "Lila. Lila. Lila."

A sob catches in my chest. It's right there at the back of my throat, trying to shove its way out. "I can't."

"Why can't you?"

"I can't...I can't...I can't."

"I got you."

"I can't sleep in a bed," I inadvertently blurt out.

He doesn't say anything. He just keeps stroking my hair back from my face.

"Not since that night he came in. He came in. He came in and he...he...put his hand over my mouth. He...he...he told me if I made a sound he'd kill me. He pulled at my clothes. He held me down. He had a knife. I let him do it. I lay there and let him. He said he'd kill me then my sister and my parents if I didn't let him. So I let him. I let him..."

15

NOLAN

I can't untie her fast enough. My hands are shaky and clumsy. Her eyes are bright with unshed tears. She doesn't say anything about my bumbling, just watches me. I can feel her anger and resentment. It fills the room around us. I forced her to tell me something she didn't want to tell me. My selfishness might have cost me the sexiest, most interesting woman I've ever met. I don't know how to fix this or what to say to her. Any apology I could make would be weak and worthless.

When I finally free her I expect her to bolt or to lash out at me, but she doesn't move. Her arms and legs remain splayed as though she were still tied to the bed. I kneel next to her on the mattress, looking down at her. My mind is blank. No words come. I feel like I need to say something or do something, but I have no idea what. What does she want? What does she need from me? Does she even want or need me at all? Am I useless to her?

"Lila." Is all I can mange to get out as I lower myself next to her and hold her.

She doesn't move. I can't tell what is going on inside her head.

"I don't care that you know I was raped," she finally says. "It's the other part... Why did you make me tell you that?"

"I thought there might be someone else or you had a kid or something you were trying to hide from me that would keep us apart. I just wanted you next to me tonight. I'm sorry."

I can feel her nodding. "I get that. Do you get that I *can't*?"

"Honestly?"

"Always."

"No. I don't. I mean I do, but I don't. Can you explain it to me?"

"I just did."

"But where do you sleep?"

"What does it matter?" She's irritated with me.

"I just does."

"I think it's time for me to go." She starts to roll away from me off the bed, but I catch her around the waist and bring her back against me. "Nolan, don't."

"Forget I asked and stay a little longer. We can get some dinner."

"And have sex again?"

"Only if you want to."

She looks back at me over her shoulder. "Stop being weird and treating me like I'm fragile. Two minutes ago you had me tied to your bed."

"I'm not." *Am I?*

"Prove it."

"How?"

She shifts so that she's on her back again, her arms and legs spread. "Tie me up again."

"You can give me the intimacy of your body, but not your mind?"

"You are the strangest man I've ever met. Most guys would have me half tied up already."

She's right, but I'm not going to let her shame me into carrying on with something I'm just not in the mood for right now. "Later. I'm hungry."

"I told you to be honest with me."

"I am."

"Fuck me, Nolan. Right now."

When I don't respond she gets off the bed. I don't stop her this time. She's messed with my head. I don't know how to deal with her and what she told me. Maybe she's right. We should just go back to being colleagues. As soon as that thought forms I'm off the bed and after her. I don't want to go back to being coworkers. I can deal with the limits she's put on our relationship or whatever it is we're doing. If she just wants me for a fuck buddy I can do that.

I catch up to her in my office where she's stepping into her underwear.

"Don't," I say, making her look up at me. "Turn around and put your hands on the desk." My voice is rough and not my own. "*Now*."

She doesn't hesitate. She drops her underwear and steps out of them as she turns around and does what I told her to do.

"If this is all you want from me you've got it, but you're going to get it my way. Understand?"

She nods and looks over her shoulder at me. I shouldn't want to do this. The sight of her bent over my desk, her breasts swaying, her ass presented to me, does something primal to me. I won't say it's resentment. It's too complicated to call it that. My hand goes to my cock and I stroke it until it's hard. Watching me, she lowers herself until her tits rest on the keyboard of my computer. Fuck that's hot. How does she do this to me? She twists me up until I don't know right from wrong, good from bad.

I don't think about how I shouldn't be doing this, I shouldn't be giving her what she wants the way she wants it. If I do, I'm never going to get my way with her. But right now I don't care as I pull the strip of condoms from the pocket of my pants on the floor where I'd dropped them during our last round. The image of her reclined in my office chair, her legs spread open for me overlaps with her bent over my desk.

I have to be inside her.

I roll on a condom and stalk toward her. Somewhere in my brain I register my anger. She makes me so fucking mad. At the same time she makes me so fucking hot for her I can't think of anything else, including how wrong all of this is.

I shove a hand between her legs. She's wet. *Of course* she is. This kind of fucked up thing is her catnip. I put a hand on her back and rub the tip of my dick through her slickness, then shove in deep. She jolts and moans like it's the hottest damn thing in the world, this cold, emotionless fucking. I don't think about her pleasure as I drive into her. It's payback. She knows it and she welcomes it. She craves it. I shove hard into her, ruthlessly pushing her into the desk. Her cries become frantic as she gets close to orgasm.

I can't let her get there. That's part of the twisted bullshit we're wrapped up in.

Changing the pace, I focus on her ass and how her pussy holds onto me as I move in and out of her. I grip her shoulder and hip. My thrusts become rougher less coordinated. I don't care about her, I tell myself. Fuck her. I don't need this. My life is complicated enough without her screwing with it. I come on a backwards movement like a goddamn teenager who can't control his shit. Pulling out all the way, I roll the condom off and shoot my cum all over her. Some of it lands on the carpet and my hand.

I don't care. I make this my mantra as I walk out of the room. Turning in the doorway I catch her looking back at me. She smiles like she had the best time.

"Get dressed," I force myself to say. "And go home. I'm done with you."

Surprise flickers across her face for a moment, then she bends down and picks up my shirt from the floor and uses it to wipe the cum off of her. I ignore her satisfied smile and go down the hall to my bathroom. Behind the closed door, I listen to her movements until the front door closes behind her. She doesn't slam it. There's not enough emotion in her for that or for me. I pound my forehead against the door.

I'm going to fuck her again. I know I will. She's too much of a temptation to refuse. All she'll have to do is ask and I'll be whipping my dick out ready to stick it wherever she wants. I put all of my frustrations on her, but the truth is some of them should be on me. She's right. Most guys would take what she's offering and be glad. Hell, they'd be ecstatic about it. No strings attached sex. That's a dude's dream come true. I should want it too. I probably would with someone else.

But she's not like anyone else.

As I clean myself up it occurs to me that I'm living a cliché. I want what I can't have and don't want what I can have. I wasn't even thinking about a relationship with her until she totally shut down that possibility. That's messed up. *I'm* messed up. She's got me so twisted around I don't know which way is up and which is sideways.

I can't say she's not honest though. In fact, I wish she

were a little *less* honest. It was me who pushed the point. I shouldn't be mad at her for giving it to me straight. I'm upset with myself, I realize, and I took it out on her. I own her an apology. I shouldn't have left things with her that way. I should've walked her to her car like a gentleman and made sure she was safe.

I calculate how long it's been since she left and the distance to her apartment. She's probably home or about to get home. Getting dressed, I wait a few more minutes to be sure. I start to text her, then realize that's the chicken shit way out and call her instead. Will she even answer when she sees it's me calling?

"Nolan." I should've known she's not the type of person to shrink away from anything difficult or awkward. "What is it?"

"I just wanted to be sure you got home safe."

"I did."

The apology I owe her sits unsaid in my mouth. I don't know why. The words just won't leave.

"Are you going to do any more work tonight?" she asks and the moment is gone.

"I was going to check out Billits's background, see if anything changed in his life around the time of Carla's trial. That strangers on a train theory you came up with."

"I have a friend who was an intern in his office. I was thinking of contacting her to get her take on him."

"That's a good idea, but be careful where her loyalties lie," I tell her. "She could tip him off that we're looking into his background."

"I will."

"What time are we meeting tomorrow? Or are we meeting?"

"I can break away around three."

"Meet me here?"

"Yeah." There's a long pause on her end. "Don't watch the office tape without me." Her hoarsely whispered command licks up my dick like a tongue stroke.

I forgot all about the camera being on when we were having sex earlier. Both times. I'd like to forget that last humiliating round, but I can't. It's going to stick with me and wake me up at night.

"I should erase them," I tell her.

"Don't."

"Why?"

"I want to see them."

"Why? What's the point?" But I know what the point is. She wants to have sex again and watching us is foreplay for her. Shit if it isn't for me too.

"I'll see you tomorrow. Text me if you find anything out about Billits."

"I will."

"Goodnight." She hangs up before I can respond.

This girl is going to lead me around by the dick until she gets bored and lets go and I'm going to let her. That's damn depressing. I need to stop thinking about her. The case should be the priority here. I fix myself a sandwich and force my tortured thoughts off Lila and back onto finding out what the deal was between Billits and Martin. What did Billits do for Martin?

I start as any good skip tracer would by pulling both of their credit reports. Without their written permission it's actually illegal for me to do this, but I get around that by using the generic sounding name of the company I made up just for this purpose. My old boss did a lot of work for insurance companies and some not so much on the up and up individuals who ran off the books businesses aka loan sharks and bookmakers. Since I'm not putting together a criminal case against these guys I'm not too worried about a fake soft inquiry that won't affect their ability to buy a house or a car showing up on their credit report. Most likely they'll never notice. If they do, my tracks are well covered.

I start with Martin. I'm looking for anything that happened both before he disappeared and after. Before will tell me where he might have gone. After will tell me if he's still alive and where he might be now.

As I suspected there's a couple of inquiries for property management companies in Wichita, Kansas of all places. He even went so far as to apply for a couple of utilities. But those don't concern me. What catches my eye is a soft inquiry on his credit report by an innocuous sounding company called Recruit Safe. Most people would think it was just a background check by a potential employer except there's another one from a company called Secure Employ that occurred around the same time. One of them Martin set up and the other is someone doing exactly what I'm doing—trying to figure out what Martin was up to around the time he vanished.

It takes a few seconds to figure out that Secure Employ is a legit company that does background checks for employers whereas Recruit Safe has a pretty convincing splash page, but there are red flags all over it. It takes a skip tracer to recognize a fellow skip tracer. Who hired them? My first guess would be Debbie Martin. She was already suspicious of her husband. I wouldn't put it past her to hire a private investigator to check up on her husband.

I wonder how far they followed Martin and how much money whoever hired them threw at the chase. I'd bet that the trail in Wichita is like a two-headed octopus with long tentacles that all lead to dead ends. He's definitely not in

Kansas and there's nothing on this report that gives a clue as
to where he actually might be.

There's not much else on his credit report after his
disappearance other than his mortgage was paid off. That
could be his wife refinancing the house or it could be her
paying the loan off with mysteriously gotten gains. I make a
note to call the lender to find out what happened there.

Next I pull Billits's credit report. I don't know how much
money a district attorney makes, but his report is suspiciously void of all of the normal accounts like bank loans,
credit cards, and car loans. Either this guy pays cash for
everything or he gets everything for free. Nobody lives this
squeaky clean unless they're living off an inheritance or
their spouse's family's money.

I shouldn't do it, but there are just too many inconsisten-
cies. So I pull both of their wives' credit reports. Mrs. Billits
has the same eerily clean credit report. She doesn't have a
job and she hasn't applied for credit in the past seven years
just like her husband. Not even to cosign for a college
tuition loan for the two out of three kids who are attending
private colleges. My spidey senses tingle. There's something
very wrong here.

Debbie Martin's credit report is pretty much normal
except for the lack of a mortgage loan. So she paid her
house off. She didn't refinance it. Where did the money
come from? I place all four reports side by side. It's always
about the money. Who has it and who needs it. There's no
doubt where the money came from that Debbie used to pay
off her house and I know why Billits gave Martin the money.
What I don't know is how Debbie got her hands on it.

The private investigator. *Of course.* Debbie was on to
Martin the whole time hence the camera in his office. As
soon as he took off she could've swept his financial rug right

out from under him. I would've loved to see his face when he found out what Debbie did to him. Karma is a bitch and so is his wife.

My impulse is to pick up the phone and call Lila, but after the last phone call I think we're due for a break. Tomorrow will come soon enough. Meanwhile I have a lot more work to do. I only hope it will keep my mind off of her.

16

LILA

I can't stop thinking about the look on Nolan's face as he told me to get dressed and get out. It kept me up half the night. I don't know how to be what he wants. I don't know how to explain to him all of the things that are wrong with me and why I won't ever be normal. It's not just the rape. There are things that go back much deeper into my childhood. They're as much a part of me as the color of my eyes. I can't change who I am or the coping techniques I've adopted over the years. Not sleeping in my bed is just one of them.

The least shameful one.

On the outside I project confidence and assertiveness. On the inside I'm a walled off mess. I say it's not the rape, but that's not entirely true. That was the tipping point and it changed me in ways I still don't fully understand. I know I'm not normal. I *know* it. No one who lives like I do is normal. I've seen TV shows and read articles about people like me. It's not that I don't see it. I live it. I can't *not* see it. But there's nothing I can do about it. Over the years I've tried. Every once in a while I make another attempt, but they always fail. I fail. Only now I'm not just failing myself I'm failing Nolan.

I don't know what to do about that.

I fill up the coffee carafe from the bathroom sink because the kitchen sink is broken. I'd stop and get coffee, but that gets expensive. I have student loans to pay off and rent to make. I should call the landlord to come and fix the faucet, but I don't like people in my space. I'd much rather put up with the inconvenience.

Last night I emailed my friend Anna who interned in Billits's office and asked if she could meet today. Luckily she said yes. We have an appointment this afternoon to meet for coffee. Hence my struggle with broken plumbing. I was also able to contact Carla's neighbor, Inez Torres. I'll stop by her place after my meeting with Anna. There's too much to do and not enough hours in the day to do it.

My phone rings and my heart does a little flip at the thought that it might be Nolan. Which is dumb. It's not like I can have him.

I groan at the name that pops up. I knew I'd have to deal with this sometime, but I've been putting it off for so long I was hoping it would eventually take care of itself.

"Hi, Kurt," I answer, picturing him already sitting in his office at Kellen, Van Buren, Ahuja, Gill, and Foley. He's Kellen.

"I was beginning to think you were avoiding me."

"Just busy."

"I was wondering if you had any plans tomorrow night. It's been a while since we went to that jazz club you like downtown."

"I'm so busy with this new case I don't think I'll have time to go out for quite a while." *If ever.*

"How's it going? Have any new leads?"

"A few."

"Tell me about them."

I pause uncertain, which is weird because I've always shared my work with Kurt. It was our thing. He has a way of seeing a case from angles I don't even know exist. I respect his opinion. Our conversations never drifted into the personal. That was one of the things I liked about Kurt. It was easy, never messy. It never tore me open and made me *feel*. It was also boring, but it was predictable, and I liked that about it, about him. He never made me want things I can't ever have.

He also never gave me orgasms that made every cell in my body buzz like I'd been electrocuted.

Which brings my thoughts back to Nolan. I can't imagine having sex with Kurt after what I've experienced with Nolan. That would be like choosing frozen single-serve dinners after dining at a five star restaurant every night. *Nolan.* His name does something funny to my insides. He makes me nervous yet comfortable all at the same time. I've been more myself with him than with anyone else, including my friends and family. I'm not sure that admission is a good reflection on me.

Why am I hesitating with Kurt? It's not like me and Nolan are exclusive—I really don't know what we are or even if we're anything at all—but somehow the thought of being with another man feels wrong. Going back to Kurt feels wrong.

"I wish I had the time," I lie. I've always made time for him and him for me. "In fact I'm running late to an appointment."

"You? Running late?" He chuckles, not buying my excuse. "Now I'm *really* starting think you're avoiding me."

"I'm not. I swear."

"What's going on with you?"

"Nothing."

"Why don't you stop by tonight. I have a great new bottle of wine, highly recommended..."

That's code for we'll have sex. Not very subtle code, but then Kurt's never had to try very hard with me. The only time I've put him off was if I was sick. Not even my period kept me from going over to his place and fooling around. By being so *available* have I lead him to believe that we're more than we really are?

"I can't," I say, hoping he'll take the no graciously and let it go.

"You *are* avoiding me. Are you seeing someone else?"

No is right there, trying to push past my teeth, but yes shoves it out of the way and storms forward. "Yes, I am." *No, I'm not. What is wrong with me?*

"Oh. Well. How long?" He sounds hurt.

"Not long. It was kind of sudden."

"He's a lucky guy."

He *is* hurt. It's strange to be having this conversation. I've never stuck with a guy long enough for it to get to this stage. Usually we just stop calling each other and if either of us notices it's weeks later and easily shrugged off.

"I'm sorry," I tell him.

"Don't be. I guess all good things must come to an end eventually."

"I guess so."

"This is going to sound pathetic, but if it doesn't work out will you give me a call?"

I won't, but I tell him I will. I say something about valuing his friendship, but it sounds stupid and false. We were never friends. We just...were. I end the call with the sense that I made the right choice, but it doesn't sit entirely comfortable with me. Kurt is a good man. I could've been happy going along the way we had been indefinitely. That's a sad but true admission. I never wanted much. What I had was enough. Now it's not.

I stare off, absorbed in those thoughts. They tumble and dive around in my brain like dice in a cup. I wish they'd just stop and give me some kind of result, some direction to take. I've never been this person. I always knew what I wanted and how to get it. But now I want something that will forever be out of my reach and I don't care what I have to do to hold onto what little of it I can for as long as I can.

The phone rings again, jolting me out of those thoughts. It's the office. I check the time. *Shoot.* I was supposed to be there twenty minutes ago. What is wrong with me? I haven't been on time in weeks. Ever since I met Nolan, I realize.

Emily, the assistant I share with two other attorneys called to remind me that I was supposed to be in the staff meeting that starts in ten minutes. I hang up with her, dash out the door, and run right into a wall of chest.

Nolan.

The panic bubbles and fizzes inside me. I keep a hand on the doorknob of my front door and lean back against the doorframe.

"What are you doing here? How did you find me?"

"We have a problem," he says, running a hand through his hair. He looks terrible, like he didn't sleep all night. "I think Martin is dead."

"*What?* How?"

He looks around the hallway and lowers his voice. "Can we go inside and talk?"

"You can't. I mean, *I* can't. I'm late for an important meet-ing." I lock my front door and turn around to find him staring at me with a strange expression. "I can't miss it," I explain.

"Okay. I guess this can keep. When is the soonest we can meet?"

"I'm meeting my friend Anna, who interned with the DA's office and Inez Torres this afternoon. I can come over after that." I say all of this on the way out to my car with Nolan following me.

"Fine. I'll see you then. And Lila—" He grabs me around the waist and hauls me into him, crushing his mouth to mine. When he lets me go I stagger back a step. "Miss me." With that he's gone, walking across the parking lot to where he parked his car without a backward glance.

It takes me a full minute, long enough for him to drive away, before I regain my wits. With a kiss like that how can I do anything else *but* miss him?

My morning is a blur of catching up and taking care of things I'm normally on top of. I was late to the meeting, which earned me a glare from the lead partner. I want to remind him that I'm never late, but he won't care. I'm late today and that's all that matters. I'm so behind that I eat lunch at my desk with the phone pressed to my ear while I answer emails. If it weren't for the alert on my phone to remind me about meeting Anna I would've forgotten. *What is wrong with me lately?*

I pull up to the coffee place near the courthouse where I'm supposed to meet Anna. I splurge on a small cup of coffee and wait in an out of the way corner. A few moments later she comes in, places her order, and joins me. She looks different than I remember, softer somehow. Have the years been as kind to me as they've been to her? Normally it wouldn't occur to me to have those kinds of thoughts. I don't usually compare myself to other women mostly because I don't imagine myself in a competition with them. I haven't had any reason to, but recently I've starting to notice the differences between them and me.

What does that mean? Why do I suddenly care about how I measure up?

"How have you been?" Anna asks and I realize I was staring at her like some crazy lady.

"Good. Busy. How are you?"

"We're pregnant," she blurts out in the way women do when they're really happy about their news. "We just started to tell people. We wanted to wait to make sure everything was going well. You know how it is." Her use of the word *we* is blunt force trauma, cracking open the gaping hole in my life where all the things a *him and me*—a *we*—would live, forcing me to face the fact that I will never use the pronoun *we* the way she does.

"Congratulations." I force a smile because it's expected. Not that I'm not happy for her—I am—but I'm also inexplicably jealous. It's an odd tasting emotion that I've never experienced before.

"It was kind of a surprise. We weren't even trying, but you know, newlyweds." If possible her smile grows wider.

"Your wedding was beautiful and so were you."

"Thank you. It was a really great day." She's so twisted up in her happiness it's hard not to be drawn in too. We chat for a little while longer—mostly about her—and then she sits back in her chair and says, "I know you didn't call me to meet me here for me to bore you with my personal life. What can I do for you?"

"No, I didn't, but I'm always glad to hear about what's going on with you. I wanted to ask you about your internship with the DA's office. I'm working on a case and I had a few questions I'm hoping you can answer. What I'm looking for is a sense of how the office was run. I can't get into specifics of the case, but I was wondering in what instances DA Billits would get personally involved in a case."

"Hmm, well, he knew about the status of nearly every case. He was and probably still is very hands on. There were several cases in which he worked closely with the attorneys prosecuting the case, usually the higher the profile the more he was involved."

"How was he to work for?"

"Not bad. He knew all of the intern's names. Not all of the prosecutors took the time to do that. He was nice, polite. Always in meetings or on the phone, but he'd stop and ask about your day as he passed by."

"I know you're not someone who participates in office gossip but..."

She nods, getting my meaning and leans in closer. "There was never any indication of an affair, at least not in the office or with anyone associated with the office. And I'd know. People treated us like furniture a lot of the time so we overheard a lot of conversations we probably shouldn't have. There were a couple of guys who met with him regularly who weren't attorneys at least none that us interns recognized. We used to joke around and call them his mafia goons. You know, big guys kind of rough. They looked more like guys he'd prosecute than associate with."

"Did you ever get their names?"

"No. They'd come in and go straight to his office without knocking, like he was expecting them. They'd stay ten or fifteen minutes then leave. They never spoke to anyone not even his assistant." She makes a *straight on through* gesture. "In and out like a surgical strike."

"What did they look like?"

"Big. Both of them had dark hair. One looked like a

boxer, you know, with a messed up nose. The other one was missing the last two fingers on his left hand. We called him Lefty and the other guy Bruiser. Not guys you'd want to owe money to or get caught alone with in a parking garage."

We talk a little more, but she doesn't have anything more to tell me that might be useful. We part, promising to get together soon. My meeting with Anna makes me late to meet Inez Torres, Carla's neighbor and babysitter. I don't glean much new information from Inez, but she backs up Carla's story, including her asshole of a landlord. She insists I stay for a cup of very strong coffee and sweet *empanadas*, which are filled pastries she made herself. The taste reminds me of the ones my grandma used to make when I was kid.

I text Nolan as I leave Inez's house with a bag full of empanadas to let him know I'm on my way. Once again I'm late. It's nearly dinnertime and way past the time I thought I'd be heading over to his house. I hadn't thought much about what he told me about Martin possibly being dead when he showed up at my apartment. I was too busy panicking at his unexpected arrival. Since then I've been running from meeting to meeting all day with hardly any time to catch my breath in between.

On the drive over what he said really hits me. If Martin is dead then there is something much bigger going on here than any conspiracy theory I might come up with. What happened to him? How did he die? How did Nolan figure it out he was dead when the authorities didn't? How does this affect Carla's case?

And the most perplexing question of all, what am I going to do about Nolan?

17

NOLAN

I left Lila's condo with the same sensation I've been having about her almost since the moment I met her —she's hiding something. What I don't know. Even after doing some minor checking into her background I can't figure it out. She's not married. She doesn't have a child. As far as I can tell she's squeaky clean and exactly who and what she says she is. So why don't I believe her?

What is it about her that creates more questions than answers? Will she ever confide in me and if not, can I live with it? Maybe I should just take what she's offering for however long it's offered and stop trying to figure her out. The truth is most guys would. They'd accept the crazy no strings attached sex without question. I need to start being one of those guys, I decide. The only other option is to keep things strictly professional. No more naked Lila. No more recording our sex acts. No more of the best sex I've ever had.

Well, that's not going to happen. The mere thought of giving up being with Lila is so ridiculous I laugh out loud, earning me a questioning glance from Cora as she looks up from the report I handed in about the updates on Carla's case.

"You okay?"

"Sorry. Ignore me. What do you think of my theory?"

"I think it has merit. The similarities in the description and composite drawing on the medical examiner's website to John Martin are striking. Contact the Spokane police department and let them know what you suspect. If this is Martin his family might finally get some closure. Good work."

"It doesn't help Carla's case. If anything it creates more questions than answers."

"Have you shown Lila what you discovered? She's the legal expert here. She'd know how or even if Martin's death affects the case. The witnesses you've found and the information you've gathered might already be enough to bring the case before a judge."

"What about the DA's connection?"

"Those are some strong accusations to bring forward without anything concrete to back them up. Sit on them until we're absolutely sure we have enough to bring to the authorities. We'll want to run this by Mr. Nash before we do anything. The DA's not someone you can throw baseless allegations at. We need to make sure we're not setting ourselves up for a lawsuit. Be careful. Don't let him get wind that you suspect him of anything."

"I won't." I can't screw this up, I remind myself. There's too much at stake for all of us.

"How's the Lasiter case going?"

I'm glad to move on to surer footing. No one's career is going to get ruined over a wife cheating on her husband with her personal trainer. So cliché and yet most of the cheating spouse cases we work on are. It's rare that a suspicious spouse is wrong. It happens, but not often. Usually their hunches are right. Which brings me right back to Lila and my hunches about her.

I push those thoughts away...again, and focus on reporting the status of the other cases I'm working on for Nash Security and Investigations. Cora seems satisfied with my work, but she's distracted. I've been so consumed with my own problems that I haven't been paying much attention to the people around me. My mom reminded me of that with her guilt-laced phone call earlier today. I missed the last couple of weekly dinners with my parents because I've been so wrapped up with Carla's case and my issues with Lila.

I force myself to once again put Lila out of my mind and ask Cora if everything's okay with her.

"Yeah. I guess. Mostly."

"Anything I can help with?"

"Nah. I'm just being paranoid."

"About what?"

She makes a face and shakes her head. I recognize something in her expression. It's the same look I get when I'm trying to figure Lila out.

"Want me to do a little digging on Leo for you?" I joke. "I could run the basics see if there's anything unusual going on."

"No." She adamantly shakes her head. "Absolutely not. I'm sure everything's fine."

I make a mental note to ignore her protest and run the check anyway. *I* want to make sure everything's as fine as she's insisting it is. I'm not sure what I'd do if I found out the boss's son was messing around on Cora, but if I was her I'd want to know.

"Okay. Just let me know if you change your mind. The offer stands."

"Thanks. I could do it myself, but..."

"It feels invasive and distrustful. Like a line you don't want to cross." Like the line I crossed with Lila.

She nods. "Exactly like that. Relationships should be built on trust. Thanks for the offer though."

"No worries. Any time."

As soon as she leaves I run the usual on her boyfriend even though she told me not to. It doesn't take me long to figure out why she's sensing something's off with him. I smile to myself and close out of the programs I was running and shut down my computer for the day. She's got a mighty big surprise headed her way. Good for her. Good for them. They deserve to be happy. I hope someday I find someone to make suspicious and then surprise. Again my thoughts turn to Lila. She's pretty much a constant pop up window in my head, frequently interrupting whatever I'm doing.

Speaking of... My phone pings with a text. Lila's running late. She'll meet me in an hour at my place. On the way home I stop at the store and pick up something for dinner. I have no doubt she'll be hungry and maybe sitting down across from her at the table will help me get some kind of perspective and put some distance between us. I can calmly lay out the ground rules I've been mulling over in my head all day during dinner.

Rule number one: This is just about sex. No emotions. No expectations. No commitment.

Rule number two: No spending the night. No cuddling. Sex and then gone.

Rule number three: Work and sex and that's it. No texts or emails about anything except work. No making plans to get together unless it's about the case.

Rule number four: No meeting each other's friends and family. No personal talk. No questions. Keep it business only.

Rule number five: Discretion. No one is to ever know about our arrangement.

Rule number six: Either one of us can end the sex at any time for any reason. No questions asked. No recrimination. No looking back. Once it's over it's over whether the case is or not.

I feel confidant she'll agree to my terms and that we both can abide by them without anyone getting hurt. I know it's what she wants and it's what I can live with.

She knocks on my door just as I finish setting the food on the table. Food, work, sex (if she's amenable), and then goodbye. In that order. Structure and perspective. That's what's going to keep everything on track here.

I open the door and all of my careful planning and promises to myself scatter like leaves in the wind. I'm momentarily stuck dumb. How could I forget how gorgeous she is? How did I not anticipate this would happen?

She slips by me without a word or invitation and then she's on me, grabbing me in that very direct way she has that leaves me with no choice, kissing me like she needs me to live. She tastes like coffee and something sweet. Her fingers twine through my hair, tugging it in a way that is part pleasure part pain. Any thoughts to stop her before things get out of control get overridden by her hand on my dick. My brain fizzles and fries. We're all urgent, fumbling hands and hot seeking mouths.

There are no rules. There is no order. There sure as hell is no perspective.

Clothes get ripped off and thrown. We leave a trail from the front door down the hall. I grope for the nightstand drawer and find a condom, not wanting to take my mouth off of her. She takes it from my hand and I groan as she rolls it down. I love the way she touches me. No hesitation. No uncertainty. She takes what she wants from me and I like it. I pull her legs until she's at the edge of the bed. She's hot and wet. I thrust easily into her with her feet on my shoulders. Using her legs for leverage, I pound into her. Her cries echo around the room. The louder she gets the wilder I get until she grips my forearms, digging her fingernails into my flesh as she throws her head back. I can't hold back and plunge deep, pushing into her as far I can. I come yelling her name.

She opens her legs and I fall on top of her, catching myself so I don't crush her. Her arms legs wrap around me. In the quiet that follows I realize I'm in trouble. It wasn't supposed to happen like this. We didn't have dinner. We didn't do any work. We haven't even said anything to each other unless you count the words *harder*, *faster*, and *fuck you're hot* as an exchange of pleasantries.

I force myself to disentangle from her. Her limbs fall away from me and she stares up at me with a satisfied smirk. I think I actually might hate her in this moment. She punched through all of my carefully laid plans, all of the roadblocks and slow signs I posted, like they weren't even there. Some of the blame falls on me. It's not like I stopped her from taking my pants off or paused for thought when I had my fingers inside her and my mouth on her tit.

I'm so disgusted with both of us I pull out of her and turn away without a word to dispose of the condom. When I get back she's lying exactly where I left her, her legs dangling over the edge of the bed like she's ready for round two. *Perspective*, I remind myself, *rules*, *order*, *control*.

But she looks so inviting as she gazes down her naked

body at me and crooks her finger for me to come to her. I can't resist. She's a siren and I answer her call. I lay down on top of her, between her parted thighs. This, I realize, is where I want to be and I'd do anything to get here again and again. *Anything.*

It's not her I hate. It's me.

She puts a hand on my cheek. "I know you're mad at me."

"I'm not mad at you," I say a little too harshly to be believable.

"Then who are you mad at?"

I take her hands off me and hold them above her head. Her eyes widen a fraction and then she rotates her pelvis, rubbing her pussy against me. I use my other hand to still her.

"Let's get some things straight," I say. "This is only sex. We work and we fuck and that's it. We don't spend the night together. We don't cuddle. We don't touch each other like we care. You don't ask about me and I don't ask about you. We don't date. No one can know we're fucking. You don't call me and I don't call you unless it's to work or to fuck or both. We fuck until we don't feel like fucking each other anymore and we work until the case is over. And that's it. Got it?"

She nods a little too eagerly.

"And you don't ever, and I mean *ever*, fuck anyone while you're fucking me. That is non-negotiable."

"The same goes for you."

"Fine."

"Fine."

I force myself to get off of her. "We eat, work, and fuck in that order and then you leave. No more coming at me like you did at the door ever again. Are we clear?"

"I didn't hear you complaining."

"I'm complaining now."

"I'll follow all of your rules except one—we fuck whenever we want. If that's before work or before we eat then so be it. But I'm not going to fuck on demand like some sex slave."

"That's not the way I meant it."

"No?"

"No."

"Then get rid of the orderly eat, work, then fuck rule."

"Fine," I grind out.

She holds out her hand. "We have a deal."

I shake her hand, thinking I've made the worst bargain in the world. This is never going to work.

18

LILA

This is never going to work.

I know why Nolan wants what's going on between us to be only about sex and work. Keeping them separate from each other is a good idea. I can compartmentalize that way and I know he can too. What I can't seem to do is remain detached in a way that will make this deal feasible. By the angry way he offered the bargain I don't think Nolan can't either. So why are we doing this? I know why I'm doing it, but why is he? What does he have to hide?

We eat at the table in silence. I could ask Nolan about why he thinks Martin is dead. I can tell him what Anna told me and about my visit with Inez. We can talk about the next step in the case and plan a new course of action. We can go over the rest of the stuff we found in Martin's office. We can do a whole bunch of things we aren't doing to get past the scene in his bedroom. Instead we focus on our food and let the silence hang over our heads like a guillotine blade. I'm beginning to think that we masochistically like it this way when Nolan finally breaks through the quiet.

"I think Martin's body is in the Spokane County unidentified remains storage locker. I think he was murdered and I think I know who did it."

As dropping bombs go that's a big one. An atomic sized explosive. It shakes everything in me. I swivel my head his direction. He's not looking at me. Something on his plate has his attention. My mouth flaps open, closed, open, closed. That's a doozy of a conversation starter.

I finally force words past the clog in my throat. "What? How? Who? Why?"

He glances up at me. "You forgot *where*."

"You just told me where. Washington."

"I did like I said I would. I followed his addiction. Idiot kept the same user name with his favorite sites, but used a different method of payment. It tied him to Spokane. He kept his same steady diet of live porn for about a month and then all of a sudden it stopped. Cold turkey. No one does that unless they suddenly found God or was somehow incapacitated.

"I searched the records of the Spokane County Medical Examiner's unidentified bodies web page and found a postmortem drawing of a man who resembles Martin and who was found a few weeks after Martin stopped visiting the porn sites," he finishes, leaving me gaping at him.

"But...who...?"

"My money's on Debbie Martin. Remember when we visited with her? Something about the way she talked about him—in the past tense—stuck with me. She said, "It was one of the things I really *loved* about him, his devotion to his clients." *Loved*. Past tense."

"She could've just resigned herself to his being gone and referring to him in the past tense could be her way of dealing with it."

"Could be," he concedes. "But I found a hit on her husband's credit report that led me to a local PI. We know she was already onto whatever he was doing when he disappeared. It's not too far fetched that the PI Debbie hired would've done what I did in tracking Martin down for her. I checked and Debbie took some time off from work right before Martin's sudden departure from porn. I bet if I dig deeper I can show that she traveled to Spokane."

"Now I really want to know what was in that box at the back of his bookcase and if Debbie got a hold of it, why would she kill him?"

"Hell hath no fury...?"

"Maybe."

"Could be Billits or someone he hired," he continues. "Maybe the deal between them didn't go as smoothly as it looks. Maybe Martin tried to shake him down for money after the fact. I'm looking at Billits's whereabouts around the time Martin stopped visiting those sites."

"Are you going to contact the authorities here or in Spokane about you suspicions?"

"Already did. Anonymously from a burner phone. I don't want any of this to come back on us, Nash or the Freedom Project. I gave them enough that they could try to match Martin's missing persons report with the remains in their morgue. We'll see what comes of it. I could be totally wrong and it's not Martin at all."

"I want to see this post-mortem drawing."

He pulls out his phone and taps the screen, then hands it to me. He put Martin's DMV photo side by side with the drawing. It's close. Very close.

"They'll likely do a DNA test if they can't get dental records," Nolan says. "It'll be interesting to see how cooperative Debbie is."

"Do you have any idea what Billits might have done for Martin or what Billits might have had on him?"

"Funny you should ask. I found a sealed arrest record on Martin. No charges were ever filed, something the DA has discretion over."

"Is there any way to find out what those charges were for?"

"Not without some hacking into a government data base, which I'm not willing to do. It might be something the police will want to follow up on while trying to figure out what happened to Martin. One of the first things they'll do is look at his record."

"My friend Anna told me something very interesting about Billits."

I fill him in on Billits's daily visitors and the rest of what Anna told me. By the time I'm done, Nolan is sitting back in his seat, a deep line of concentration between his brows.

"We need to get a look at these guys," he finally says. "What are you doing tomorrow?"

"Work. I'm very behind." Embarrassingly so. Between my newfound chronic lateness and the time I've taken away from my regular workload to work on this case it's a wonder I haven't been fired.

"I can do the stakeout alone I guess."

"Stakeout?"

"I want to know who those guys are who are visiting Billits, get photos of them."

"Oh. You don't need to do that." I bring up the photos Anna sent me. "My friend took pictures of them when they first started coming in. They made her nervous. She joked that those men are the kind that made people disappear. I guess she wanted a record of them just in case. She sent me the pics she took. Here's the first one." I hand him my phone.

He takes a look and then taps on the screen of his phone. He holds our phones side-by-side. "Please tell me they look nothing alike."

I point to the picture on Nolan's phone. "When did you take this and why? How did you already know about this guy?"

"He was one of the guys guarding the Lucky Inn Motel the other day when I went by for a look. There's no doubt they're running a prostitution ring out of there." He swipes his screen and brings up the next pic. "And here's the other guy."

I flick my finger across my screen and bring up the photo of the second guy Anna sent me. Another match. We turn in unison toward each other, mirroring the same look of shock and disbelief on our faces. This isn't just a can of worms we've opened. It's a giant festering, puss-filled, maggot swarming wound. The connections click into place. Billits and Carla. Carla and Martin. Martin and Billits. The DA ties everything and everyone together. There's no way Carla didn't know who Billits was to her even if she didn't know who he was to Martin.

She lied.

I turn my attention back to the photos on our phones. These men are the links tying Billits to a prostitution ring. A ring that Carla was a part of. Billits wasn't a just a random customer, he was likely her pimp. Why didn't she tell us that? Why did she pretend that she didn't know whom he was other than some guy who paid to have sex with her, some ordinary john?

"We need to talk to Carla again," I say. "We're missing something here. Something she knows."

"So much for that photo array with Billits in it that I made to show her."

"She probably thought we wouldn't make the connection between her mystery man and the DA."

"No. I think she *wanted* us to make the connection. Why else would she give us just enough information to identify him without giving up his real name? Her description of his tattoos was very specific. She had to know we'd find him and discover who he really is. I think she knew all along who was behind Martin tanking her case. But *why*? Why would a man like Billits care about whether or not one of his prostitutes was convicted of murder or not? If anything I'd think that he'd want her cleared so she could keep working for him."

A terrible thought occurs to me. So terrible I can't voice it. I get up from the table on shaky legs and go into Nolan's office where I left my files. I feel him follow me, but he doesn't say anything. I go straight for my file on Diego and open it. Right on top is a picture of the preschooler with his beautiful blue eyes. I put the photo of Billits that Nolan printed out right beside Diego's. Cold dread seeps into me. Their eyes are the same color, the same turquoise blue.

"Oh, shit," Nolan breaths. "You don't think..."

He doesn't finish the sentence for the same reason I can't answer him out loud. It's too horrific to bear. Carla was fifteen when she had Diego. *Fifteen*. That means she was fourteen when she got pregnant.

I push the pics aside and read Diego's birth certificate with new eyes. There's no father listed, but the names of the hospital where he was born and the doctor who delivered him are.

I point to the names. "Is there..." I can hardly push the

words out of my mouth. "Is there a way to find out who paid the hospital and doctor bills?"

Nolan is already in his computer chair, hands on the keyboard before I can finish my sentence. I pace the small room while he does his magic. The constant whir and hum of his machines aren't soothing me the way they usually do. The longer it takes the more my agitation grows until I'm shaking with it. Carla wanted me to know, but she couldn't tell me. She couldn't tell anyone. She was a victim long before the justice system got a hold of her.

"Cash," Nolan says. "All of her bills were paid in cash, including the hospital."

I nod, knowing he can't see me. It confirms everything. But I need to hear it from Carla. I need to look her in the eyes and have her tell me the truth and then I need her to tell me what she wants me to do with it. Why did she write to the Freedom Project? Why is she willing to go up against Billits now when she wasn't then? What changed? Or did anything change? Has she been planning this from the start? Is that what *all* of this is about—revenge?

Nolan turns toward me in his seat. "We need to talk to Carla," he says, echoing my thoughts. "We're in much deeper waters than she warned us about."

"Revenge. It's a game of revenge. Billits tampered with Carla's case to get back at her for his son's death. She's using us to expose his criminal activities. It's pay back for putting her away. This isn't about getting her freedom at all." *How did I not see this sooner?*

"What do you want to do? We could walk away from all of this, tell Carla that we didn't find anything new that would help her. *Or*...we could go balls to the wall with it. Mr. Nash has FBI connections. We could turn over everything we have to them and see how it shakes out. Step totally out of the picture. You'd still need to decide what to do about Carla—leave her in prison or try to free her."

"Carla is a victim here. Many times over. The fact still remains that she didn't kill her son. Yes, she was negligent, but his death was a tragic accident. How and when and in what order do we make the attempt to exonerate her? If we do it too soon Billits will be tipped off if he's not already. If we wait, that's however many more days she sits in prison for a crime she didn't commit.

"I get it now. I get *her* now. Like really, *really* get her. I thought I knew what it was like to have no power as an undocumented immigrant. I knew nothing. Carla was taken advantage of in the most reprehensible ways possible. I'm proud of her for trying to get back some dominance here even if she's using us to do it."

"So we're doing this."

Squaring my shoulders, I confirm it with a nod. "We're doing this."

He gives me the flashy grin that struck me from the start. "That's my girl."

I don't think about how much I want to be just that—his girl. We have so many hurdles to cross, not just with the case, but ones he can never know about. I blink rapidly and look away from him, trying to hold in the tears stinging the backs of my eyes. It's not fair. Any of it. I won't get a fairytale ending, but maybe Carla can. Or at least a happy one. I renew my promise to Carla and to myself to free her once and for all. Maybe she can create the life she should've had. The life she was promised when she crossed the boarder all those years ago with her father and brother. The life all immigrants dream of.

All of them except me.

19

NOLAN

The discovery about Billits and Carla seems to have stripped something from Lila. There's a shadow in her eyes that wasn't there before. Just thinking about everything Carla went through at the hands of Billits makes my stomach grind. Predators like Billits prey on the vulnerable and a fourteen-year-old undocumented immigrant would definitely be defenseless against someone with the kind of power he has. Billits is in a unique position as DA to be in control of who gets prosecuted or not. It's genius really.

If any of his sex workers got arrested he would be in on the decision about things like taking a case to trial and plea deals. I'd bet money that a lot of his victims got off easier than his competition's. Going to the FBI with what we know will shake up the entire San Diego legal system. I'm overwhelmed with what's in front of us. By Lila's frantic back and forth pacing and twisting fingers she's just as overcome as I am. Maybe more. She was invested in Carla's story in a way I never was.

Finding out Carla is using us has to hurt. I want to go to

her and tell her everything will be okay, but the words would be useless platitudes. She knows it won't. We're in so deep here. Too deep. And we're all alone in this with no back up at all. If what we think happed did in fact happen and Billits gets wind that we're piecing things together we could be in some real trouble, the kind you don't come back from.

Focusing on the things I can do, I turn back to my computer. I've taken the precaution of running my searches through a network that doesn't write my work onto the main drive of my computer, making it untraceable. The operating system on a thumb drive came with encryption tools and secure erase tools for maximum privacy. If anyone were to log into my computers normally they would think that I never used it. There's no way to trace my work back to me. Even though I know it's secure, I can't help but worry that someone's been watching us and knows what we know.

I pull the thumb drive with the self-contained operating system out of my computer and run checks just to be sure. Browser history, cookies, the whole lot. Nothing just like I expected. It's secure. Even if somebody knew what we've been doing there is no way they could trace it back to us. We're safe at least in that regard. As for Lila's friend who interned at the DA's office, Carla, the Freedom Project, Nash Security and Investigations, and everyone else we've talked to about the case...not so much. There are a lot of loose threads dangling.

"Is it too late to call Mr. Nash?" Lila asks.

"Probably. I'll put a call into him first thing in the morning. Are you available to meet with him right away?"

"I'll have to clear a couple of things, but yes, I can do that." She rubs her arms as though she's chilled. "How safe are we? Be honest."

"Right now? As safe as we were before we figured out what all of this is about. We've done everything we can to keep it as quiet as possible. If Billits knows about us and what we're doing he hasn't made any move to tip us off." I let out a breath. She's not going to like what I have to say next. "That said, I don't think you should be alone tonight. I have security here that you don't have at your place. Stay. Stay with me tonight."

She's already shaking her head before I finish. "I can't do that. I *told* you."

"I know you did and I'm struggling to understand exactly why. I really am."

"I...I don't expect you to understand. Especially when I don't quite understand it myself."

"We could hang out in the living room, on the couch..."

"I don't have any of my things here."

"We could stop by your place and pick up a few things."

"No."

"I could stay at your pla—"

"*No.*" She puts her hands up and takes a step back. Her rejection is not just emphatic it's panicked.

I take slow, measured breaths, trying to tamp down my anger. I'm not struggling to understand her I'm *battling*. This is a fight with a faceless, nameless foe. Whatever she's hiding terrifies her and she won't let me near it.

"Okaaayyy. Then we'll go to the store and buy you what you need. You can sleep anywhere you want *here*, wherever you're comfortable. *But you will not be alone tonight.*"

"I don't want to be alone."

The way she says it I know she's not just talking about tonight, that maybe she's talking about whatever it is she's fighting against, because she looks like a solitary woman at war. She hugs herself, swaying back and forth a little, her body turning in on itself. Her gaze doesn't meet mine the way it normally does. I hate the way she looks right now—small and defeated. And alone. So alone.

I hold a hand out to her half expecting her to reject the gesture the way she normally does. My hand hangs out there open to her for so long that my arm turns leaden and I have a hard time keeping it up, but I refuse to put it down. This feels like a moment and if I give up I may never get back here to try again with her. We'll never move beyond what we are to each other right now and, eventually, we won't be anything at all. I won't give up on her, on us. I'm starting to see that I might be the only one in her life who never has and never will.

Finally her gaze tracks slowly from my hand up my arm to my face. Her fingers are cold against my palm. I clasp her hand and something settles inside me. She takes a step forward then another until she steps between my legs and lowers into my lap. I wrap my arms around her. The tension in her is strung tight, but she gradually relaxes and even puts her head on my shoulder.

"I'll stay here," she whispers almost too quietly to be heard. "On the couch, but you have to sleep in your room."

"I can do that."

She traces a pattern I can't make out in my palm. I wonder if she knows what she does to me when she's quiet and vulnerable like this. Puffing my chest out and making me want to slay dragons for her. I don't remember ever having this sensation with anyone else. What is it about her that does this to me? Do I matter to her? Or am I just what's happening right now? Will she always keep a part of herself walled off from me or will I eventually break through to the other side?

"Thank you," she says in that same small voice. "I know this isn't normal, I'm not normal."

"Normal's boring."

"You're just being nice."

"We all have our things. Yours might be too big to see around right now, but eventually it won't be."

"I want to believe that."

"Then believe it. You come from fighters, Lila. Anyone who went through what your parents did to get here is tough. It's in you to do more, be more."

"I think you have too much faith in me. I'm not like my parents. I never would've done what they did."

"Because you didn't have to. They did it for you."

"They got their green cards because of me."

"Yeah? Because of your work with the Freedom Project?"

"No. Because they cooperated with the police when I was raped."

I try not to tense or have any reaction at all at the thought of someone hurting her. It makes me want to punch something. Preferably the son of a bitch who violated her. But she doesn't need that from me right now. She's opening up and I have to listen to what she's saying because it's important. She's important.

"That's how I got my green card too," she continues. "Because of a loop hole in the system that gives legal status to undocumented immigrants if they're a victim of a crime. So you see, I'm not tough." Her laugh has a brittle, resentful edge to it. "I didn't do anything to make that happen for my family. I just lay there and waited for it to be over, hoping he wouldn't kill my family and me."

No words. I have no words.

Swallowing back the golf ball that's suddenly lodged in my throat, I search for something to say, something that might take away her pain and her shame. It's the shame that guts me. She survived because she's strong. She's a fighter. That she thinks less of herself because her protective instincts toward her family ended up having a side benefit for her *and* her family tears me up. I have a newfound respect and admiration for her. I tell her, but she pushes it away like she's done with every other compliment I've given her.

"Anyone can lay there and take it," she says. "There's nothing noble about being frozen with fear. *Why didn't you scream? Why didn't you make him stop?* I got asked that over and over. Yeah, *why didn't I?* Why couldn't I move? Why didn't I scream or try to push him away? Why did I just *let* him?"

"You did what you had to do in order to survive." I can't help the anger that seeps into my words. It pisses me off that anyone would say that to her let alone think it. "You don't owe anybody anything."

"I wish I had fought back or screamed or something."

"Whatever you did or didn't do was the right thing. You survived."

"He died, you know. In prison. Right after the trial. Had a heart attack and died instantly. Didn't feel a thing. Sometimes I think about doing to him what he did to me. And sometimes I wish it were me who died instead of him. Mostly I want to cut up my green card and reapply based on my accomplishments as a person and not what happened to me." She looks up at me, her dark eyes calmer than the storm roaring through me. "Isn't that dumb?"

"I don't think so."

"I said that to my mom once. She told me I should be grateful something good came out of something so bad. I don't know how to be that kind of grateful."

Again she's got me searching for the right words to say. And once again none come. I ease her a little closer, needing the contact more than she seems to. She rests her head on my shoulder, her sigh heavy with the burden she's carried around for her family. She saved them twice. Once from the man who terrorized her and a second time by changing their legal status. That's a lot for someone who barely tops out at five feet tall.

"Well. It's late." She pops up and off me. "We should get to bed if we're going to get an early start tomorrow. Lots to do like bring down a DA and his prostitution ring."

"You're amazing."

She looks at me sharply. "Don't say that."

"Why not? It's true."

"Do you have an extra toothbrush I could borrow?"

"Come back here." I pat my lap.

"It's late."

"I'm not coming onto you."

"Maybe you should be."

"Why? So you can distract me from giving you compliments?"

"Because this is only supposed to be about sex."

"Except that it's not."

There's a war in her eyes. She wants to deny it, but there's too much evidence to the contrary. Instead she does what she does best, her expression morphing from challenging to seductive. Her hips have an extra sway as she walks back to me. She straddles my lap and tangles her fingers in my hair. I'm going to give in to her because I can't stop myself from doing anything else. My want for her is a constant thing, buzzing through my veins and clouding my head.

She grinds her pussy against the zipper of my jeans and

that buzz becomes a roar. She's going to make this, like everything else, about sex, but she's not fooling either of us. I play along, kissing her deep and long like I've fallen for her trap when in reality I willingly tipped head first into it. She exposes herself to me in inches. This ploy is her not being able to say what she's feeling so she shows me. I watch and learn and give her what she wants, while getting what I want —more of her.

I undo my pants, lifting her as I raise up to shove them down my legs. She makes a move to drop to the floor like she's going to suck me off, but I catch her.

"Ride me," I command, handing her a condom from the stash I now keep in the office. "Backward."

She smiles at me like she's won. I let her think that as she climbs off me and strips. Her body is a wonder to me, all roundness and curves. I could stare at her forever. She pulls my pants the rest of the way off and then bends forward. Her tits brush my thighs as she licks me, swirling her tongue around the head of my dick. I make an approving sound that comes out as more of a growl. She laughs and places a chaste kiss on the tip before rolling the condom on. There's no shyness in the way she turns around and presents her ass to me. I guide her down onto me, watching the way my cock disappears and then reappears with each movement.

Gripping her hips, I glide in and out of her, keeping the pace slow and steady. I fight the urge to thrust high and hard into her. This is about and what I need to show her. We're not just screwing. You don't share the things she's shared with a fuck buddy. It doesn't matter how she thinks she's cataloged me. I'm more. *We're* more.

Her fingers dig into my thighs. She's close. Very close and so am I. I give her want she wants. Her first orgasm nearly strangles me with its intensity. I can't hold on.

Thrusting deep, I empty myself inside her. For a flash of a second all I am is where I'm connected to her. Everything else blacks out, then refires like the staccato of gunfire. I'm hyper conscious of everything about her. The way her hair drapes across my chest, her heavy breaths, how hot and alive she feels around me, and how necessary she's become to me.

I have to make her want me the way I want her, show her we can be more than this animalistic rutting. Pulling her back against me, I use my fingers on her clit and tit to make her come again. Her head falls back onto my shoulder as she cries out.

In her ear I urgently whisper, "*You're mine.*"

He's not playing fair. Doesn't he understand that this can't be what he wants? It's already more than it should be. I went too far sharing those things with him. Instead of pushing him away it had the opposite effect. He sees my confession as proof that we can be a real couple in a real relationship, that there's hope for a future. There is no hope. There is no future.

Even as I tell myself these things his insistent words pulse through me with the last waves of my orgasm. *You're mine.*

This round was supposed to be me showing him what we are. Instead he showed me what we could be and I *want* it. I want it more than I want to fight against it. But he doesn't know everything about me. The truth looms large over everything else—I'm deeply, *deeply* flawed. He only sees the scars on the surface, only has a hint of the shame. The secret is too big. It's just too big.

He's going to keep pushing, keep trying to get me to see what I already know. I'll have to show him. Vomit crawls up the back of my throat at the thought of it. I imagine myself opening the door, revealing everything to him a little at a time. As we go through it I picture his disbelief, then revulsion, and finally his rejection. It's too overwhelming. He won't be able to handle it.

Suddenly feeling claustrophobic, I push against his arms tightly banded around me. His hold is too tight. It's too much. He makes me *feel* too much.

"Let me go."

"Why? So you can seduce me again?" The bitterness in his laugh makes me flinch. "That's going to take a while. I can rebound pretty fast for you, but not fast enough for you to be able to distract me from getting the answers I want *right now*."

"You don't understand."

"Make me."

I shake my head.

"Lila." He shifts so we're a little more reclined in the chair. "You don't get it, do you? I'm not going anywhere. We can keep playing these games, hell, a sick part of me actually *likes* them. It's like my goddamned catnip. But we'll just keep coming right back to this point."

He's right. I know he's right. I can see us months from now. Every time he gets an inch too close I'll ripe my clothes off or drop to my knees in front of him and then we'll be right back where we started. The thought of it makes my breath catch. I can't keep doing this to him, to us, but I'm not brave enough to make it stop. Selfishly I don't want this to be over. I'm not any happier than he is with the situation, but when faced with the choice I'd keep things exactly they way they are. The only other alternative is to lose him.

"I know," I tell him. "I know."

"What is it? Are you not who you say you are? Did you

kill someone? What? What could be so bad that you can't share it with me?"

"You're not going to understand."

"Try me."

My heart speeds up. The panic crawls over me like a million tiny ants. Sweat pops out all over my body and I shiver, suddenly cold despite his warmth at my back. If I show him I have to face it, really face it. The enormity of it all is too much. I'm overwhelmed. It's too big. I try to lick my lips to talk, but my mouth is dry and the words stick.

"I...I have to show you." My mouth suddenly fills with saliva. I can't believe I'm doing this.

"Okay. Show me."

I push at his arms. This time he releases me and I bolt for the bathroom. I barely make it in time to throw up. He gathers my hair and holds it, while I shake over the bowl. Rubbing my back, he murmurs words that don't soothe me. I close the lid and lay my head on my arms, trying to catch my breath. The plastic is cold and a new shiver runs through me.

"I'm sorry." He presses his face against my back and holds me. "Forget everything I said. You don't have to do this."

"No." My voice comes out as a rough rasp. "I need to. I need to show you."

He helps me stand and waits while I rinse out my mouth, then hands me a new toothbrush and toothpaste. I wish I knew what he was thinking. I'm a freak. I know I am. I must look like a crazy lady to him. He has no idea just how crazy my life is. I try to steal myself against his reaction while we dress and get in the car. I tell him to take me to my place.

He doesn't say a word on the drive over. He doesn't

extend a second offer to give me way out. He doesn't want to let me off the hook. He wants to know what I'm hiding more than he wants to hold on to what little we have now. I childishly cling to that, turning it into resentment against him that morphs into anger. He's doing this to us. He's the one pushing, looking for a way out. Well, I'm going to give it to him. He'll realize I was right all along. He can't handle it. He can't handle me. We should've just kept it about sex and nothing else.

I'm out of the car before it comes to a complete stop. He catches up to me just as I unlock my front door.

"You want to know what my big secret is well, here you go." I push the door open as far as it will go and flip on the light.

There's enough room for me to slip past him and inside. I don't turn back to see if he's following. I know he is. I stop a few feet away and turn to look at him. He maneuvers through the entrance and then halts. His gaze roams the room, taking everything in. There's a lot to see. The stacks of things are nearly as tall as he is. I stand at the end of the narrow path that branches out to the bathroom and kitchen. He says nothing, but his expression says everything. Just as I'd feared—shock, disbelief, revulsion. All of it flashes across his face. He doesn't even try to hide it. I'm not sure he could.

His hands fist in his pockets and his jaw hardens. He doesn't look at me. I'm not going to cry, I tell myself even as the first tear falls. Despite the way it looks I feel safe here. This is my cocoon, my place to hide from the world. It might look like piles and piles of junk, but these things—my things—mean more to me than anyone or anything in the world.

I know what he's thinking. I know what I am. There are

shows about my condition that people watch for entertainment. They laugh and make fun of it. They think the people they see living in houses packed to the rafters with stuff are crazy. They don't understand. *This* I control. Everything outside of here is completely out of my control. I've built walls both mental and physical, barricading myself against the world. I *know* all of this about myself. I *know* what all of this looks like to other people. But to me, it's a haven. It's safe. It's the one thing that makes me feel like I have some sense of power.

Nolan's really making an effort. I'll give him that. He hasn't blurted out the first thing that came to mind. He hasn't asked me *why* or *how could I?* He didn't even gasp. He just stands there, taking it all in. When his gaze finally lands on me what I see in his dark gaze is pity. It makes me take a step back. That's the last thing I want from him. His anger and frustration I can handle. His quiet disappointment and sympathy is more than I can deal with.

"Now do you see?" I lash out. "Now do you see why we can't be together?"

He shakes his head. I'm not sure if he doesn't know what to say or if he doesn't quite trust himself to say the right thing.

"This is what you wanted," I taunt. "Now you know my secret. Happy now?"

More head shaking.

"Get out." I point at the open door. "Just get out."

His head still moves back and forth, but he doesn't say anything. He just keeps staring at me like I let him down. He feels sorry for me. I can't take that. It makes my skin feel itchy and too tight.

"Get out!"

"No," he finally says.

"Stop looking at me like that!"

My face and neck are wet from the tears I don't hold back. He may as well see all of it, all of me. I don't have anything else left to hide. I open my arms as wide as I can, accidentally hitting a stack of stuff and ironically knocking a box of trash bags into the cleared path.

"This is it," I yell. "This is what you wanted to see. You made me do this. Don't stand there and say nothing. Not now. Where are all of your *you can tell me anything's* and *there's nothing you could do or say to drive me away's*? The *it won't change the way I feel about you's*? I *told* you that you couldn't handle it, but you kept insisting. Well, *here it is*. Here it *all* is."

"Just give me a goddamned minute, okay?"

"No. Tell me we're possible now, Nolan. Tell me how none of this matters. Go on, do it."

"It doesn't matter."

I laugh. "Who are you trying to convince, me or you? Because I'm not convinced, Nolan. I never was. I told you from the beginning this would never work, but you had to push it, didn't you?"

He runs a hand through his hair and looks around the room again like he's searching for an answer. "It *doesn't* matter."

"You were more believable the first time you said it."

"What do you want from me?" He makes an angry, all-encompassing gesture. "Would you just give me a fucking minute here? This is a lot to take in."

"Take your time. Nothing's going to change."

I swipe at my face, angry with myself for holding out the smallest, barest hint of hope that we can somehow work through this. I hug myself and glare at him, watching him, waiting for the questions I know will come. Questions I don't have any answers for.

"How long?" he asks.

"I don't know."

"Does your family know about this?"

"No. No one knows. Except you."

"You're so on top of everything else..."

Like I can stop this at any time, like I would *want* to stop it.

"Maybe if you saw a counselor or talked to someone..." He's trying to fix this, fix me.

I don't give him any hope or make promises I can't keep.

He picks up a stack of junk mail. "Aren't there specialists...organizers...something that could help?"

I give him a shrug. There probably is, but I don't know that I want anyone in here telling me what to do. He sets the mail back down and I let out the breath I was holding. I don't like people touching my things.

He turns in a tight circle, still trying to take everything in. "Is the whole place like this?"

When he faces me again I give him a curt nod.

"Show me."

I carefully step into the path to the bedroom and motion for him to go ahead of me toward the kitchen. He picks his way forward. I try to see it through his eyes. There's a small spot cleared on the counter that's big enough to put a bowl or plate down. The rest of the kitchen is cluttered and dirty and basically unusable. The stove broke and I never had it fixed. The sink is unusable hence the reason I have to get water for the coffee pot from the bathroom.

He takes a breath through his nose and takes the same slow perusal of the space that he did in the living room. His gaze snags on the dining area where I created a small niche for myself.

He points to it. "What's that?"

"Where I sleep."

His jaw moves like he's grinding his back teeth.

"You want to see the rest?"

He gives a jerky nod and moves out of the kitchen. I follow him down the path to the bedroom and bathroom. The doors to both are open, too crammed with stuff to close. The bathroom is somewhat serviceable, but the bedroom is packed. This is where I keep things like old clothes and broken things I can't throw away, things I found and things I bought. I'm suddenly fiercely possessive of them and how he might be judging them, judging me.

"Have you seen enough?" I ask, defensive. "Are you done yet?"

He inclines his head and goes back the way he came, straight for the front door. He doesn't look back at me. He just bolts like he's suddenly been sprung free and he can't wait to get out. The door slams behind him. I give it a glance and then head to my bed and lie down. Curling up in a ball, I let the tears come. My body shakes and my throat is raw.

I told him we'd never work out. Looks like he finally believes me.

21

NOLAN

I stumble out into the parking lot and bend over, clutching my knees and trying to pull in air. I'm suffocating. Somehow I slide to the ground next to my car. It's too much. I can't take in everything I saw. There was just *so* much. Of everything. It was everywhere. I wouldn't even know where to start to clear it all out. Lila looked at all of that *junk* like it was the most important thing in the world. I'd give anything to have her look at me like that. I let out a laugh that sounds more like a sob.

Fuck that's stupid.

I press the heels of my palms into my eyes, rubbing at the unexpected wetness. I don't know what to do or say. This is so far out of my comprehension I can't grasp at any thoughts. I don't know what to make of it. *How did that happen? Why can't she make it stop? How are we going to get past this?* All of the daydreams I had of us being a couple, someday living together, come crashing down in bitter chunks around me. She warned me. She told me I shouldn't get close. I can't say she didn't. I foolishly, selfishly ignored her, pushing all of her protests away like they were puny, inconsequential objections.

I built it all up in my mind. We were bigger than any issue she had. We could get past anything together. I pull in a ragged breath. Except this, I realize. This is all her. None of it is me or *us*. There is no pushing this aside. She wants her compulsion more than she wants me. That's a hard blow to take. It knocks the wind out of me and sends me reeling. I can't fix her. Jesus. God. I was *such* an idiot. So goddamned naïve and stupid. Just *dumb*. So dumb.

I picture her face wet with tears, standing there in the middle of all of that chaos, knowing I couldn't handle what she was showing me. Why did I have to keep pushing her? What had I been thinking? I suck in deep breaths, trying to get some control. I don't know whether to punch something, go to her and demand answers or just walk away from it all. My first instinct is to get in my car and leave. I tamp it down, ashamed at the thought.

I should go to her. Maybe we *can* work this out. Maybe I can talk her into getting help. Maybe if she had enough support... Those are all lies. We can't work this out. If she wanted help she would've already gotten it regardless of how much support she had. She's not a weak willed person...and yet she is. There's a whole house packed full of shit to prove it.

I picture her on that makeshift bed in the dining area and I want to hit something. When she said she didn't sleep in a bed I thought it was because of the rape, like maybe it gave her flashbacks or something. I don't know. I don't know anything. I'm grasping at wisps of smoke. She's given me no indication that there's anything to hold onto here. It was all built up in my mind despite her protests that we didn't have a relationship. We had sex. That was it. Just fucking.

I got so frustrated at how she held herself away from me. The more she did it the more I wanted her. I wanted to know her, every part of her. Now I've seen it all and I'm not sure I can handle it. I'm ashamed of that weakness, ashamed that I'm reacting exactly the way she thought I would. I'm failing the same way so many others in her life have. She expected I would and I didn't disappoint.

I don't know what to do. Do I tell her it doesn't matter, that we can keep going like we are with no long-term future? Do I go in there and fight for us, try to convince her to get some help and tell I'll be there every step of the way? Or do I end it?

I know what she expects me to do. But what do *I* want?

If I'd been asked that question before walking into her apartment I would've answered unequivocally *her*. Now? Now I just don't know. I can't pin any hope on her changing. I have to accept that she might never get better. We'd never be able to live together. That's hard constraint to put on a relationship. Marriage would be out of the question. I mean, what married couple doesn't live together?

If she gets help it has to be because *she* wants it. Am I strong enough to go through that with her? I wish I could say that I am, but I honestly have no idea.

The one thing I do know is that I can't walk away. The thought of never getting to talk with her or touch her is... unimaginable. That hasn't changed.

So I guess I have my answer.

But there are a thousand other questions rolling around in my head that I can't answer, like what do I say to her? How do I make her believe I want the possibility of us? How do I get her to see that there *can* be an us? Where do we go from here?

I guess the first step is getting off my ass and getting back in there.

Hauling myself up, I dust off and take a deep breath, then another. I check myself to be sure I'm really doing this. Yeah, I am. Her front door is a portal that once crossed will change my world and maybe Lila's too. Without knocking, I barge right on in.

"Lila," I call out. "Lila, where are you?"

There's some movement from somewhere deep in the apartment and then she appears. We stare at each other for a long moment. She's surprised to see me. On some level I'm offended. I know I shouldn't be. We haven't known each other long enough for her to realize I'm not someone who gives up. I might be a fuck up, but I'm not a quitter.

I keep my focus on her and ignore everything else around me. "Did you gather what you need?"

Her brows pull together.

"To stay at my place."

She stares at me like she doesn't understand what I'm saying.

"Nothing's changed," I tell her. "It's still not safe for you to be alone."

"*Oh.*"

"Look, I didn't handle this very well." I gesture toward the apartment in general still keeping my focus on her so I don't panic and bolt again. "I'm sorry for that. I can't promise that I'll always know the right thing to say or do. I'm bound to screw up more than get it right. If you can deal with that then I'd like to see if we could still try to figure out whatever this is between us. Because it feels big, Lila. It feels like you could change my life. And I don't know, maybe I could change yours."

My words hang in the air between us, a long bridge I

hope she'll cross. Her eyes and nose are red from crying. She's wearing her protective, fuck off expression, but it's all for show. She hugs herself like she's starving to be held, but I know if I try to touch her she'll reject me.

Her gaze turns wary. "You decide the sex was too good?"

"I'm not going to bullshit you. It's the best I've ever had, but that's not the only reason and you know it."

"I really don't."

"Now who's the bullshitter?"

"I must be a really good fuck to overlook all of this."

"You can try to make it all about sex if you want to."

"I don't know any different. That's the only kind of relationship I've ever had." She recoils at her own admission as though it embarrasses her.

I'm sad for her. She deserves so much more. I gentle my voice. "Get your things. Come back to my apartment with me. Please."

She blinks rapidly and swallows. "You sure?"

"Of what's between us? Yes. Of the future and how we'll work everything out? No."

She drops her gaze, nodding. "Give me a minute?"

"I'll wait outside for you."

I try to measure my steps so she doesn't see my panic. Now that I put it out there I can't take it back. The enormity of her problem hits me all over again. I thought I had a handle on it, but seeing her apartment again was somehow worse than the first time. I was in shock and a fair bit of denial. Knowing what to expect when I walked in there didn't make seeing it any easier a second time. If anything it was even *more* overwhelming. I'm crushed by the enormity of her problem.

I stood in the middle of all that chaos and promised to try to work through it with her, but now the doubts are back bigger and more insurmountable than before. I'm not cut out for this. I'm bound to fuck it up. I shouldn't have promised those things to her. They weren't lies at the time, but now I wonder whom I was trying to convince, her or me?

It's only when her front door closes behind me that I can pull in a full breath and the panic subsides to something close to tolerable. It's still there though, waiting to creep over me again. I hope I can hide it from Lila. The last thing she needs is me backing out on her. I should've thought this through better. I should've taken the time to live with it for a while and really go over it in my head before making that declaration to her. You'd think I'd know better, but being the fuck up that I am I dove head first without working it through first.

Leaning against my car, I wait for Lila. My thoughts are racing rats in a maze, swarming over, under, and around. I'm so caught up in my head that I don't notice it until the flash of a flame catches the corner of my eye. Turning my head, I see the dark sedan a split second before it peels away from the curb. My thoughts are slow so it takes me a moment to recognize the profile of one of the men from the Lucky Inn Motel—Billits's man.

I come off the car to get Lila just as she comes out with a bag slung over her shoulder. She locks the door and comes toward me with a wary look on her face totally unaware of what just happened. I have to get us out of here. Gripping her by the arm, I hustle her into the passenger seat and jog back around the car and climb in.

"What's wrong," she asks.

I tear off down the street in the opposite direction the sedan went without a word. All I'm thinking about is getting Lila somewhere safe.

"Nolan, what's going on?"

"Billits had a guy out in front of your apartment."

"*What?*"

"He's onto us. I gotta get you somewhere safe."

I take the next turn practically on two wheels. Lila screeches and clings to her door. In my head I'm running through the possibilities of how they found us when my phone dings.

I hand my phone to Lila as I blow through a yellow light. "What does it say?"

"Side window breech."

"Shit."

"What does that mean?"

"It means we can't go back to my place."

"Where are we going?"

The sedan pulls out onto the street half a block behind us, but doesn't try to catch up. How in the...? *Stupid*. Of *course*. *Think*, I tell myself. Taking the next turn, I speed up the next traffic light, then suddenly jerk to a stop and climb out. Dropping to my belly on the pavement, I search underneath the car. There. At the back near the left wheel a red light blinks on a black box. I pry it off and climb back into the car before the sedan rounds the corner.

I hand it to Lila. "Here. When I tell you to you're going to get out of the car and follow my instructions." I take off at the green light.

"What is this?"

"A tracking device. Don't turn around and look. We're being followed."

To her credit she doesn't look behind us. She stares down at the blinking light on the tracker. "Tell me what to do and I'll do it."

"I just have to find the right... There." I change lanes just in time. "When we stop at the light, get out and attach the tracker to that silver car." I point to a car two car lengths ahead of us.

"It looks just like your car."

"Exactly. Put it under the bumper, but don't let the two passengers see you. When you get back in, slide down in your seat so you can't be seen." I keep an eye on my rearview mirror, watching for the sedan, but it hasn't caught up to us yet. He's not in a hurry. After all he's got the advantage with the tracker.

"Oh, I get—"

"Now! Go! Hurry!"

22

LILA

I jump out of the car, slap the tracker under the lookalike car, and leap back in. Crouching in the foot well, I glance up at Nolan who is now wearing a cowboy hat and grinning at me like he's having a fantastic time.

"That was awesome! Way to go, babe."

His endearment slides through me like warm milk.

He looks back at the road. "The people in that other car didn't even flinch."

When the light turns green he eases us through the intersection and makes a left, his gaze flickering back and forth between the road and his rearview mirror. I can't tell where we are, but it's darker here. Maybe a residential street? He turns the car in a wide arc, then puts it in park and turns it off.

"What's happening?" I ask.

He flashes me the quick smile that drew me from the first time I met him. "I think you did it. Come on out of there."

I climb back up into my seat. We're parked on a street

with houses all around. In front of us is the main road we were just on.

"There." He points to a black sedan that drives right in front us on the road we were just on. "It worked. They're following the other car."

He gives me a quick kiss, then another. Just like all of the other times we've gotten physical it quickly gets away from us. We've got out hands in each other's pants when a car alarm goes off nearby startling us apart. Panting, we stare at each other in the dimly lit car.

"We need to find somewhere safe." He tucks himself back into his pants. "I need to get you under me as soon as possible."

I rebutton my jeans and press my legs together, trying to quell the throbbing between them. "Or over you."

He glances up at me, his eyes heavy with desire. "That would work too."

"Where are we going to go?"

"Give me a second to think."

He watches the traffic go past the little street we're on, his wrist hooked over the steering wheel. There's something about his profile backlit by the streetlamp across the street that makes me feel safe. Not just in a physical sense—he's already proven himself in there—but emotionally. He already knows the worst about me. Why he didn't run the first chance he got I don't know.

When he came back inside and gave his speech about me possibly changing his life I didn't know what to say. His thoughts so closely echoed mine about him it scared me. It terrifies me as much as showing him my apartment. He *could* change my life. He might be the only person who can. His words stormed the walls of my resistance and gave me something I've never had—hope. He makes me want to try and that's something I've never felt before. As much as my hoarding was a comfort it was also a trap. It wasn't that I didn't see it that way, it's just that I see it much more clearly now.

I don't have Pollyanna thoughts about his love changing me in some magical way like a hundred and ninety pound fairy godmother waving his wand and making all of my issues go away. I'm pretty sure he doesn't see it that way either. Behind the incredible things he said to me were tiny seeds of doubt and a heavy dose of incredulousness. Taking me on with all of my baggage is daunting to him and I'm apprehensive about letting him.

None of what we're considering here is going to be easy. I know that. I already harbor a tremendous amount of guilt over what I'll likely put him through and for not cutting him loose altogether. He shouldn't have to deal with me and my problems. He should be dating someone who can throw away junk instead of holding onto it like a life preserver. Someone he can think about a future with not someone who may never be normal and who can't give him normal things.

Why he would want me I don't know. I'm not sure I would take him on if our roles were reversed. That not only makes him better than me, but better than I deserve. I don't know what it is he sees in me that's bigger than my problems. It has to go beyond chemistry. There's no way he's so desperate for hot sex he's willing to overlook something as huge as my issues. Nobody's that good. I'm certainly not.

He starts the car. "I know where we should go."

"Where?"

"If you don't mind roughing it a bit my friend has an RV parked on the side of his house. It's in a fenced off carport. I stayed there a couple days when I had my floors redone. It's not fancy, but it'll be secure and off the grid so to speak."

"You mean no credit card charges for a hotel."

"Right. And he won't care if we just show up."

"Sounds perfect. You know I live in a constant state of *roughing it*."

He gives me a quick glance. "Shit. That's not what I meant."

"I know it's not. You've been really good about it. Maybe too good."

"What's that supposed to mean?"

"I don't know. Never mind."

"No. Say what you want to say."

"It's just that the sex can't be *that* good."

At a light he turns to me. "You tell me how good it is."

I look away from him out the side window. "It's amazing."

"Is that all it is for you?"

"No."

"Then why do you assume that's all it is for me?"

I shrug, then realize he can't see me. His gaze is back on the road as we make our way through the intersection.

"I don't know. I don't know how to do this."

"Neither do I. Right now I'm just trying to keep us safe until we can talk to Mr. Nash's FBI contact."

"And we can fuck."

"You're really starting to piss me off."

"You can't tell me that's not what this is about. You honestly can't be this hard up. No one is."

"Goddamn it!"

He jerks the wheel and we come to an abrupt stop at the side of the road. The seatbelt halts my lunge forward. When he turns to me his face is in shadow so I can't see his expression, but his breathing is rapid and harsh sounding in the cocoon of the car.

"Are we going to have this out right now, right here?" he asks.

I tilt my chin up in defense. "I guess so."

"You've made this about sex from the start. I went along with it because I didn't see any other way to have you, but I'm done with you setting the limits here. Here's how it's going to go. Yeah, we're gonna fuck because it's what we do best. The rest of the time we're going to try to figure out how to make the in between times work. It's going to suck sometimes. It's going to be just okay other times and then there will be pockets of *holy fuck this is good* because that's how relationships go. If you want out, if you can't handle that then say so right now and I'll let you go."

His eyes shine in the darkened interior. I've never had what he's talking about. My parents had it. I saw it everyday and wanted it for myself. And then everything collapsed and it was me at the bottom of the avalanche trying to dig myself out. I'm still trying to tunnel out with my bare hands. They're bruised and raw and I'm tired. So tired. It feels like he's handing me a shovel, but I don't know what to do with it. I don't know how to make this work the way he wants it to. I'm scared.

I don't realize I said the last out loud until he cups my cheek with his hand. "I know you are. So am I."

"You?"

"It's fucking overwhelming, Lila. All of it. Your apartment. The way we connect. The way I feel about you. I'm out of my depth here."

"It was easier when I didn't like you."

He lets out a self-deprecating laugh. "Yeah, it was."

"I might not ever be the person you want me to be. I might never be normal. That's not fair to you."

"No, it's not. But who ever said life was fair?"

"I'm going to hold you back. You could have someone so much better than me."

"Here's the thing... I don't *want* anyone else."

"I can't do this to you." I don't know how to make him understand what I'm trying to say. "I can't be the person who contorts your future into an approximation of what it should be."

"What if I was in an accident and I ended up in a wheelchair. Would you stay with me?"

His question throws me off guard, but it only takes me a moment to come up with an answer. "Yes."

"Your life would never be normal. I'd hold you back."

"But it wouldn't change who you are."

"Would it change how you feel about me?"

"No."

He doesn't say anything for a long time. "I don't know how to help you or if I even can. You might never change. I'm working on coming to terms with that and what it means for us. It's not easy. I'm not going to sit here and tell you that I'm not pissed as hell at you or that I understand and accept your...compulsion. I don't. I don't get it. *At all.* I might never get it. But here's the thing. I get *you*. Do you understand what I'm trying to say?"

"Yes, but I'm afraid to believe it."

"I can't make you any promises. I don't know what's going to happen. But I'm here now and I'm trying."

"I guess that's all I can ask. It's certainly more than I've ever hoped for." More than I deserve.

We fall quiet. The only noise is from the traffic around us. He shifts the car into gear and pulls back out into traffic.

We don't speak the whole way to his friend's house. I wait in the car while he grabs the key to the RV and his friend opens the gate. Nolan drives the car inside and his friend closes it behind us. When I climb out, Nolan makes the introductions. His friend's name is Fred and if I think I'm awkward in social situations, Fred makes me look like an extrovert.

Fred closes the gate, sealing us away from the road, and goes back in the house mumbling something about leaving some food and beer in the RV for us. Nolan grabs a couple of bags out of the trunk of his car. Mine is slung over my shoulder. I wait for him near the door of the RV. Things are supposed to be settled with us, but it feels weird that Nolan knows my secret. He's the only person in the whole world. I want to tell him that fact, but I don't want to bring it up and rehash everything all over again.

Instead I hold my hand out to him and try to pretend we're a normal couple hiding out from a corrupt DA in an RV in the backyard of a friend. Nothing unusual going on here. He catches my hand in his and opens the door for me to go inside. It's very RV-ish with lots of brown splashed here and there with orange and red. It might be unattractive, but it's clean. Not that I have room to complain. Most of all it's safe. At least I hope so.

Nolan closes the door behind him and sets one of his bags down on the table. He pulls a cell phone out and punches in a number.

"Burner phone," he tells me as he waits for the other person to pick up. "Sorry to bother you so late, Mr. Nash. I need to talk to you about the case I'm working on for the Freedom Project."

He lays it all out for Mr. Nash, leaving out the part about how we're hiding out in his friend's RV. The fact that we're sleeping together is probably something he wouldn't want his boss to know either. After a lot of back and forth, Nolan hangs up and turns to me.

"He's going to call his contact and get back to me." He opens the mini fridge. "Are you hungry? I'm starved. Looks like Fred left us some sandwich makings." He starts pulling everything out and sets it on the table, moving his bags to the floor.

He hands me a beer and I watch in silence while he makes us a couple of sandwiches. Everything we've been through tonight hits me all at once. I take a long pull off my beer, trying not to freak out. When I took this case I thought I might get the opportunity to change Carla's life, but my life's changed in ways I never could've imagined. The man in front of me is a huge part of that change. I've shared more with him than with anyone else in my life. That's no small thing.

I'm grateful to him and *for* him in ways I can't quite express. He settles the mad rush of emotions that I can't control on my own. At the same time he makes me feel things I've never felt before. He's sexy as hell. I want him every time I look at him. Like now. The way the muscles on his forearms flex reminds me of when he holds himself above me while thrusting deep. I cross my legs under the table, trying to curb my reaction to those thoughts. That's the one part of our relationship or whatever it is we have going on that comes easy. There's no thinking at all when he touches me. Only action and reaction.

I need that most from him—to not think, to not let the thoughts take over. He gives me something else I need, but don't feel like I deserve—quiet acceptance. I know he's struggling with my issues, but he does it without judgment. He's extraordinary in that way and a lot of other ways. I don't know what he sees in me that makes it all worthwhile for him or what makes him want me warts and all.

I make a vow to him and to myself to look into getting help as soon as we wrap up this case. I want to discover the part of me that only he sees. I have a feeling I buried it along with all of the things in my apartment. It won't be easy. Just thinking about throwing anything away makes my palms sweat and my pulse race. I don't have any idea how I'm going to do it, but I want to try. That has to count for something, right?

He slides a plated sandwich my way and takes a seat across from me. "You okay? You're kind of quiet."

"Just thinking."

"About?"

"A lot of things." I pause. "Mostly about how soon I can get you naked."

He sputters his beer and wipes his mouth with a napkin. "The answer is as soon as we finish eating."

"What did Mr. Nash say when you told him about Billits?" I ask, needing to change the subject.

"He was shocked at first. Then pissed that Billits could be running a prostitution ring right under the noses of the state attorney general and the FBI. I figure we'll tell him about our suspicions that Billits might be Diego's father and if he is then he had sex with Carla when she was underage. She's probably not the first or the last. Guys like Billits usually have more than one victim."

"I wonder how many other children he may have fathered. If Carla confirms paternity they may have to exhume Diego to compare his DNA to Billits. That will be the smoking gun." An awful thought suddenly occurs to me. "Do you think Carla's safe? If Billits is onto us then he has to know who we're helping."

"I don't know. When Mr. Nash calls me back I'll ask him. Maybe the FBI can set something up for her. Some sort of protection on the inside."

"I hope she's okay. What if something happens to her?"

"It's not like the movies and TV. It's not as easy to get to a prisoner. There are cameras and security everywhere."

"I hope you're right."

He puts his hand over mine. "It won't be long now before Billits gets what's coming to him and Carla is freed."

"And we stop working together."

He threads his fingers through mine. "Yeah, that too."

"We won't spend as much time together."

"No."

"I'm going to miss that."

"Me too."

"Maybe we'll work together on a new case."

"Maybe."

I rise from the bench and go to him. He shifts so that I can step between his parted legs. I put my hands on his shoulders and look down at him. His hands go to my waist, his eyes full of all of the things he wants me to do to me. I lean down for a kiss. Instead of coming at him like a starved, crazed animal as I usually do, I take it slow with gentle, coaxing kisses. He responds by running his hands up my back and drawing me closer. I melt into the ease of being with him. He's all I can see, hear, touch, taste, and smell. He's all I want filling up my senses.

He stands slowing, melding his body to mine. The feel of him up against me and around me always shocks me with how damn good it is. It's like his body was made to fit mine. We connect at every important point in a way that is at once overwhelming and intoxicating. When we're like this I wonder why we're ever apart. I know it will feel even better skin-to-skin. The memory makes me want to rush to get to that part like I would normally do, but I force myself to go slow, to enjoy *this* moment, *this* kiss.

A growl rumbles from his throat and vibrates through every part of me. He takes his time, kissing me thoroughly, leaving me panting and clinging to him. This is what I missed all of those other times in my hurry to get to the good stuff—the anticipation, the leisurely build up. I let him control the pace. He's good at the slow stuff. He doesn't go for the cheap grope, touching me in a way that's both intimate and chaste. It's a slow burn and I'm dying to be consumed.

We peel each other's clothes away a piece at a time with long intervals in between. That feel of his bare chest against mine makes me tremble. It feels like this is our first time, which is silly because we've already done all manner of things to each other. I'm learning his body in new, unexpected ways with my hands and my mouth. A shudder goes through him and his fingers flex into my flesh when I lick a sensitive spot just below his ear. So many new discoveries.

We topple onto the bed at the back of the RV, our limbs tangled together. Touches become more desperate and demanding. I'm going to die if I don't get him inside of me soon. I tell him that and he chuckles darkly as he dips his head to take my nipple in his mouth. I can't stop telling him how I feel and what I want him to do to me. The words just pour out, becoming dirtier and dirtier. I'm shocked at myself.

Nolan makes a deep, throaty noise at the back of his throat and looks up at me from between my legs. "You're making me crazy here, woman."

"Your mouth should be a registered weapon." I widen

my legs, inviting him to finish what he's started. "You're killing me."

"I've barely gotten started." The end of his sentence is a rumble on my over sensitized flesh.

He's good at a lot of things, but he's a fucking master at oral. By the time he lets me come legs are shaking and I'm begging him for release. My orgasm slams into me sideways and a scream rips from my throat. He kisses his way up my body and opens his mouth over mine in an intense, soul-surrendering kiss. I'm his. I'm owned and he lets me know it as he eases inside me, his mouth fused to mine. He rocks into me as though he has all day. Lifting my leg, he changes the angle and hits deep.

I cling to him, wrapping around him. I need something from him, but I don't know what. Everything he's doing isn't enough and yet it's too much. Our bodies become slick with sweat and still he thrusts in and out slowly as though he's memorizing every inch of me. I bow under him, craving something that doesn't have a name, chasing it as though my life depended on it. Digging my fingers into his flesh, I throw my head back. He hooks his arms under my legs, forcing them up, driving even deeper into me.

I'm crazed now. My screams echo off the walls and mingle with his grunts and the slap of flesh on flesh. I come on a hoarse cry. Burrowing his face in my neck, he follows, pressing me down hard into the thin mattress. My heartbeat is a throb through my whole body. Running my hands everywhere I can reach, I can't stop caressing him. He moves his head and finds my mouth. Something's changed between us. I can't put my finger on exactly what, but it's a subtle shift, hardly noticeable except that the ground is more even and I can breathe a little easier. Does he feel it too? I don't dare ask. Maybe I'm making more of it than I should. It could just be my imagination.

He leans up on his elbows and looks down at me. His gaze traces the lines of my face like a touch. I try not to squirm under his scrutiny and smile up at him. He smiles back. We stare at each other for a long minute. He looks different to me somehow. More attractive maybe or more familiar. I don't know. I feel like I know more about him than any other man I've ever been with. That's a strange thought to have and not at all appropriate with him naked on top of me and still inside me.

He lifts a lock of hair from the corner of my eye with a finger. "You're really beautiful."

I find that hard to believe with my makeup all sweated off and my hair a rat's next under my head, but I can tell he means it. Knowing that turns my insides all melty and liquid. I'm practically a puddle beneath him. I can only stare up at him doe-eyed and a little awe-struck. He makes me feel things I've never felt before. Mostly he makes me want things I never believed I could have.

He shifts to pull out of me and stills. "Shit. No condom."

"Oh." I look down between us. "That's okay. I'm on birth control."

"I'm clean. Just got tested a few months ago."

"Me too. I'm all good."

He flashes me that quick luminescent smile. "Thank god cause that was amazing."

"It really was."

"So are we going without from now on?"

"We can. I want to. I mean, we're exclusive, right? So it should be okay."

"More than okay."

"All right then."

He rolls off me and gathers me against him. We lay in silence for a while. An odd emotion has lodged itself under my ribcage. I want to give it a name, but I'm afraid. It feels like happiness. I've learned the hard way that it doesn't last. So I ignore it and snuggle deeper against Nolan's warm, hard body. I'll stick to the physical. The emotional is too fraught with changes and disappointment. I drift off to sleep, not at all confident that I can maintain that distance.

I don't know what's come over Lila. She seems—I don't know—calmer somehow. We're in the middle of all of this chaos, but she's gone strangely Zen on me. I don't know if I should be wary or glad. I'm kind of a strange combination of both. She settles in the bed next to me with a content sigh like we didn't just out run the bad guys and are hiding from them. Like we're not going to talk to the FBI about a possibly corrupt DA and she didn't just reveal her biggest, darkest secret to me. Like we didn't just have earth shattering, life-altering sex, deeply committed sex.

Maybe this is the calm before the storm.

I wish I could crack her head open and peer inside to find out what she's thinking and get a glimpse of how her mind really works. Just when I think I've got her figured out she throws me a curve. She didn't come at me like she usually does when she wants sex. She let me have the lead and set the pace. That's new. Maybe she finally accepted the fact that we have something here that demands our attention. She can't keep ignoring it or pretending it's only about sex.

She shifts closer to me, her body growing heavy. This too is new. We've never lain together like this before. Our post sex routine has always been about her re-establishing boundaries and putting space between us. She's definitely not doing that now. Her breathing grows even and steady. She's falling asleep. Next to me. In a bed. Must be exhaustion. It's been a bitch of a day. I can't pay too much attention to what's happening. It's likely a one off and the build up of everything we've been through. It doesn't mean anything, I tell myself. Don't read too much into it just enjoy it for however long it lasts.

And then there's the condom thing. I nearly blew it there. Her behavior shocked me so much that common sense totally left my head and all I could think about was how to keep things going exactly the way they were. She didn't freak out the way I thought she might. Thank god she's on birth control. My screw up could've been a total fuck up. I can't predict how she'd react if she got pregnant, what she'd decide or what would happen to us. We need to take this very, very slowly. Any jumps ahead could scare her away permanently.

If we're going to end I'd rather it not be over an unplanned pregnancy or other scare—something *I* could've prevented.

When I'm sure she's asleep I let myself drift off. It occurs to me just before all conscious thought stops that I'm falling for her and that might be my biggest fuck up yet.

～

THE RINGING of a cell phone jolts me awake. I don't recognize the ring and then I remember that Mr. Nash was supposed to call on the burner phone. Lila shifts in my arms. Her warm naked body wakes up other parts of my anatomy. I want to forget the phone call and roll her over onto her stomach and enter her from behind. Unfortunately that's not going to happen.

Sitting up, she flips her hair out of her face and squints down at me like she can't quite believe I'm there. She glances around the cramped space of the RV. I can see the moment her memory clicks everything into place for her. She yawns and stretches, her breasts lifting invitingly. I ignore the siren call of her body and flip back the covers to get out of bed.

I answer the phone call on what has to be the last ring. "Hello?"

"Nolan." It's Mr. Nash. "I have some news."

"Yeah?" I stifle a yawn and turn to watch Lila climb out of bed. Damn she's gorgeous.

"Carla Ruiz was found hanging in her cell."

His words jolt me fully awake. "What? When?"

"Last night. She's in ICU. It doesn't look good. They were able to bring back her heartbeat, but they don't know how long her brain was deprived of oxygen."

"Jesus. How did that happen?"

Lila comes to my side and looks up at me with a concerned frown. "What happened?"

I hold up a finger for her to wait so I can hear what Mr. Nash is saying.

"Suicide attempt," he says.

"No. That can't be. There's no way."

"Tore a strip of her bed sheet and fashioned a noose. They only found her when they did because the woman in the next cell from hers had the flu and was throwing up. Her yelling for a guard is what alerted them. When they walked past Carla's cell that's when they saw her. They cut her down right away and started CPR. Her cellmate claimed she was asleep and didn't hear anything."

"You don't believe that?"

"Do you? The other end of the sheet was tied to the top bunk. Someone's kicking and flailing and hitting your bed and you don't wake up? No. I don't buy it."

"You think her cellmate might've had something to do with it?"

Lila grabs onto my arm and goes to her toes to get my attention. "Is it about Carla?"

I nod.

"What happened?" she demands.

"She's in ICU. They think she tried to commit suicide."

She shakes her head. "No. No way. There's no way she'd do that."

"Her cellmate's been questioned and released back to her cell," Mr. Nash says. "There's nothing to prove she was involved. All the same the prison officials aren't convinced."

"What was her cellmate in for?"

"I don't know."

"Can you find out and let me know?"

"I can try. You think this might have something to do with the DA?"

"I'm wondering if she got a deal or is in some way connected to Billits."

Mr. Nash lets out a low whistle. "That's some accusation you're making, son."

"The timing of it's suspicious, don't you think?"

"It's awfully convenient for him, yes." After a pause he says, "I got you a meeting with the Special Agent in Charge at the San Diego FBI office at eight sharp. Bring everything you have on the case."

"Wow. I was expecting to meet with an agent not the man in charge."

"Let's just say he owes us after what went down with Beau and Vera and we have a strong track record with him. Plus this is a *very* delicate situation you two stumbled on. It needs to be handled cautiously. There's a lot more at stake here than what's going on with Carla Ruiz. Every case Billits's office prosecuted will get looked at. The FBI has some skin in the game. Billits's office handled some pretty high profile federal cases. The Feds are going to want those convictions to stick."

"We'll meet you there with everything we've got on the case."

"See you at eight." Mr. Nash says and ends the call.

Lila immediately throws one question after the other at me. I fill her in on everything Mr. Nash said. When I'm done she wraps her arms around me.

"I don't believe she did this," Lila says. "There's no way. She wouldn't give up so easily. Carla's a fighter. She knew what we'd find. Why would she go through everything she did to get her case considered by the Freedom Project and then give up before we've even started the legal process to free her? We didn't tell her what we've found out about Billits or our suspicions about Diego. No. She didn't do this. Something's very wrong here."

"I agree."

"What if Billits goes for her again at the hospital?"

"She's under guard."

"A fake nurse or doctor could get into her room. The guards aren't going to check out medical personnel. Their job is to make sure she doesn't escape. They're not there to protect her."

"I'm sure Mr. Nash has thought of that. Just to be sure I'll call him back. Why don't you get dressed? We have to be at the FBI office in a little over an hour."

She gives me a quick squeeze, then gathers her stuff and goes into the shower. I throw on some boxers and sit at the table going over everything we have on Carla's case, adding new notes about what happened last night and the phone call this morning on the tablet I keep in my bag in my car. I already had Fred's wifi password keyed in from when I stayed here before so I add the notes to the copy of the case file I keep in my cloud server. We should have everything we need to convince the FBI to look at Billits's business dealings along with what happened in Carla's case.

Lila comes out of the tiny bathroom with a towel wrapped around her that barely meets. I get a glimpse of bare thigh and hip before she heads back to the bedroom to put her clothes on. I wish we didn't have such a tight schedule. I'd rip that towel off and tumble her back down onto the bed. Instead I take my turn in the shower. By the time I get out Lila is dressed and waiting for me in the dinette area munching on a granola bar. She hands one to me and we gather up what we need to take with us. It's not much. All of our physical files are at my place, but we have enough stored in my cloud server to present our case to the FBI.

I just hope they see it the way we do.

Lila's quiet on the drive to meet Mr. Nash as the FBI building, but as soon as we got in the car she grabbed my hand and hasn't let go. That's a bold move for her. She's not the most demonstrative person. I try not to think about what it might mean for us, if it means anything at all. She could just be scared and looking for comfort and I happen to be handy and willing.

The FBI building looks like a normal multi-story office building. I don't know what I was expecting. Maybe something less ordinary and ugly. Something fortress like and impenetrable. Instead it looks like a bunch of accountants and lawyers lease the place. If Lila has an opinion on the building and what we're about to do she's not giving it. She's stayed fairly quiet and to herself since we got the phone call about Carla. She took the news hard, like she blamed herself. I'd tell her it's not her fault, but I know her well enough to know it would be a wasted effort.

I catch her hand as we walk side by side. She gives me a quick surprised glance, but doesn't pull her hand away. I could be in some trouble with Mr. Nash over it. I'll find a way around it if I am.

Mr. Nash is already in the reception area when we walk in. He takes in our clasped hands. His face reveals nothing. I don't know him well enough to know if that's a good thing or a bad thing. His son and Cora met during a case as did Beau and Vera so there's some precedence here. Plus she's not a client. That will hopefully work in our favor.

"You must be Lila Garcia," Mr. Nash says, extending his hand and forcing me to drop Lila's so she can take his. "It's a pleasure to meet you. I've heard a lot about you from Brent McMahon."

I don't know if Mr. Nash is making a point about mentioning Lila's boss at the Freedom Project or if he's just making conversation.

"He's had a lot of great things to say about you and your agency as well," Lila tells him. "From my experience on this case it's all true and more. Nolan's been a tremendous help. I don't know where we'd be without him."

"I only hire the best." He turns his attention to me. "Bet you never thought taking this case would lead to being questioned by the FBI. Great work, Nolan. Really great work." He shakes my hand and claps me on the back. "I'm proud of you, son."

"Thanks. We got more than we bargained on for sure. I just hope Carla is okay." I glance at Lila, then back to Mr. Nash. "We'd really like to see her get her freedom."

A woman opens the door that leads to the offices. "Mr. Nash? The Special Agent in Charge will see you now. Please follow me."

We trailed behind her to a set of elevators. Lila put her hand in mine as we rode up to the fifth floor and didn't let go until we were escorted into a conference room. We took our seats and waited. A few minutes later an older Asian gentleman joined us. Mr. Nash stood up and shook his hand, then introduced us to SAC Charles Fung.

"Thank you for seeing us Agent Fung," Mr. Nash began. "I told you a little bit about what Nolan and Miss Garcia found. I'm going to hand it off to them to tell you the rest. Nolan?"

I began and then Lila joined in. We took everyone through the steps we went through and how we connected the dots from the information Carla gave us to Martin's disappearance and possible death to Lila's friend who intervened at the DA's office and everything we discovered on our own. SAC Fung and Mr. Nash asked questions along the way. I didn't hold back about how we obtained some of the information even if it might get me in trouble. When we finished SAC Fung sat back in his seat, rubbing his chin. Lila and I exchanged worried glances. He must be killer at poker because his face betrayed nothing. Mr. Nash however was beaming like a proud papa.

"You skirted the law pretty cleverly," Fung finally says to me. "We won't be able to use some of what you found in our investigation because of how it was obtained." He glances at

Mr. Nash who shrugs as though he doesn't care that my tactics weren't entirely on the up and up. "But we'll eventually get it and more by other means. We've got someone on the inside of his organization and have managed to connect it to Billits. But we don't have enough for an arrest. None of the people we've picked up will talk. I don't know what Billits did or is doing to engender that kind of loyalty, but we've been unable to break it.

"We've got Carla Ruiz under restricted guard. Only pre-approved medical personnel are allowed into her room with law enforcement present. Her statement would give us the link we need to get Billits. Even if statutory rape is the only charge we can get him on it's a start. Once we have that we can get a warrant to exhume Miss Ruiz's son's body for a DNA sample to prove paternity. We're hoping she'll be the break we need to tie Billits to the prostitution ring and will give us enough to make some arrests.

"Miss Ruiz is the first person to break ranks with Billits. There's no doubt in my mind that he tried have her killed. Her cellmate was transferred into Miss Ruiz's cell the day before she allegedly tried to hang herself," Fung continues. "We're looking into how that happened and who made it happen. We're hoping to catch a break there."

Fung glances between Lila and me. "Do the two of you have a safe place to stay until this is all over?"

"Yes," I say. "It's not fancy, but we'll be okay."

"I've got a car I want you to drive," Mr. Nash says. "They're going to be looking for yours. We need to make it as difficult as possible for them to find you. You should also change your appearances and try not to go out in public as much as possible." He directs his next comment to Fung. "I'd hoped the FBI would approve some protection for you, but apparently that isn't going to happen."

Fung gives a *what can I do* gesture. "It's out of my hands. Neither one of them are material witnesses. I won't be able to use the majority of the information they provided when this case goes to trial. I don't have the budget to assign an agent to them or put them up in a safe house." He turns to Lila and me. "I'm sorry, but you're on your own."

24

LILA

Fung's words run on a loop in my head. *You're on your own.*

I've been on my own for a long time, but it never felt like this. There've been times when my fears felt like they were devouring me from the inside out or like I was drowning in them. I've felt helpless and inconsequential. I've been overwhelmed, overburdened, and overpowered. During all of those times I was utterly and completely alone. I think it was that loneliness, of being isolated in my experiences that did the most damage.

Glancing at Nolan as he concentrates on the road driving the car Mr. Nash loaned us, I realize I'm not alone anymore. For whatever reason I now have him. What I did to deserve him I don't know. I'm surprised at how he somehow managed to slip past all of my defenses and offensives. We're something more than we were before, more than I thought I deserved. I'm ashamed of that. I habitually held people away—lovers, friends, and family. I thought distance was protection. I see now that it didn't make me stronger. It made me weaker.

I think of Carla and how very, very similar we are in that way. She had no one then. She has us now. I want to go to her and tell her she's no longer alone. We've worked hard on her behalf, harder than I've ever worked on anything, including myself. I don't know what I'll do if she doesn't pull through. She deserves the life she should've had. I really hope she gets it.

After checking the car for trackers, Nolan drove a circuitous route back to Fred's house. He said he was watching for anyone tailing us. We finally pull up the driveway of Fred's house pretty sure we're in the clear. Nolan gets out to open, then shut the gate after us. He turns the engine off, but we don't get out right away. The tick of the engine is the only sound as we sit there waiting for what I don't know. We've come to a point where there's nothing more for us to do for Carla. We can't go home and we can't go to work. We're in a sort of holding pattern with no end in sight.

Oh, and we're on our own.

"What's going to happen if Carla doesn't pull through?" The question pops out before I can think to ask it.

"I don't know, but I imagine they'll get Billits...eventually."

"That's not very reassuring."

"No. It's not."

"So in the mean time we're *on our own* for an unknown amount of time."

"Pretty much." There's something about his tone that says he's not going to just sit by and wait it out.

"What are you thinking?"

"I'm thinking that although I really like the idea of having nothing to do but make love to you day and night, we need to be proactive here. We're missing something..."

"What?"

"I don't know, but it feels like there's a thread dangling that isn't going to get snipped unless we do it."

"I have the same feeling. It's incomplete, unfinished." I turn to him. "What do you usually do when you hit a wall in a case?"

"Go back to the beginning. Start from scratch and go through it all over again, trying to look at it from different angles. See if I missed anything or if something didn't fit in with the rest of the case. Sometimes there's a clue that seems inconsequential at the time that can break a case open and take it in a new direction."

"That's what we'll do then. Go back over everything. Do we have everything we need to do that?"

He looks out the windshield, his wrist hanging over the steering wheel. "Most of it." He taps the dashboard with the blunt end of his fingers, then reaches under his seat with both hands and pulls out a small box. He turns to me. "Do you know how to shoot a gun?"

"What?"

"Like you said, we're on our own, which means we're left to defend ourselves."

I stare at the box as though is holds a cobra prepared to strike. I've never seen a gun in person let alone touched one. I wouldn't know what to do with it. I tell him this.

He opens the box. Inside are two small guns. He takes one out and holds it in his palm. "It's easy. Point and shoot." He tucks it into his sock, then hands me the other one.

"Where do I put it?"

"Wherever you can easily access it."

I open the neck of my shirt and tuck it in my bra between my arm and my breast. "This isn't going to accidentally go off and shoot my boob off, is it?"

He laughs. "No, but be careful that's my favorite of your boobs. Come on. Let's go inside."

We climb out of the car. I wait while Nolan unlocks the RV. He pulls the door open, steps up, then stops.

"What?" I ask.

"Come on in," a male voice I don't recognize says. "And bring the lovely Miss Garcia with you."

Nolan turns to me and mouths *run*.

"You wouldn't want anything bad to happen to your lover, would you Miss Garcia?"

Nolan silently pleads with me to do what he said. He glances toward the gate and his gaze freezes. I turn to see what he's looking at. One of the men from the Lucky Inn motel—Billits's man—leans against Nolan's car, his arms crossed over his chest, a gun in one hand. My attention snaps back to Nolan. His lips are pressed into a grim line. He takes my hand and leads me up into the RV.

Billits sits at the dining table. His other man leans against the door to the bathroom, blocking the way to the bedroom, in the same pose as the man outside complete with a nasty looking gun.

Billits extends his hand to the empty bench across from him in invitation. "Have a seat."

Nolan slides into the bench across from Billits. I sit next to Nolan, unable to keep my eyes off Billits. *How did he find us? What does he want?*

"You're good," Billits says to Nolan. "You covered your tracks very well."

"Not well enough apparently."

Billits inclines his head, then turns his attention to me. "Miss Garcia. How nice to finally meet you. You're even prettier in person."

"What do you want?" Nolan interjects.

Billits ignores him, keeping his focus on me. "So noble too, helping those who can't help themselves. But you're wasting your time."

"What's this about?" Nolan interrupts again. "What do you want?"

Billits lazily flicks his hand toward Nolan like he's an annoying insect buzzing around him. The big man behind us moves so fast I don't see him coming until his fist connects with Nolan's face. Nolan's head snaps back, then he slumps in his seat out cold. I scream. I'm suddenly cut off by the big man slapping a meaty hand on the tabletop in front of me. The threat is clear. I'm next if I don't shut up. I turn to Nolan. Blood seeps out of his nose. It doesn't look right. It's swollen and off center. I shake him, but he doesn't respond.

"Forget him," Billits commands, his voice agitated and annoyed.

"He's hurt."

"He'll live. I said *forget him*."

I clasp Nolan's limp hand under the table and turn my attention to Billits. "What do you want?" My voice comes out a lot stronger than I feel. I grip Nolan's hand tighter.

"Drop the case. It's not going anywhere anyway."

"Thanks to you. How did you get to Carla?"

"*I* didn't do anything."

"You got someone to do your dirty work for you. Martin, corrupt cops, these goons here, and Carla's new cellmate. How could you? What did she ever do to you?"

"She got what she had coming."

"She's the mother of your child."

The minute widening of his eyes betrays him. "She was a meth whore who opened her legs to anyone for a hit."

"What do you mean *was*?"

"Whores don't last long. Whores who use have the life span of a fruit fly."

Everything in me goes cold. "What did you do to her?"

"You shouldn't have gone to the FBI." He shakes his head sadly. "I'm very disappointed in you." He reaches out to touch my face, but I move out of reach. "It'll be a shame to see you go."

His meaning sinks in and the bottom drops out of my world. He's going to kill us. Our bodies will never be found. Our families will never know what happened to us. I grip Nolan's hand tighter. His twitches in response, then squeezes mine right back just as hard. He breaks my hold and taps something out on my palm that I don't understand. I resist the urge to look at him, keeping my focus on Billits, and wait for Nolan to give me more. He folds down all of my fingers except my index finger and thumb. I finally get what he's telling me. Gun.

I lick my suddenly dry lips, trying to come up with something that will buy Nolan some time to recover and me a chance to figure out how to pull the gun from my bra. "That was a nice headstone you had made for your son, Diego," I say to Billits. "You must've loved him a great deal."

"His whore mother took the money I gave her for him and shot it into her veins. He died while she fucked her landlord because she blew the money I gave her for rent."

"But you made her a whore. *Your* whore."

His laugh is thick and sick. "Is that what she told you? My guys picked her up trying to turn her first trick in my territory and brought her to me. I liked the looks of her. She was happy to take my money for her time. Happier still after she developed a meth habit. I cut her loose then. I don't do junkies. That's when she turned whore." His greasy gaze slides over me, lingering on my breasts. "I like the looks of you. You remind me of her only older and not all tweaked out."

"When she wakes up she's going to tell the FBI what you did."

"She's not going to wake up. Even if she did, I've got something that will insure her silence."

"What could you possibly have that would keep her from telling the world what you are?"

"I've got you." He pulls his phone from his pocket and taps the screen, then turns it my direction. "And I've got her little sister." He shows me the image of a young girl maybe sixteen, seventeen tied to a chair, gaged and blindfolded. "I like the looks of her too."

"You're disgusting. You're never going to get away with it."

"I already did."

Under the table Nolan taps my hand three times. I still don't know what he wants me to do. *How do I get to the gun? What is* he *going to do?*

"The FBI is onto you," I tell Billits. "Your arrogance will be your downfall."

His laugh sends chills through me. "Ah, sweet girl, my arrogance is what got me where I am. Enough of this."

He makes a gesture with his hand and his goon grips me by the arm, yanking me out of the bench in one swift motion. My hand slips from Nolan's and he collapses onto the bench where I was just sitting. I yelp and turn toward the big man, pretending to try to wriggle free. My body blocks my movement for the gun. I don't quite get it free of my shirt before it goes off, hitting the henchman in the shoulder. My finger spasms on the trigger and it fires again. The bullet grazes the bad guy's chin, but it's enough that he lets go of me. I squeeze the trigger a third time. A shot to the gut. The guy goes down.

Behind me a gun goes off and I spin around, gun raised to find Billits slumped over the table blood oozing from his head and Nolan gun in hand.

"Get down," Nolan shouts at me. "The door."

I hit the floor just as the second goon comes through the door. Both Nolan and I get shots off, but I'm pretty sure his is the only one that hits the guy. The force of the shot knocks the bad guy off the step. Nolan is up and after him before I can get my feet under me. The door slams shut after him. There's another shot. I burst through the door not thinking about anything except getting to Nolan. He's standing over the man, chest heaving.

He turns to me, blood from his nose running down his face. "I told you to be careful with my favorite boob."

I look down at myself. My bra strap snapped, peeling back the cup. Through the hole in my blouse my breast hangs out, a thick crimson gash is gouged out of the top of it and blood runs down the front of me. My whole breast is red. The world suddenly spins too fast and I fall. Somewhere in the darkness I hear Nolan's muffled curse and then nothing.

25

NOLAN

I managed to catch Lila before she hit the ground. Just barely. She lies on a stretcher in the back of an ambulance still out cold. They tell me she's in shock. They want to put me in a different ambulance, but I won't let them. I won't leave her. I can't believe what she did. She nearly killed herself saving us. Thankfully the wound isn't deep enough to be life threatening, but she'll have a nasty looking scar and a messed up story about how she got it.

I blame myself. I should've told her to put the gun somewhere else. Somewhere safer. She was nervous about the gun. I shouldn't have given it to her until she was familiar with it. They tell me that man she shot will likely live. He was rushed to the hospital for surgery. Billits is dead and it doesn't look good for the other bad guy I shot. When I came up off the bench after pretending to slump over so I could get the gun out of my sock, Billits had his gun out and aimed at Lila. I pulled the trigger knowing that if I didn't Billits would've killed her.

My whole face throbs like a son of a bitch. They packed my face with ice so I can't see anything. I can barely breathe.

But Lila's hand is warm in mine and I can hear the steady, reassuring bleep of her heart monitor. I don't know what I would've done if I'd lost her.

"Are you two all right?" It sounds like Mr. Nash's voice, but I can't see him.

"Nolan." Cora's voice sounds panicked. "Oh my god."

I lower the ice pack. "We're okay." My voice comes out thick and stuffed up sounding due to my broken nose. "Mostly." Through my swollen, blurry eyes I see Cora recoil. I can only imagine what I look like. That asshole packed one hell of a punch.

"Your face," Cora whispers.

"I may never be pretty again," I try to laugh, but it hurts too damn much.

SAC Fung comes up behind Mr. Nash. "Thought you should know that Carla Ruiz is awake and talking."

"We really need to get her to the hospital," the paramedic tells me.

"Let's go then. I'm sure I'll see you all later." I put a hand up to wave as the ambulance doors slam shut.

I turn my attention back to Lila. She looks so pale. I wish she'd wake up. She'd hate that they cut her shirt off of her to bandage her up even though she's covered up now. Other than the nasty gash on her chest there doesn't seem to be anything else wrong with her. They keep telling me she'll be okay, but the only way I'll believe that is if she tells me that herself. I kiss the back of her hand.

"You should really keep ice on that," the paramedic says. "It's swelling right before my eyes. Next time duck, huh?"

"Hahaha," I answer sarcastically. "Thanks for the advice. A little late though."

I'm just about to cover my face again when Lila stirs.

She blinks up at me and frowns. "What happened to

your face?" We hit a bump and she looks around, her eyes growing wider and wider. She tries to sit up even though she's strapped down.

The paramedic and I put hands on her shoulders. "Be still," I tell her. "Or you'll start bleeding again."

"Blee—" She looks down at the bandage across her chest. "Oh." Then as she remembers what happened. "*Ooohhh*."

"You're going to be okay," I reassure her. "Probably need some stitches and antibiotics. You're better off than me." I point to my nose. "I'll probably need surgery to set this. Will you still like me if I don't look the same?"

"Will you still like me now that I've damaged your favorite boob?"

I kiss the back of her hand. "I'll kiss it and make it better."

WE BOTH ENDED up staying the night at the hospital in separate rooms. I hated that. Cora reassured me that Lila was fine and said that she had to give Lila the same reassurance about me. That was the only thing that kept me from climbing out of my hospital bed and going to find her. That and the pain.

I didn't end up needing surgery. The doctor reset my nose under local anesthetic. Hurt like a son of a bitch. It throbbed for days afterward. The FBI interrogated Lila and me for hours. They don't like it when you kill their lead suspect in a major case, but I don't much care. Seeing Billits point a gun at Lila's back broke open a rage in me that I didn't know I was capable of. I'd shoot him again if given the chance. I'd do anything to save her.

We realized after being released from the hospital that we'd gone about having a relationship all backward. It was actually Lila's new therapist who pointed it out. So we're dating and learning about each other in the usual way. I thought I knew most everything about her. I was wrong. First of all she's funny. She can cook and she likes horror movies. Twice a week we have movie night and I've been sharing my horror B movie collection with her.

She's working on getting better. There's been some forward progress. I think Lila is more frustrated than I am that there hasn't been more. She doesn't know it, but I've talked to her therapist to help me find the patience I sometimes lack and to see if there are any ways that I can help. Mostly I've learned about all the ways that I'm *not* helping. But I'm learning and that has to count, right? I don't know where we'll end up, but I have no doubt we'll get there together.

The FBI was instrumental in getting a court date just a few weeks after Carla was released from the hospital. Carla is cooperating in their investigation and in return they've assisted in Lila's and the Freedom Project's efforts to free her. Lila sits at a table at the front of the courtroom with Carla and a man who she introduced as her boss and the director of the Freedom Project.

I sit at the back with Cora, Leo, and Mr. Nash. It's crowded. There's a lot of press. Billits death and the scandal that followed was big news. Members of several different activist groups have also crowded in. Carla's story struck a nerve in the community and highlighted the plight of undocumented immigrants. The FBI hasn't allowed her to be interviewed by the media because she's a material witness so they turned their attention to Lila, who's become a fine representative of the immigrant community and has been asked to speak for groups and schools.

It's all over Lila's face how badly she wants this hearing to go well for Carla. All three of us—Lila, Carla, and I—have the scars both physical and mental as proof of how hard and tirelessly we worked to get to this day. I hope it goes the way it should.

The judge finishes reading the paperwork she's been studying for what seems like hours and sets it aside. Her focus goes to Carla who sits quietly with her hands in her lap, her head slightly bent. Lila whispers to her and Carla's head comes up.

The judge addresses Carla. "It's clear to this court that a grave injustice was done to you Ms. Ruiz. Our justice system was perverted and misused for individual gain and revenge. For that the court sincerely apologize. I cannot give you the years of your life back, but I hope you find meaning in the years ahead and have a life filled with all of the things that bring you happiness and contentment. It is my honor to reverse the verdict set down by this court. You are a free woman, Ms. Ruiz. God bless you and god bless the United States of America." She bangs the gavel. "Court dismissed."

Cheers and applause breaks out. Carla turns to Lila, her eyes wide, and says something to her. Lila responds with a lot of nodding and a huge smile. Carla's face blooms with disbelief, then joy. She throws her arms around Lila and gives her a big hug. They both dissolve into tears. Eventually Carla is taken away, back to prison where she'll wait for the paperwork to come through for her release. Lila watches her go, a bittersweet smile on her face. I know she wishes Carla could walk out of the courtroom with us, but that's not how things work.

During their celebration I managed to fight my way to

the front of the courtroom. I wait as Lila shakes her boss's hand and gathers her things.

The first thing I do is give her a big hug. "You did it," I tell her. "You did it."

"*We* did it. I couldn't have done it without you and Nash Security and Investigations. Especially you." She kisses me. "Thank you for everything. Carla thanks you too."

"Please tell her it was my pleasure. I was glad to help."

"I will."

"Hey, you two," Cora says. "Congratulations. We're having a little celebration back at the office. You *have* to come. Mr. Nash won't take no for an answer."

"We'll be there," Lila tells her.

I glance down at Cora's hand. "Something else we're celebrating?"

"Oh." She looks down at the sapphire ring on her hand with what can only be described as a *dreamy* expression. "Leo asked me to marry him."

Leo steps up behind her and puts an arm around her. "And lucky for me she said *yes*."

"That's wonderful," Lila beams. "Congratulations."

As we exchange hugs and handshakes I whisper to Cora, "I guess now you know why things were a little off with Leo."

"I'm so embarrassed that I dragged you into that."

"Don't be." I wink at her. "I knew everything would work out."

Lila and I follow them out of the courtroom. Reporters try to get Lila's attention, but she tells them that today is about Carla not her and refers them to the Freedom Project. As we make our way through the doors into the sunlight I can't help, but feel like the luckiest man in the world. I might fuck up now and then, but as long as I have Lila I know everything will be okay.

THANK YOU FOR READING RECLAIM!

If you loved RECLAIM, you'll love the sexy, funny, award nominated DANGEROUS LINES series. Someone is stalking Miyuki Price-Jones and it's up to former Navy SEAL, Lucas Vega, to protect her.

Turn the page to read an excerpt from **LOST** now!

If you enjoyed RECLAIM, please consider leaving a review on your favorite book site. Reviews help readers find books!

➤RECLAIM (RECOVERED INNOCENCE novel)

➤GOODREADS

Join my VIP Facebook group Babes with Books for exclusive sneak peeks at my upcoming books & other, members only, perks:

➤www.facebook.com/groups/BabesWithBooksReaderGroup

Sign up to receive my newsletter for new release alerts, exclusive bonus content, and giveaways!

➤**www.bethyarnall.com/newsletter**

Turn the page to read an excerpt from **LOST** now!

EXCERPT FROM LOST

Miyuki Price-Jones held up the shocking pink Multiple O vibrator, flipped the switch and... nothing. No reversible rotating head, no quivering bunny ears and no massaging beads. For the third time this week she'd turned on a toy only to end up frustrated.

"Davy!" Crosby yelled from somewhere in the darkened television studio.

The young man in the corner jumped, then shuffled over to the man sitting in a faded director's chair. "Yes, Mr. Crosby?"

"Your job is simple. Put the batteries in the toys, test them to make sure they work and don't give me a reason to kick your ass all the way to Tuscaloosa!" Rob Crosby, the director of the adult home shopping show, *Pleasure at Home*, pinched the bridge of his nose.

All Miyuki, or Mi, could see was the top of Crosby's balding head, but she could tell he'd had it with Davy. He was going to fire him even though none of this was his fault. It was sabotage... again. She set the Multiple O vibrator down on the faux walnut coffee table next to the other sex toys she would be showcasing today and stood to get Crosby's attention. "I'm sure it's not Davy's fault. Maybe we got a bad batch of batteries. Or—"

"Or more likely Davy is an incompetent idiot who couldn't find his own ass with both hands and a map!" Crosby shouted. Crosby was always shouting. It had taken Mi three weeks to stop flinching every time he opened his mouth. Crosby turned on Davy. "Did you even *put* batteries in it?"

Davy bobbed his head. "Yes, sir."

Without wavering his glare at Davy, Crosby barked, "Check it, Mi. And so help me, Davy." Crosby pointed a finger at the young man. "If four double A's don't pop out the bottom of that thing your ass is grass." Someone's ass was always grass or otherwise in jeopardy with Crosby.

Mi picked up the Multiple O and opened the bottom of it. Four batteries sat there, nestled properly with the plus and minus ends exactly as they should be. "Davy's right. There must be something wrong with the batteries." She tipped the device upright and switched it on. Still nothing. "Or the vibrator."

Crosby threw the sheaf of papers in his hands, sending them floating down around him. "God damn it! Somebody get me some goddamned batteries that work! Of all the incompetent, backwoods, inbred—"

"Crosby?" Mi interrupted. "Why don't I just take the batteries from one of the other—"

"Davy can do it!" Crosby stood up. "Take five, everybody. When I get back every single one of those goddamned things better work. Or your ass is hitting the pavement. Hear me, Davy? And somebody pick up those goddamned papers." He turned and stormed off in the direction of the studio offices. "Mi! With me."

Mi handed the Multiple O to Davy with a mumbled apology. Even though there was often no good excuse for Crosby's bad behavior, she still felt like she had to apologize for him.

Davy waved it off as most did when she made the gesture, his long blond hair hanging like a curtain as he bent over his task. "Ain't your fault, Miss Mi. Better catch up before he starts threatenin' you, too."

Mi turned to follow Crosby and caught sight of a man she'd never seen before, standing against the wall just out of the reach of the stage lights, his face fully shadowed. He was large—well over six feet tall and as broad as a doublewide. Something about the way he stoodstill, yet humming with energy caused an answering rhythm to thrum from deep inside her. Her pulse kicked up, generating a near fight or flight sensation that sent her senses into overdrive. Who was he? What was he doing here?

"Mi!"

She jumped, her focus flickering to Crosby, then back to the man. "Coming," she answered, keeping her gaze on the man.

She rounded the end of the stage opposite him and stepped down. The man made no move, but she knew he watched her. Turning down the hall after Crosby, she should have felt relieved to be out of the man's sight and yet she instantly missed the extra beat his attention had caused.

Crosby sat at his desk, pulling a long drink from the flask he kept in his bottom drawer. He wiped away the bright pink drop from his bottom lip, but not before Mi had seen it. He thought he was fooling everyone by putting stomach medicine in a container meant for alcohol. And he was. Everyone, but Mi.

He looked up at her with blurry, red eyes. "Third time this week." He held up a hand. "Before you say it, I know. It's not Davy. But goddamn it, I hate this shit." He leaned back in his chair and waved for Mi to sit down, so she did. "The police don't have one single lead and I know you're not going to like it, but Sellers hired you a bodyguard."

She opened her mouth to protest, but was cut off.

"Goddamn it, don't fight me on this. It's a done deal. With Lucy out on maternity leave, you're all we've got. And there's no way Sellers is going to stop shooting the show for one single goddamned day. You got me? You're cash in the bank. Ratings haven't budged an inch since Lucy got too big to hock dildos, proving you're the real draw, not her." He waved an idle hand around. "Must be that ancient Chinese secret thing or something. Hell, I don't know. All I know is that Sellers protects his investments and right now, you're investment number one."

Mi would have corrected him that she was one-quarter *Japanese*. The rest of her heritage was comprised of a mixed bag of European descendents, but she knew Crosby didn't care. That wasn't the point. A bodyguard. She didn't like the sound of that. A bodyguard meant real danger and she didn't think a handful of threatening letters and one or two random acts of vandalism warranted a rent-a-cop.

"But Detective Rolls said it was probably a couple of over zealous members of that religious group, C.A.L.M. Unless something's changed that I don't know about." She searched Crosby's face and instantly knew she hadn't been fully informed. "What aren't you telling me?"

"Shit." Crosby dropped his gaze to a paper on his desk, pausing for a moment like he was making an important decision. "I don't want to scare you, kid, but I suppose you'd find out about it sooner or later." He lifted the top couple of papers, then carefully slid out an envelope and handed it to her. "These are copies of what was handed over to the police."

Mi didn't comment on how much his hand shook when she took the envelope from him. That small tremor sent her nerves jangling. If Crosby was this upset over what was inside the envelope, then it had to be bad. Very bad.

She braced for it, but the reality of what she had to face was worse than she ever could have imagined. She flipped through the photos, one after the other, caught by the snippets of her life that had been well documented on film. Her unlocking her car in front of her house, in the produce section of the grocery store, in line at the dry cleaners, sitting in a church pew, holding a box of tampons in the drug store, having lunch with Lucy. And the final one—the one that had her clutching at her chest—was of her and her mother, feeding the ducks in the park under a hot Texas sun with the baby stroller parked close by.

She looked up to find Crosby watching her closely. "Are you okay, kid?"

She shook her head, unable to form the words she had for the emotions welling up inside her, trying to claw their way out.

"In that case, let me introduce Lucas Vega. Your bodyguard."

She jerked in surprise, turning her head to the side, then up, way up. That low hum started again at the sight of the still man from the studio. He stood feet above her, looking down at her with no emotion. Certainly, nothing like the sensations clanging around inside her caused by his nearness. He was dark, like a shadow, dressed in all black with black hair and near black eyes. And not at all handsome. Which strangely made him more attractive to her.

Mi clutched the photos tighter. "No."

"Sellers owns this station and all our asses. There is no 'no.'" And then Crosby said something he avoided as though it gave him a violent rash. "Sorry, kid."

She knew there was no way out. Those two simple words sounded with a thud in her head, like a trunk lid closing with her inside.

"She's a peach once you get to know her," Crosby said to Lucas, standing. "I'll leave you two to get acquainted and to make sure Davy's finally unscrewed his screw up." Crosby pointed at Mi. "Three minutes and then I want you back on set twirling dildos. Jesus, if my mother could see me," Crosby mumbled to the ceiling as he left the room.

*

Lucas wasn't sure what to say. Miyuki Price-Jones off camera was nothing like he'd thought she'd be. First off, she was small, too small, looking more like a teenager than the twenty-eight her file said she was. He knew she wore the glasses for the sex-kitten effect on the show, but what the file hadn't said was what a strange color her eyes were, gold, like an old coin.

The file also hadn't said anything about her having a kid. He wondered why. It wasn't like her reputation would be compromised. She sold sex toys for fuck's sake. Something told him that her having a kid would add a complication he wasn't sure he wanted to deal with. Must have been why Cal Sellers had left that bit of information out of the file. And why Lucas would look into it as soon as he got the chance.

She didn't speak or pay him any attention at all as she shoved the photos back into the envelope, her movements jerky and rushed. Then she sat there, holding the envelope, staring at it as though she didn't know what to do with it.

"May I?"

She jolted at his question, spinning in her chair. She eyed his outstretched hand as if he'd strike her with it. That thought made him frown.

She clasped the photos to her chest. "No."

He withdrew his hand, disguising his uneasiness at her reaction to him with a careless shrug. He was used to people making judgments about him. Usually he spun those misconceptions to his advantage, but for some reason her negative assessment of him rankled. He told himself it was better this way. Her discomfort meant she'd take direction from him if things got bad. And that was good.

"I'm sorry, Mr. Vega." She rose to face him.

The first thing he noticed was that she was a little taller than she first appeared. The next thing he noticed was that despite her paleness from shock, her spine was straight, her chin high. It would take a lot to really rattle Ms. Price-Jones. That, too, was good. Maybe this favor he was doing for Cal wouldn't be so bad.

"I didn't mean to be rude." She indicated the pictures. "It's just that these are personal."

"It would help me to know what we're dealing with." The truth was he wanted to study them more closely than the glimpse he'd gotten over her shoulder. He told himself they would tell him more about who might be after Ms. Price-Jones, but the real truth was he wanted to know more about *her*.

She frowned down at the envelope. "Oh."

"And please, call me Lucas."

"Lucas." She said it as if she were trying it out to see how the letters felt on her tongue. Which brought his attention to her mouth and its fullness. Her tongue darted out, leaving her lower lip wet.

He had the strongest urge to run his thumb across it just to see how it felt.

"How does this work? This bodyguard thing?"

Lucas brought his attention back to her eyes, which were wide behind her fake glasses. With fear or something else? He couldn't be sure. He wanted to put her at ease. He almost reached out to touch her, but wasn't entirely sure she wouldn't bolt if he did. Instead he shifted his stance, trying for reassuring.

"I'm with you twenty-four seven. I go where you go."

"Oh." She didn't look reassured. If anything she looked more agitated.

"You won't even know I'm there."

She gave a shaky laugh. "I seriously doubt that. You're awfully hard to miss."

"What I mean is, you'll go about your day same as always."

"Except for my very large shadow."

He cracked a hint of a smile. "Yes."

She smiled in return and then the most remarkable thing happened. She touched him, taking his hand in hers. "Well, then, nice to meet you, Lucas. Please, call me Mi."

"Mi." It was his turn to try out her name, and he liked the way it made him feel.

She released his hand. He missed the contact.

"I'd better get back before Crosby starts yelling." She looked at the envelope again, a frown creasing her brow. And then she thrust it at him, hitting him mid chest. "Here." She released it without waiting for him to bring his hand up. He grabbed it before it hit the ground. "When you're done, burn them. Shred them. I don't care." But she didn't look at them as though she didn't care. "I don't want to see them again."

That he believed, and he wanted to be the one to make them go away for her. He wasn't sure why he felt a protectiveness toward her that went beyond his job description. A protectiveness that was entirely personal. He wanted to be the shield that separated her from the things that made her eyes wide with fear and had her flinching at an outstretched hand.

Lucas tucked the envelope into the inside pocket of his leather jacket and followed Mi back to the studio where it looked as though they had gotten everything straightened out. People milled about, checking or testing things, shouting out and answering commands. He felt out of place here. Everything was so fake: the seating group meant to look like anyone's living room, the backdrop with a windowed view of anyone's neighborhood, and the woman standing in the midst of it all, getting her hair and makeup touched up. Mi.

Gone was the reserved, almost shy, woman he'd met earlier. In her place was the on-camera siren who sold sex toys, handling them like a pro. That thought made his shoulders twitch. Would he be the first to assume a woman who sold sex toys also had vast intimate knowledge of how to use them? What kind of crazy kink would a woman like her be into? Watching her switch on a vibrator and stroke the shaft while extolling its virtues affected him more than he wanted it to. More than it should have. He wondered if he was the only one getting turned on by her display. He'd bet not. A woman like her would have men tripping themselves to get to her.

But there had been no reference of a husband, boyfriend, or any other kind of personal relationship in her file. Maybe there were too many to mention. He shifted his feet, more uncomfortable with that notion than he had a right to be. He thought again of the photo of Mi and another woman by a lake with a baby stroller. The other woman looked too old to be the mother of an infant. So if the baby wasn't Mi's, whose was it? And where was the baby's father?

Mi held up two odd looking things with small clamps. "Next up we have a beautiful set of cordless vibrating nipple clamps from Love's Slave. Foreplay fun or masturbation enhancement, these lovely vibrating clamps are made of soft, supple rubber and are adjustable for your pleasure. Tickle, tease, and please your perky tips hands-free, batteries included…"

Jesus. Lucas's gaze immediately dropped to Mi's breasts as she spoke. He first imagined using the nipple clamps on her, but quickly discarded that image, replacing it with his hands and mouth, licking and coaxing her nipples to stiff peaks…

"Increase your orgasmic pleasure by combining your Love's Slave vibrating nipple clamps with the vibrator or dildo of your choice. Only twenty-nine, ninety-nine and available in three colors: pink, purple and silver…"

He'd like to increase *her* orgasmic pleasure and not with some battery operated contraption, but the old fashioned way with hands and tongue and the slide of skin on skin. He pictured his hands pressed to her small breasts, his thumbs tracing circles around her aroused flesh…

"Also from Love's Slave we have the Ride 'Em Cowgirl, a stationary ride-on vibe with three speeds. Just place the Ride 'Em Cowgirl on your bed or floor and set your own pace, slow and sensual or fast and hard. However you like it, you decide…"

A fine sweat coated Lucas's forehead and upper lip. He

adjusted the front of his pants, picturing Mi naked, rising over him, riding *him* like a cowgirl...

"This bubble gum pink ride-on vibe has adjustable speeds and a strong suction cup attachable to any surface for when you want to ride doggie-style..."

Fuck. His hands flexed at his sides as he pictured Mi on all fours in front of him. He gripped her hips, taking her hard and fast from behind just the way he'd like...

"Don't forget tonight's show special: Decadence's Heart-on For You, a beautiful hand-blown glass phallus with a heart shaped handle and sensual beads for added stimulation. And *Pleasure at Home's* own Slippery When Whet, a water-based, non-stain lubricant to enhance your sexual experience. Regularly fifty-nine..."

Was she wet right now? Did she get turned on, handling the long hard shafts, describing how to use them? Did she pleasure herself in the darkness of her bedroom late at night?

"We also have some wonderful products for gentlemen, beginning with the Super Stroker 3000 from Midnight Embrace." Mi held up some kind of tube-looking device. "Extra long to accommodate any sized man, this deep throated stroker will bring you to completion and beyond. Soft, full lips wrap around your shaft, gently sucking..."

He'd experienced less painful torture in the Navy. He didn't get why people bought those things, but watching Mi's sales pitch was the most erotic thing he'd seen in a long time. And it had been way too long since he'd had anything but his own hand to slake his lust. Needing another focus for his attention, he shifted his feet and looked around. He was thirty-two, not a fifteen year-old boy unable to control himself for fuck's sake. He wanted to fill a sink and dunk his head, give it a good solid soak for the things he'd been thinking. Instead he let his gaze wander the studio, studying the layout, the exits, and the people. He catalogued every-thing, storing the knowledge away. He was here to protect Mi, nothing more. If only he could erase the erotic images that flickered across his mind like a porno movie.

Damn Cal and his stupid favor.

*

An hour later, Mi wrapped up the show by repeating *Pleasure at Home's* two phone numbers—one for women and one for men—and reminded her viewers that they could view all of tonight's products and more online on *Pleasure at Home's* website.

"That's a wrap," Crosby shouted.

Mi stepped off the stage, glad to be out of the glare of the lights that seemed sharper with the headache hovering at the back of her head. Her gaze automatically wandered the far corners of the studio, looking for Lucas. She found him near the door, arms folded over his chest. She could just make out his dark shape in the shadows. He looked more imposing than ever. She remembered how gentle, almost kind, he'd been with her earlier. The contrast in him gave her shivers.

She handed Tracey, the makeup artist, her on-show, trademark eye-glasses. It had been Mr. Sellers's idea for her to wear them even though she had perfect eyesight. He'd thought the sexy librarian look would be a perfect contrast to Lucy's blond bombshell. She missed Lucy. Doing the show without her wasn't as much fun, but with just weeks left of her pregnancy, Lucy didn't fit *Pleasure at Home's* provocative image. A hugely pregnant woman wasn't sexy, according to Mr. Sellers.

Mi and Tracey headed to the makeup room just off the main studio. *Pleasure at Home* was wildly successful, but not successful enough for anything more than a glorified closet as a makeup room. Tracey pulled the bobby pins from Mi's hair while Mi attacked her face with a baby wipe. She hated the thick pancake makeup required for on-camera work. Tracey finished brushing out Mi's hair just as Mi wiped the last of the makeup and cold cream off with a tissue.

Tracey set down the hairbrush and began cleaning up the makeup counter. "You're all set, Mi."

"Thanks, Tracey," Mi said as she gathered her things. "I'll see you tomorrow." She turned to find Lucas crowding the doorway. "Oh! Hello." Had he been there the whole time?

He examined her face as though it was a riddle that needed solving. "You have freckles," he whispered more to himself than her.

Mi lowered her head a little, touching a finger to her lightly speckled nose. She hated her freckles. "Yeah, since I was a kid," she answered just as quietly.

"Hmm."

She couldn't tell if that was a good 'hmm' or a bad 'hmm.' He continued to study her face, his gaze tracing over every inch as though it intrigued him. She knew she looked much different without the makeup, which exaggerated the almond shape of her eyes, the fullness of her lips and the sharpness of her cheekbones. Most men only saw the sex kitten who sold personal pleasure devices, expecting her to be wild in bed. Her on-camera self was sexy and sought after, but her off-camera self was freckled and easily skipped over.

She didn't know why the way he looked at her now made her feel apologetic, it just did. And it annoyed her. "It's the makeup. I'm supposed to look the part." She dropped her voice further until it was barely audible. "You know, seductive and alluring."

He frowned, a deep V forming between his brows.

"Mi, you forgot this." Tracey held out Mi's cell phone, angling herself for an introduction to Lucas.

"Thank you. Tracey Casey, meet Lucas Vega, my—" And then it slipped out, catching Mi as unaware as anyone. "—boyfriend," she finished, not daring to look at Lucas. What had she just done?

"Pleased to meet you," Lucas said smoothly as though it were true.

"Boyfriend?" She could feel Tracey's questioning stare, but she didn't dare look up.

"Yes, ah—"

Lucas cut in. "We've just made it official."

And then Lucas draped his arm across her shoulders, bringing her up against his side. A decidedly hot and altogether hard side. She could smell the leather of his coat mixed with the fundamental scent of warm male. It was all she could do to not turn her head and rub her face against his chest, luxuriating in his scent like a bitch in heat. Instead she brought her arm up and under his jacket, laying her hand flat on his lower back just above the hard ridge of what was probably a gun. More heat. His muscles twitched under her palm.

Tracey tipped her head back and to one side. "Well then, congratulations. I suppose."

Mi was surprised at the tone Tracey used. If she didn't know better, she would have thought Tracey was being catty.

"Thank you. Well, we'd better go. See you tomorrow," Mi told her.

Lucas navigated them through the doorway. Mi bunched

a handful of his t-shirt in her fist to keep up with him. Once they were clear of Tracey, Lucas leaned down and whispered in her ear, his lips brushing her hair. "Nice explanation."

"I didn't know what to say. How to explain."

"I'm not complaining. It's the perfect excuse for us to be together twenty-four seven."

She could have sworn he smoothed his cheek away more slowly than necessary. And he might have taken an extra deep breath while he did so.

"So you're okay with that?" She hoped he was because they were getting looks on their way back through the studio, walking with their arms around each other.

"Sure. Unless you already have a boyfriend."

Her answer came out rushed. "No. No boyfriend."

"What the hell?" Crosby said from behind them.

They'd almost made it to the door when Crosby called them back. "Mi, in my office. Now!"

Mi would have dropped her arm—turning to go back was the perfect excuse—but Lucas still held her to him.

"Get in here and close the door." Crosby waited while they crowded into his office, which wasn't much bigger than the makeup room. Crosby gestured back and forth between them. "What the hell is all this?"

Lucas dropped his arm, forcing Mi to do the same. "Appearances. Unless you want everyone to know Mi has a bodyguard?"

"No. I suppose not." Crosby never looked happy, but this was a new level of displeasure even for Crosby. "You're gonna watch where you put your hands. You get me?"

Lucas tucked his hands in his pockets. "Yes, sir."

"Crosby." Mi's cheeks heated. She felt about sixteen, going on her first date.

"There are a bunch of goddamned protesters out front, more than usual," Crosby said. "Sellers hired a couple of guards for outside, but I wanted to give you the heads up. The lady from C.A.L.M. is out there with a goddamned megaphone, stirring up all kinds of shit."

"C.A.L.M.?" Lucas asked.

"Christians Against Loose Morals," Mi explained. She tried not to show how much it bothered her that Cookie Dixon and her group picketed every show taping or that their numbers seemed to be growing every week. When she met Crosby's eyes and saw the softening of his expression, she knew she hadn't pulled it off.

"It'll be all right, kid. You're well protected." Crosby sent Lucas a look, communicating something Mi didn't catch. "Investment number one, remember? Here's your mail." He handed a stack of envelopes to Lucas. "I know you like to answer your fan mail, but from here on out, he goes through it with you. Anything that's off gets bagged and goes to Detective Rolls. Got it?" Crosby said more to Lucas than Mi. "Now get out of here."

They did as Crosby said, exiting the building through a side entrance near where Mi had parked her car. The building that housed the *Pleasure at Home* studio and offices looked like every other building in the huge industrial complex just outside of Dallas.

The air hung heavy with the heat of the dying day. The last rays of the sun slashed the sky orange and red, foretelling another day of oppressive summer tomorrow. They could hear the crowd on the other side of the building, sending up cheers after everything Cookie Dixon said through the megaphone. Mi tried to not let the negativity and hatred get to her, but it was hard when so much of it was often directed at her as one of the faces of *Pleasure at Home*.

Lucas held out his hand. "Give me your keys."

"Why?"

They'd reached Mi's car, a compact sedan that looked like every other vehicle in the parking lot, and faced off on the driver's side of the car.

"I drive," Lucas insisted.

"This is my car."

"For me to do my job I'm going to need you to do what I say. Sometimes I'll be able to give you a reason, sometimes not."

"So what's your reason?"

He looked at her for a moment like he wouldn't answer, challenging her to go along without having to give her a reason. Then he seemed to come to some kind of decision. "I'd feel weird having you drive me around."

She dropped the keys into his palm. "That's as good a reason as any, I suppose."

He walked her around to her side of the car and opened the door for her. She saw him flick a look at the car seat in the back and cringed inside, anticipating his questions. Instead he closed the door without comment, which felt almost like he'd closed off a part of himself.

He climbed into the driver's seat with difficulty, his knees up near his chin. Mi smothered a laugh. He finally got the seat adjusted as far back as it would go, but his legs were still too long.

"Damn compacts," he muttered.

This time Mi didn't bother hiding her chuckle. "I can drive."

"We'll be taking my truck going forward."

He pulled out of the parking space. They drove around

the building and got their first look at the mass of people gathered outside the gates of the parking lot. Cookie stood on something to make her taller than the crowd that jabbed picket signs in the air, shouting in response to the things she said. There were more than ever before and their signs were more sophisticated. This was a new kind of crowd—organized and more dangerous than the Sunday school teachers and PTA parents who usually protested.

Suddenly a loud crack rent the air. The back window exploded behind them, pelting them with glass.

"Get down!" Lucas ordered, shoving Mi's head between her knees. He hit the gas pedal, sending them straight at the crowd blocking their exit.

WANT TO READ MORE?

➤One-click LOST Now➤

Looking for something lighter and funny? Check out THE MISADVENTURES OF MAGGIE MAE series, starting with WAKE UP, MAGGIE, available now! Maggie has to keep her very inappropriate thoughts to herself about the FBI Special Agent assigned to protect her from a murderer.

➤One-click WAKE UP, MAGGIE Now➤

ALSO BY BETH YARNALL

Dangerous Lines

Lost

Saved

Fake

Real

Urge

Rare

Betray

Recovered Innocence

Vindicate

Atone

Reclaim

The Misadventures of Maggie Mae

Wake Up, Maggie

You're Mine, Maggie

Find Me, Maggie

Azalea March Mysteries

Killing It In Vegas

Beth Writing as Betty Paper

Crazy On You

Captive

Tinsel

Piano Lessons

BETH'S BOOKS FOR WRITERS

Crafting Unputdownable Fiction series

Going Deep Into Deep Point of View

Making Description Work Hard For You

Some Like It Hot: Writing Sex and Romance

ABOUT THE AUTHOR

USA Today best selling author and Rita® finalist, Beth Yarnall, writes mysteries, romantic suspense, and the occasional hilarious tweet. She lives in Southern California with her husband, two sons, and their rescue dogs where she is hard at work on her next novel. For more information about Beth and her novels please visit her website- www.beth-yarnall.com